JOAN BISSONNETTE EDDY

THE BRAIDING MAN
AND OTHER
STORIES

P.D.SMITH

TRAFFORD
PUBLISHING

For John Ivor

Note for Librarians: A cataloguing record for this book is available from Library and Archives
Canada at www.collectionscanada.ca/amicus/index-e.html
ISBN 1-4251-0581-5

Printed in Victoria, BC, Canada. Printed on paper with minimum 30% recycled fibre.
Trafford's print shop runs on "green energy" from solar, wind and other environmentally-friendly power sources.

TRAFFORD
PUBLISHING™

Offices in Canada, USA, Ireland and UK

Book sales for North America and international:
Trafford Publishing, 6E–2333 Government St.,
Victoria, BC V8T 4P4 CANADA
phone 250 383 6864 (toll-free 1 888 232 4444)
fax 250 383 6804; email to orders@trafford.com
Book sales in Europe:
Trafford Publishing (UK) Limited, 9 Park End Street, 2nd Floor
Oxford, UK OX1 1HH UNITED KINGDOM
phone +44 (0)1865 722 113 (local rate 0845 230 9601)
facsimile +44 (0)1865 722 868; info.uk@trafford.com
Order online at:
trafford.com/06-2339

10 9 8 7 6 5 4 3 2

Contents

THE WALLET

The Dog and Gun. What more plebby name could a pub have? Didn't it conjure up the image of a hostelry where one could drop in wearing one's old Mac and Wellies? It used to be like that in the old days, in the days when Tommy Moore was a lad and living in the Fens.

The old pub was situated at Wicken Fen near the confluence of the Cam and the New River where he fished as a boy, and within sight of Devil's Ditch. Some time before, a visiting American, much taken with the romance of the fenlands, bought the property and converted it into an hotel, incorporating a restaurant which drew the sort of clientele one would expect to see in Simpson's on the Strand, or Café Mozart on the Upper West Side.

It riled Tommy Moore that in order to have a meal at his former stamping ground he was forced to wear a jacket and tie. In the living section of their get-away van he whinged and grumbled as he dressed in what passed in his life for formal attire. There was very little room to maneuver especially with

Jan trying to get herself ready at the same time. They bickered away, as usual, despite it being their tenth anniversary and this special evening a celebration of that date. Wriggling into the only dress she now possessed and drinking a gin and tonic, not her first, Jan reminded him that he was the one who insisted on making a reservation at the Dog and Gun while she would have been much happier going into Cambridge for a Big Mac. That only spurred Tommy to rant even louder about how he was buggered if he was going to be kept out of his old haunt by some upstart Yank who was following in the footsteps of his antecedents by invading British Territory.

"Funny, I thought they came here to rescue you," Jan sniped.

At that Tommy exploded, which is exactly the result Jan wanted. Jan was only twenty-nine, too young to know anything, never mind anything about the war. For so many nowadays the war was a distant memory or no memory at all, not that at sixty Tommy had any personal wartime experience of the American troops in East Anglia but his father and grandfather had made sure that he understood their impact on the local towns and villages, and what bastards they were with their chewing gun and nylons.

Ready at last Tommy went forward and slid into the driver's seat. The old vehicle wheezed and complained when he turned the key, and it didn't look any better than it sounded. It was a broken-down old rust bucket and one of Tommy's conceits, which he insisted on using for their summer touring around the English countryside. This exercise was to enable him to make the sketches he would use as a basis for his painting when they returned to Paris where they lived from October until April. This peregrination had been their routine for the last five years, and each year Tommy said it was the last, claiming that the disruption of their lives twice a year was becoming intolerably tedious. Quirkishly, this why he refused to buy a decent van for them to live in for six months, because they wouldn't be needing it after the current year – but they always did need it, and as a result were still stuck in a rattletrap on its last wheels about which Jan never failed to remind him at every opportunity.

And then there were her parents who lived on inherited money in Esher. Their young daughter's relationship with him was bad enough, a man old enough to be her father, but to live half the year in a broken down van using ditches as loos like the ancients of the Dark Ages, was disgusting, outrageous and unhealthy, they informed him. When they first knew Tommy they had accepted his eccentricities because he was a well-respected artist, but now they didn't accept him or his eccentricities, not since, ten years ago he had seduced their nineteen year old daughter whom they expected to fulfill the destiny for which she had been bred, namely, to make a good marriage and settle into a stately home, or the modern day equivalent.

Tommy wasn't even free when they had shacked up together, as Jan's brother so inelegantly but accurately described it. Tommy had been married for twenty-seven years to Brenda, a woman who had supported him financially and in every other way while he struggled to find a place for himself in the art world.

Long before he dumped Brenda for Jan, Tommy had acquired a reputation for his expressionistic canvases and was selling everything he painted. Success did not go to his head. Instead, as Brenda was fond of telling their friends, it went to his dick. As soon as Tom Moore became a celebrity within the cloistered world of highly regarded artists, young women began emerging from the woodwork eager to offer themselves as muses to the master. Brenda was confident that her and Tommy's happy years together, their warm, close relationship, made even closer perhaps because they had no children, together with the sacrifices she had made to support and promote him in the early years and bad times, was enough to ensure her security. Alas, it was a confidence sadly misplaced.

Tommy had insouciantly disregarded the nymphets until Jan Mattingly appeared in the master class he had agreed to give at the Logan School of Fine Art in Surrey. He fell hard for the haughty deb who swanned about with her nose in the air. It was unknown to Tommy that this teenager, whose daubs were so terrible they offended the eye, had paid the two hundred pounds to attend the day long session simply in order to seduce him. Jan Mattingly had seen Tommy at the opening of his one-man show at the Style Gallery in Knightsbridge. It was a high profile, social affair. Jan's parents were patrons of the gallery and she had gone along because she had nothing better to do. She hadn't spoken to Tommy that night. In fact, she had not even tried to get near him, but from that moment she was determined to have him, married man or not. She didn't give a hoot for his wife. As soon as she got home she logged onto the Internet and researched his background. Without any trouble at all she was able to discover where he lived and the places he could be found. She followed him around, went to events where he was scheduled to be, but stayed in the background, never revealing herself to him. She intended choosing the right moment to make her advance and it was a moment which came when she learned that he was to give that master class.

At nineteen Jan Mattingly was a beauty. She was blessed with strongly defined features, brilliant blue eyes under winging brows, and long rich brown hair with highlights of gold. Her body was lithe, bosomy and suntanned from holidays at the family villa in Las Palmas, the immediate focus of all eyes. No-one at the Logan master class would have guessed that Jan had ever seen Tommy Moore before in her life, never mind that she had been stalking him for two months. When he came to her easel she treated him with cold respect. Her cool detachment so enchanted Tommy that he did not even stop to consider why someone whose offering was so abhorrent to an artist's eye would pay a goodly sum to attend a class which was so patently out of her league. But then, it wasn't in Tommy's psyche to consider anyone else or their motives. He had been too well spoiled by Brenda, and his mother before her. A more aware person, aware of others, that is, would have seen that no-one one with the remotest interest in art could have produced the hideous renderings which materialized from the end of Jan's brush. But Tommy wasn't looking at the canvas. He was looking at Jan, at the beautiful, supercilious face, the perfectly proportioned, arrogantly poised body, the youth, and the challenge.

It wouldn't be true to say that Tommy never gave Brenda another thought. One didn't just dump a wife of more than a quarter century without at least a passing reflection, not even Tommy. He recognized that there had to be some compensation for Brenda in the divorce he intended to have. Therefore, in addition to her half of their accumulated assets, he made a provision that she would receive a percentage of all his future sales. Money would solve the difficulties.

Had Brenda not loved Tommy with all her heart and soul she would have considered this a fair deal. It was a horrible thing to be bought off but this pay-off was considerable. It would ensure her comfort for the rest of her days. The problem was she did love Tommy with all her heart and soul, and no amount of money would ever compensate for his betrayal. To be rejected after all those years, to be unceremoniously dumped at the age of fifty-three by a husband of fifty-five for a girl of nineteen would have been painful and humiliating if the marriage had not been good, but to have it happen when the union was so long and happy made no sense to her, or anyone they knew, except, of course, for it being a common enough case of an old man lusting after a young girl. What Tommy didn't seem to grasp, or didn't care about, was that if he had not been a well-known artist Jan would not have given him a second glance, and if he had tried anything on with her she would have called him a dirty old man.

But he *was* a well-known artist so she didn't.

Brenda begged and pleaded. It would have seemed degrading to some but if you couldn't beg and plead with your husband of so many years not to break up your marriage whom could you beg and plead with? In the event, it had no affect. Tommy cried a lot but didn't back down. People need different things at different times in their lives, he told her. That this different thing would demolish the life of another didn't factor into the equation, apparently. 'One flesh' he had called them all their married life. One flesh, the bible said. His words, never hers. Cleaving that one flesh asunder was easily accomplished for him. He took the action. He did it. Twenty-seven years of blood was spilled, blood representing love, companionship, friendship, trust – trust! His response to this argument was simple. If you love me let me go.

Cue for a song?

Brenda didn't let him go, but he went anyway.

Had the emotions of those years been so shallow that he could walk away from them without a backward glance?

When Jan informed her parents that she was moving in with Tommy Moore, age fifty-five, as if they didn't already know what was in the wind from the publicity machine, they were appalled. They forbade it, naturally, but Jan went anyway. She was over eighteen, and there was nothing they could do about it.

Both Tommy and Jan were appallingly brash. They carried on their affair in public as well as private, heedless of the anguish it caused Brenda. Still, shattered as she was she continued to hope that Tommy would come to his senses and return to his home and his marriage.

He did neither.

A year passed, then two, three, and four. Tommy's sales accelerated, especially when he began his nude studies of Jan, not that most viewers would have recognized her. Her hair was instantly recognizable, however, and so was her naked body to anyone who knew it, but the face was always obscured.

Jan's parents were not amused. Not for a moment over the years, did they stop campaigning to retrieve their daughter. They continued to have hope that she would come to *her* senses and marry a stockbroker.

Neither was Tommy amused.

Not only did he have the ongoing pressure to give Jan up from a prospective father-in-law three years younger than himself, he had the same aggravation from Brenda. There was only one way to put a stop to it. Leave the country. That is how he and Jan came to move to Paris, but Paris in the summer was too much. It was hot and overrun by tourists and if there was one thing Tommy could not abide, one among many, it was tourists. Besides, he missed the fens. The fens were his inspiration. This led to the getaway van and the summers spent on caravan sites in East Anglia.

This new arrangement was a bit tricky with Brenda still living in their old home in Ely, but she'd paid him for his share of the property so they didn't have to sell, and was stubbornly hanging on. He formulated a plan to get her out of there. Without telling Jan, who had made it her business to oversee his finances, necessitating some secrecy on his part so that she didn't know the full extent of his wealth, Tommy made an offer to Brenda. If she would sell the house and move to the States where she had dual citizenship, and some relatives, he would pay her fifty thousand pounds. Considering the amount of time which had passed even Brenda had to concede that it was unlikely her husband would return to her, despite not having made a move to marry Jan. Now Brenda wasn't even sure she wanted him. After the shock, the sorrow, and the period of mourning all she had lost, time began to press the wounds down deeply and cover them over. She recognized that for the first time in her life she could consider her own desires. She could organize her life to suit herself not Tommy, and she had the financial resources to do it.

She accepted Tommy's offer.

Brenda listed the Ely house. The real estate market was beginning to burgeon and it sold within the month at a highly inflated price. She added that to Tommy's bribe of fifty thousand, and making sure that the legalities of her financial arrangements vis-à-vis Tommy's future sales were still intact, she flew first class to the United States.

The following year Jan's father died of a massive heart attack alleged by the family and his doctor to have been precipitated by his long worry over the fate of his daughter. Mrs. Mattingly, who had begun to drink when it became clear that there was not going to be a stockbroker son-in-law and grandchildren to comfort her in her old age, sank into dipsomania from which she never emerged.

Tommy and Jan thrived, but no-one would have guessed it from the way they lived. Tommy remained a prolific and popular artist. In fact his reputation grew. The prices of his paintings soared, and his financial portfolios bulged. Despite this Tommy stayed true to type and they lived modestly. He bought an apartment on the Left Bank which was expensive, but nothing special. It was a typical artist's den and looked like it because neither Tommy nor Jan was interested in domestic chores. He did not, however, replace the old van. By the fifth year of their relationship, spending the winter in Paris and the summer in the van in England had become an inflexible routine with the van one bone of contention among many. It would have eased the situation if he'd agreed to buy a top of the line model with a fitted bathroom to spare them the discomfort with which they were plagued in their life on the road, but that was too easy for Tommy.

As time passed Jan took over the handling of Tommy's

business affairs, as Brenda had done, but in Jan's case, perhaps because of Tommy's advancing age, she gradually became a go-between – between him and everyone else, including his dealer. This was a source of great annoyance to his dealer who needed personal contact with all his clients in order to do a proper job of selling their work.

Tommy didn't have a wide social circle owing to a lifetime spent in the studio, the only place where he was really content, but those friends he did have were of long-standing and far pre-dated Jan Mattingly, so the resentment engendered when they were unable to speak to or see Tommy without being screened by the young upstart was profound. When alone with his cronies, an event which became less and less frequent, Tommy would claim that it was news to him that Jan was blocking his friends, and obstructing his dealer, fighting with his bank, and generally keeping all and sundry at bay, but no-one believed that for a minute. It seemed obvious to all who knew him that he had inveigled Jan into taking the same position in his life as Brenda had occupied, a front woman to deal with all the aggravations, to fend off all interruptions; skirts to shield him when he didn't want to be bothered. If he was challenged, all he had to do was produce his captivating smile, crinkle up his blue Santa Claus eyes and blame it all on that bloody woman, Jan.

Jan knew this but she didn't care. She loved the power and control that Tommy's acquiescence allowed her. She had no position of her own, no money, and no means to make any. She lived vicariously through Tommy and his work, assuming more and more power in the relationship, yet she was never accepted in Tommy's world in Brenda's place, and was not well liked, especially when she drank. In fact, drinking was the only diversion she had. Growing up she'd been fond of gardening and was good at it. She had tended the family garden at their summer cottage in Devon, growing all the vegetables for the house, and successfully competing against the neighbours for the prettiest garden in the village, but this hobby was denied her in her life with Tommy in the apartment on the Left Bank, and on the road in the fens.

By year seven Brenda had met an American she wished to marry and so she divorced Tommy. That it was now incumbent upon him to marry the young woman whom he had encouraged to leave her family and the comfortable, establishment life she had known, was pointed out to Tommy by a fellow artist who was sympathetic to Jan's odd position in life as nothing more than an adjunct to an aging man. Tommy was not enthralled by the notion but was finally prevailed upon to suggest it to Jan. She made an impressive show of indifference which belied the intention which had been in her mind since the day she first set eyes on Tom Moore. She may have been his token eye candy young lover at the beginning of their relationship, but now he was *her* prize.

After marriage the only real difference in their lives was an increase in Jan's aggression and Tommy's reticence. Jan drank more and Tommy drank less, and bickering had become a major part of their existence.

They bickered away that day, getting ready for their anniversary dinner. Tommy uttering curses while wrestling his tie under his collar. In between swigs from her gin glass Jan worked at a skirt zipper under pressure from the additional pounds which had accumulated around her once slender hips. They managed to arrive at the Dog and Gun only a few minutes late for their reservation which would have been lost after fifteen minutes, they were informed, such was the demand for tables. The car park was full of flash cars; Porches and Beemers being in the majority. Unimpressed, Tommy parked the rusting van in their midst and made his way towards the gracious old hostelry hitching up his pants as he went. Jan followed, lofty as ever, oblivious to her changed appearance; no longer the fetching deb whose haughty demeanor had, in earlier days, only added to her allure, but now a rather blowsy, overweight woman with a disagreeable turn to her mouth, gin breath, and a distinctly hostile attitude.

The Dog and Gun lived up to its reputation. Both service and food was exemplary. Of course, Tommy didn't like opening his wallet at any time and the anniversary dinner was no exception, especially as Jan had insisted on a bottle of Lacrima Christi instead of Spanish plonk. He attempted to retrench on the tip but Jan made him put down the full amount. Upon their departure he followed her out so involved in whining and grousing about the expense which he could well afford, that he bent to pick up the wallet lying in the parking lot without registering what he was doing. Jan was already at the van, unlocking it and climbing into the passenger seat. It was only when they were getting ready for bed, and he tossed the wallet next to his own on the shelf which passed for a dressing table within the tight confines of the van that Jan saw it.

"What's that?"

"What?"

"That," she said, seeking to aggravate him by not being specific.

Because he was tired he did not prolong the bicker, but gave in and said, "I picked it up in the parking lot."

She stretched out for it. Everything in the van was within arm's reach. She sat on the double bed she had already unfolded and opened the wallet. In the unhurried, deliberate way she did everything, and which drove the impatient artist mad, she emptied the wallet, laying the contents out on the bed; credit cards, driver's license; bank cards and cash. Lots of cash.

"There's a couple of thousand quid here," Jan gasped.

"Are you serious?"

"No, I just said that for effect." She was studying the driver's license. "Giles Michael Prentice, Drove Lodge, Sutton. That's near here, isn't it?"

"What?"

"Sutton."

"Never heard of it."

Jan pulled the road atlas from the shelf which served as a bookcase. "Yes. There it is, about six miles west of Ely. You must've heard of it, you've lived here all your life."

"Yeah, I've been through Sutton a few times. There's a sort of manor house there. Sutton House. Never heard of Drove Lodge."

Early afternoon the next day they took the A142 north to Ely and followed it west through the tranquil hedgeless fields whose rich earth had been farmed since the land was reclaimed in the seventeenth century. Sutton, like most fen villages was built on a rise in the ground as a precaution against flooding. It was not a calendar village of whitewashed cottages with thatched roofs and roses around the doors, but rather a haphazard collection of old houses dominated by St. Andrew's, a church much larger than one would expect to find in such an unimportant village, impressive but made severe by its missing icons, destroyed by Cromwell.

Tommy drove slowly around the Brook and where it joined with the High Street he turned east towards the church. He circled the churchyard and continued down Church Lane, bringing them back to their starting point at the Ely road. He started along the Brook again, repeating the circle.

"We're not likely to find Mr. Giles Michael Prentice this way," Jan sniffed.

"I thought there might a name on a gate post."

"Well, there isn't, is there? Do you propose driving round in a circle all day in hope of a messenger from the Almighty materializing from the fenland mists and handing you a piece of parchment with saintly directions upon it?"

"This messenger might be of more use." Tommy pulled up behind the post van which had stopped in front of the butcher's shop. "Go and ask."

Jan got out and Tommy watched her approach the postman. From what he could see the man was chatting her up and for a moment Tommy saw her as he remembered her that day years ago when she had walked into his master class and his heart had lurched. From that moment on there had been no more thought for Brenda and the life they had shared. He wanted beautiful, snooty, deliciously young Jan Mattingly, and if he had been in possession of three loving wives and sixteen children he would have sacrificed the lot to have her. It hadn't lasted, of course. Well, it wasn't all bad. They were happy for about three years after which it began to pall, and Jan began to drink. At that time he had hoped that Jan, still only rising twenty-three, would meet some aristocratic young blood and fulfill her family's dream of becoming a Lady. But it hadn't happened and she would be thirty on her next birthday. He doubted anyone would come along now willing to take her off his hands. She had let herself go, had gained weight, and although the bones of her face were as wonderful as ever she was no longer particularly attractive. Most of the time she wore jeans and a shapeless sweatshirt, and scraped her still rich hair back in a rubber band. The postman seemed to find her alluring, however. Perhaps he could unload her onto him, Tommy thought.

"We turn around and go to the other end of the High Street," Jan instructed, climbing into the van. "We drive along towards what they call the America. God knows why, the postman doesn't, and take the turning to Sutton Gault. Cross the Old Bedford River and make an immediate right along, guess what, a drove, and we will find Drove Lodge."

"Old family mansion, is it?"

"No, pretty new. Prentice built it about fifteen years ago. Came here from Cambridge, according to the postie."

"He does know something, then," Tommy derided.

The north turn-off from the High Street led them to the two

Bedford rivers and a straight dyke, One Hundred foot Drain, cutting through Langwood Fen. Tucked alongside the bridge was the pub made famous by Peter Scott. As promised by the postman, a drove opened up on their right. The weather had been dry and the tires of the old van raised a dust, but there was no hint of dust in the Prentice demesne. Once through the open gates they were engulfed in an oasis of greenery. A serpentine driveway led them to a replica of a Georgian manor house set in formal gardens which did not fall far short of magnificent. A three-car garage, the modern equivalent of a stable block was hung with fuchsia baskets. It was just possible to glimpse beyond the house the dappled water of a swimming pool.

Tommy drew up at the front steps. He got out and walked up to the perfectly proportioned front door, hitching up his pants as he went. When he rang the bell he fully expected it to be answered by a retainer of the Jeeves variety. What he saw was a distinguished gentleman in cords and a cardigan with a pipe in his hand.

Tommy was no more surprised than Giles Michael Prentice, whose heart sank to his leather slippers when his eyes fell on the disreputable character on his doorstep, and the equally inglorious van parked in the drive. As his eyes fastened on the grey beard and faded blue neckerchief of his visitor he feared that he had the dreaded travelers on his hands. Mavis had told him time and time again not to open the door if he didn't know who was there but he continued to do it and now her case was proven.

"Mr. Prentice?" Tommy queried, rightly speculating that this could be the owner of the wallet, or his son, or father, or even an uncle.

"Yes."

"Mr. Giles Prentice?"

"Yes."

Tommy produced the wallet from the pocket of his almost

threadbare jeans. "I believe this belongs to you."

Giles's jaw dropped. "My God! Where did you find it?"

"At the Dog and Gun. In the car park to be exact."

"I must have dropped it last night. I thought I'd left it in the restaurant and called them, but they hadn't found it. I didn't expect to see it again."

Tommy handed it over. "Well, here it is."

While they stood on the doorstep Giles went through the wallet. Everything was in it, including the cash. His surprise was insultingly evident. "Well, thank you so much. Here - " He began to extract some notes.

"No! I don't want any money."

Giles looked even more surprised, then awkward. "Well – er – would you like to come in for a coffee?"

Tommy began backing away. "No, thank you."

"But you can't go unrewarded," Giles protested. "Isn't there anything I can do for you?"

"No, thank you." Tommy nodded a farewell.

In the van Jan demanded, "How much did he give you?"

"Nothing."

"Nothing!" she screeched. If the van had been stationary she would have leapt out and challenged Giles Michael Prentice but Tommy was already roaring down the drive. "Cheeky bugger," he was growling.

"What? What happened? Tommy, you stop this van this minute and tell me what's going on."

Tommy kept driving. "The bugger had the cheek to stand there on the doorstep and count the bloody money. Do I look like a bloody thief?"

"Well, you don't look like Prince Charles."

"Who'd want to look like bloody Prince Charles? After that, I wouldn't have taken his bloody money if I were starving in the street. Who do these fucking *nouveau riche* think they are? Don't tell me that bloke has done a hands turn of honest labour in his miserable life -"

'Some people would think painting pictures was less than honest labour' is what Jan would have said if she could get a word in.

" – he probably inherited his money from his father who applied whips to the backs of hundreds of sorry individuals down a coalmine or in a bloody mill, and here he sits in the lap of luxury, not a care in the world, money piling up in a Swiss bank, counting his miserable pounds on his doorstep expecting me to take off my fucking cap and pull my fetlock!"

Fetlock? Wasn't that a tuft on the back of a horse's leg?

"Standing there in his Turnbull and Asher shirt!"

"Okay! I get the picture!" Jan shouted. "No need to keep on about it. You should have let me handle the situation. You've got no sense at all, Tommy. Dammit! A couple of hundred quid isn't to be sneezed at."

"We don't need his bloody money."

"Every little counts. He might at least have offered us a cup of tea for our trouble."

"He did."

"And you refused? For God's sake, Tommy, don't I have a say? I'd love to see the inside of that house! Shit!"

Giles watched the old van disappear down the drive and turned away from the window with a sigh of relief. When his wife got home from shopping she was astounded to hear that his wallet had been returned intact. "How extraordinary. I hope you gave the man a little reward."

"I offered, but he wouldn't take anything. There was a woman. She didn't get out of the van."

"Van? You mean a delivery van?"

"No, one of those things people live in, well, holiday in. Awful old thing."

"Really?"

"Falling apart."

"And yet he refused a reward. That was a bit odd, wasn't it?"

Giles moved uneasily. "I thought so, yes - "

"What's the matter, dear?"

"Nothing. Nothing at all." He gave his wife a reassuring pat on the shoulder and went off to his study.

Behind his closed door Giles sat in contemplation. There was something bothersome about the man who had returned his wallet. Despite his ragtaggle appearance he seemed a well-educated sort of fellow but he was bristly, as though he had a chip on his shoulder and that troubled Giles. In retrospect he was glad the man had refused his invitation to come into the house.

His relief was short-lived, however.

The following day when Giles had almost managed to put the wallet incident out of his mind he was out front examining his roses when the fenland peace was shattered by the clanking of an old engine, and the rattle of a worse exhaust pipe, and to his dismay the ghastly van of yesterday reappeared. Giles' heart sank. What fresh hell was this?

This time the woman got out of the van and was introduced to him. They said they were John and Mary Morrison from Plymouth. "Would you care to come in?" he invited nervously, and to his surprise the answer was no.

"But there is something we would like to ask of you," Tommy announced.

Oh-oh, here it comes.

"We must leave our caravan site today, and we've just had a message from our next port of call telling us that there's been a mix-up in the bookings, and they cannot have us for three days. It would help us enormously if we could park on your grounds while we wait."

There was only a moment's hesitation but plenty to rile Tommy. He kept his cool, however, and fixed Giles with a gimlet eye daring him to refuse. Giles didn't refuse but was filled with horror which he did his best to conceal. Without success. "Yes, yes, of course," he blustered. "No trouble at all. Stay as long as you want." He could have bitten his tongue off the minute he uttered those words. To cover the flush he felt rising up his neck he mumbled and muttered that they should walk to the rear of the property to look for a suitable site. He pulled the front door closed behind him and led the way around the side of the house.

In addition to the pool, there was a poolhouse, and a tennis court. Forcing conversation about lawns and herbaceous borders, Giles walked them around pointing out possible places where they might park the van. Tommy chose the spinney. Giles nodded in agreement and put the poolhouse at their disposal in case they needed to shower or use the loo.

In case? Tommy thought. Out loud he said, "Yes, it will do."

Not exactly a gracious acceptance of the huge favour Giles was doing them, Giles thought, but clearly all he was going to get. He watched Tommy staring about as if assessing – what? That worried Giles.

Giles wished he didn't have to tell his wife about their visitors and fished around in his mind for some way to avoid it but obviously it was out of the question. Once the van was moved it was out of sight of the house, but it would be difficult to explain away why there were strangers making use of their poolhouse, particularly at times when she might be entertaining her lady friends.

Mavis was not only unhappy, she was confused. "Surely there must be other caravan sites or whatever you call them in Cambridgeshire?"

"Perhaps they're all full."

Mavis was not convinced.

Giles shrugged. "How could I refuse? They wouldn't take anything for returning the wallet, and there wasn't a penny missing. Don't worry, darling, they'll be gone in a couple of days."

But they weren't.

Seven days passed. In all that time Tommy and Jan did not once approach the house, which seemed to Giles more sinister than if they had. He took to going upstairs early in the morning and peering out of a rear bedroom window. The Morrisons were not early risers. They never appeared before ten. At which time they trailed to the poolhouse with their towels and sponge bags. Twenty minutes later they emerged and returned to their van. Every morning they drove the van out of the trees and down the drive. Every afternoon they returned. Two hours later they went off again, presumably to have dinner somewhere.

Strange sort of life, Giles ruminated, from the chair he had pulled to his spying place.

Word had quickly got around to the Prentices' friends that they had a squatter on the property. "Are they travelers?" Richard Broughton asked over a pint at the Chequers on Sutton High Street.

"No, I thought so at first, but they're a couple who found my wallet and returned it. They're on holiday in their van and got turfed out of their caravan site. Least I could do was let them stay when they asked."

"How long is that going to be?"

"We didn't get into specifics."

"You should have," Richard grunted. "Take my advice and give them the boot."

"They'll be gone in a couple of days."

But they weren't

The second week arrived and there was no sign of the Morrisons moving on. Mavis became more and more nervous. "It's like living in a minefield," she fretted to her lady friends. "Everything seems so peaceful and quiet, but you know that danger lies under your feet and one false step could blow you to smithereens."

Giles attempted to conceal his edginess from Mavis. He continued to watch his unwelcome guests from his aerie on the upper floor. But all the time he observed their comings and goings he had the uncomfortable feeling that he himself was under observation. So strong did this sense become that if he and Mavis had been going off to Copenhagen as they often did at this time of year, he would have cancelled the trip. The Morrisons were up to something, he was sure of it, and whether that was a simple case of breaking and entering when the appropriate moment arose, or something much more ominous he didn't know, but he would be ready, and indeed, he loaded up his father's old army pistol and put it in the drawer of his bedside table.

One night, driven by he knew not what, except for sleeplessness, he slid carefully out of bed not wanting to disturb Mavis, and just as carefully opened the drawer of his bedside table and took out the pistol. Not bothering with slippers or robe he crossed the thick carpet and left the room. Mavis turned her head on her pillow, opened her eyes and looked at the clock. It was three a.m.

Tension grew in Drove Lodge. The former tranquility of the Prentices' lives began to disintegrate. Giles could not settle to anything. He spent his days watching and waiting. He now knew how Damocles felt sitting under that sword. When, and why, would it drop? His nights were restless. His only sense of security was the gun.

So it came as a sort of anticlimax in the fourth week, when a note was found on the floor of the hall, pushed through the letter box of the front door, saying that the Morrisons would be leaving the next day. Mavis fairly skipped with joy, but Giles was not so easily convinced. That feeling of foreboding which had gripped him when Morrisons first appeared on his doorstep had not diminished, and did not now. In fact, it intensified. He couldn't explain it. He didn't even try. There was no point in destroying Mavis's euphoria at being at last freed from the pernicious presence in the spinney. Giles himself would believe that they were free of it only when that van clanked down their drive for the last time.

As he did every morning Giles returned upstairs after breakfast to take up his position behind the soft sheer curtains of the back bedroom. It was shortly before the time that the Morrisons always trekked to the poolhouse for their daily showers, but to his surprise he saw John Morrison leaving the poolhouse with his wet towel over his shoulder. This break with the daily routine gave Giles a surge of hope that they were actually going to leave that day. He waited a while expecting to see Mary Morrison leave the poolhouse and when she didn't he assumed she had preceded her husband, and he had missed her.

Giles was uncertain what to do during the course of the day. The Morrisons had not said in the note what time they would be leaving and he wanted to be there when they did, so he loitered about the property, checking the borders, smelling the roses, watching the birds at the feeders. Just before lunch, breaking the quiet of the day, came the distant rumble of the van's engine as the ignition was engaged. Giles moved smartly to the front of the house and stood where he would be visible but not close enough to cause John Morrison to stop and speak to him. When the van rattled into view he turned as though it was a surprise to him that it was on its way, and lifted his arm in the sort of Richard Nixon salute which could be seen from that distance. Without stopping Tommy rolled down the window and stuck his arm out in response. "Thank you!" he shouted. "Stupid bugger," he muttered as he rolled the window back up.

Tommy's comment brought only blissful silence from the passenger seat. He smiled. And smiled. He hadn't felt so relaxed in seven years. His morning shower had been terrific, and he had needed it to soothe his aching back. It was a good few years since he'd dug a trench to plant potatoes, never mind excavating a hole large enough to conceal a body – bury a body. *Bury* a body. His repetition of the words was positively gleeful. So the shower was very welcome to ease his protesting muscles, even though he had had to wait several hours to have it. He couldn't very well have gone to the poolhouse directly after he'd finished filling in the grave, working in the starlight, and covering the softly turned earth with woodland detritus. Christ, but it was damned hard work! He wouldn't have been pleased if he'd wrecked his back digging that hole to bury the body – to bury Jan. *Bury Jan*. There, it was said, said and done. All over!

Tommy turned north. He was going up to Kingston-on-Hull where he would walk on the ferry to Rotterdam instead of driving south to the Chunnel. First he had to dump the van. That would take time. Knowing this county he knew exactly where he could safely rid himself of a vehicle, but first he had to remove anything which could identify him or Jan. Not difficult because they lived so simply. He stopped in towns along the way dropping off in dumpsters the plastic bin bags he had prepared during the night, one at a time. The license plates he would throw over the side of the ferry when they were well out into the North Sea. His plan was the safe thing to do even though it would take him much longer to reach home, and he longed to get back to his apartment. *His* apartment. As he drove he imagined the bliss of being alone in his apartment. Alone, in the lovely quiet.

As for Giles Michael Prentice. Tommy's smile grew even broader. It would serve him right if, no *when*, it was bound to be *when*, when sometime in the future a dog would dig up some bones and a skeleton would be discovered on the property. Some people would remember the Morrisons. When the bones were identified as a woman, Mrs. Giles Michael Prentice would remember Jan. So that is why Giles wouldn't take steps to get rid of the couple in the van, she would think, that is why he let them stay in the spinney for almost a month, he was having it off with young Mrs. Mary Morrison, and she had threatened to expose him so he had to get rid of her!

Oh yes, Mavis would remember that her husband watched the Morrisons constantly, pretending he was scared that they would do something untoward, when all the time he was peeping at the woman. 'Yes, Mrs. Morrison did often leave the poolhouse with only a towel wrapped around her', Mavis would testify, if she was asked at the Inquest, and yes, she had seen the young woman swimming nude in the pool in the moonlight. And yes, she had seen Giles leave the bedroom one night with his father's pistol in his hand.

Tommy's blue eyes sparkled. He'd teach Mr. Giles Michael Prentice who thought he had been giving hospitality to a Mr. & Mrs. Morrison from Plymouth, to count the money in his wallet on the doorstep. The discovery of Jan's body would teach him. And if it didn't, what did Tommy care? He was free, and carefree.

Giles watched the van disappear around a bend in the drive for the last time. But was it last time? It may not come back today, or next week, or next month, but as long as he lived at Drove Lodge, Giles Michael Prentice knew that he would never be released from bondage to that dropped wallet.

SET FOR LIFE

When the moment came he wasn't prepared for it. He stood like a zombie in the middle of the court acknowledging the cheering crowd; the standing crowd. How many of them? Fourteen thousand? Standing and cheering him. Well, maybe a few cheers were for his opponent; his opponent who was last year's Gentleman's Champion at the All England Club. This year HE was the Gentleman's Champion at the All England Club. GOD! He would have flung himself down and kissed the battered grass of Centre Court if someone else had not already done it. Who was that? Bjorn Borg? Andre? Someone from the dark ages.

The roar of the crowd went on and on. He kept bowing and waving. He batted a few balls up into the stands. He tossed up the damp shirt he'd ripped off. He spoke to some reporters alongside his chair. There were people who wanted interviews after the presentation. He said okay, fine, having no idea who they were or where he was to be interviewed. Now what was he supposed to do? All this was new to him. Someone had told him what would happen but because it was so totally unlikely that at forty-two in the world he would win the tournament, he hadn't taken much notice. He looked over to where his coach, Larry Grant, was standing clapping harder than anyone else. His parents hadn't come over from the States. They hadn't expected him to win. That was okay. They'd be watching on television. He looked around to find a camera so he could say, Hi Mom!

A very British man in a blazer approached. He reminded Josh that he and the runner-up would be presented with their trophies and their cheques by a Duke. The ball boys and girls were lining up to form a sort of guard of honour. In a moment the Duke and Duchess would come down from the royal box. That made Josh's blood run cold. He'd never met royalty and he didn't know what to do. "Address him as Your Royal Highness the first time you speak," the fruity Englishman said. "And after that, 'Sir'."

They gave the runner-up his trophy first. Josh strained his ears to hear what Guillermo said to the royal duke. Guillermo had taken home the big prize last year, so he would know the protocol. Suddenly it was Josh's turn. He walked forward. Terrified. He didn't see how his tired knees could hold him up. The duke held out a royal hand. "Congratulations."

"Thank you - *your royal highness.*"

"Very good game."

"Thank you, *sir*"

"This is your first win here, I believe?"

"Yes, *sir.*"

"Good luck in the next tournament."

"Thank you, *sir.*"

The duke put a cheque in his hand, and then the mighty championship cup.

Josh held the cup high. A microphone came into view. Someone from ESPN was asking him questions. He answered like an automaton. All around was a kaleidoscope of sound, colour, movement. Everything kept changing. He heard his voice echoing around the stadium, giving thanks for winning, thanks for everything. His devastated opponent stood quietly waiting for it all to end so he could get the hell out of there. Josh was pushed by one of the All England Club staff, pushed to walk around the court holding up the trophy. All around the court. Holding up the trophy to acknowledge the cheers of the crowds. Afterwards he couldn't remember a thing about it. He had to see the replay on television to be reminded. Had to look at himself walking around showing off the cup. Smiling. He couldn't believe how calm and contained he looked. His head had been in a whirl. They told him that he wouldn't be taking that particular cup home. His name would be engraved on it and it would remain there. He would be given something similar.

Larry was waiting for him in the locker room. Larry was so overcome he couldn't speak. He hugged Josh, and hugged him again and again. A few of the players called out congratulations. Others went about their business. The tournament was over. Most of them would be leaving that night, returning home, preparing for the next stop on the tour. The winners, it was hoped, would stay for the Wimbledon Ball.

"I don't have anyone to take to the frigging ball," Josh said, quaffing his beer.

"You've got to be kidding," Larry laughed. "You can have the pick of London."

They were in the Royal Oak, a pub down the road from their hotel. Their modest hotel! As an unseeded player, Josh had been a moderate success on the ATP tour, but until this moment had never come close to winning a Grand Slam. Expenses were high when one had to pay a coach and travel around the world staying in hotels. Travel was expensive. Hotels and food were expensive. That's why his Mom and Dad had not come over to Wimbledon to see him play. They both worked, but they would have made some arrangements to be covered and come to Wimbledon if anyone thought he could win, which nobody did.

Larry told him that the corner had been turned. Now the endorsements would come pouring in. Josh was young, only nineteen, nearly twenty, not the youngest Wimbledon champ, of course. Boris held that title, he thought. Larry said never mind Boris, Josh had it all. He was good looking. He had a wonderful disposition. His reputation was unblemished. Josh was the ideal role model, the sort of wholesome, clean-cut, personable, amiable young American the sponsors loved. Larry could already see Josh's image on the cereal box. Josh had - charisma!

In the pub a couple of young girls sitting nearby were eyeing Josh. He tried to ignore them but it wasn't easy. Giggling and simpering they couldn't take their eyes off him. It was embarrassing. In the end they came over and asked him for his autograph. Feeling incredibly stupid he signed the scraps of paper they held out to him. Giggling and simpering they retreated and quickly left the pub to go and brag to their friends. They had spoken to Josh Armstrong, and had his autograph to prove it!

Josh and Larry walked back to the hotel still analyzing every point in the match. A group of teenagers was waiting on the street, hanging around the inconspicuous steps which led up to the hotel lobby. Seeing Josh they surged forward and surrounded both him and Larry. They squeaked and squealed, holding out their pens and pads for his autograph. They talked about his game, talked about how cute he was, asked him if he had a girlfriend, asked him what his favourite movie was, asked him this and asked him that. He didn't answer. He didn't even speak. The girls apparently needed no response. They moved along with him as he forged towards the steps, signing his name as he went.

"You're going to have to expect a lot of that from now on," Larry told him when they were safely inside.

Well, that's all right, Josh thought, but it still didn't answer the question of whom he could take to the Wimbledon Ball. He supposed he could ask one of the Russian teenagers on the women's side to be his date but that would start a whole bunch of rumours about a tennis romance and he didn't want to get into that. There was enough gossip and innuendo in the locker rooms without adding to it just for the sake of having a woman on his arm. He would go alone.

"No way," Larry said, the next day. "Just isn't done, old boy. This is England, remember."

"The duke won't be there, will he?" Josh asked nervously.

"No, no, he'll be back in his stately home."

Josh spent the next day giving interviews for television, magazines, tabloids, answering hundreds of questions about his private life, his love life, his family, and sometimes even about his career. Again, he had no idea what he said, and had to watch himself on television to know. He thought he hadn't disgraced himself, mainly because there was nothing in his young life he had to cover up. His family background was solid. Both his parents were university professors. His siblings were working towards college. Life was not luxurious but it was comfortable, and quite ordinary by anyone's standards. Where his talent for tennis came from no-one knew. He was the first player in the family.

The following day a couple of foreign reporters, one from Hello Magazine, showed up at the hotel. "Is it true that you're taking Amanda Chela to the Wimbledon Ball?" one of them asked in perfect English.

Amanda Chela, the pop star. Were they kidding?

Larry appeared before the reporters left and immediately they jumped on him, saying wasn't it true that Josh was taking Amanda Chela to the Wimbledon Ball, and Josh's mouth fell open when Larry said, yes, that was absolutely right.

What?

"What?" Josh screeched, when he and Larry was alone.

Larry laughed and nodded. "She's in London as I'm sure you know. Her manager phoned and asked if you would take her to the Ball."

"I don't know her!"

"You soon will."

Amanda Chela was the toast of the town, the toast of the world, the latest young American pop star, the darling of that mysterious world of teens. Josh himself had been to as many of her concerts as he was able, now he was being told that she was going to be his partner at the ball. It couldn't be true. But it was.

Josh hadn't the right clothes to wear to a formal. Larry said they would go up to London, to Harrods, and get him something suitable. It had to be off-the-peg because there was no time to have something made in Savile Row. Even so, Josh protested that he couldn't afford it.

"Can't afford it," Larry chortled. "You've just been handed a cheque for over six hundred thousand pounds. POUNDS, Josh!"

"Before taxes," Josh reminded him, prudently

But they did go to Harrods, and bought a suit, and on Oxford Street some shoes that Josh could dance in.

Larry hired a chauffeured limousine for Saturday night and along with his wife, they drove with Josh to the Dorchester where Amanda and her entourage were staying. Amanda was the same age as Josh but she was light years ahead of him in sophistication. He'd known nothing but tennis courts from seven years old, and she'd been streetwise since she was eleven. On the stage she looked eight feet tall, but thankfully he discovered that she was of average height, and even in her incredibly high heels she was still half a head shorter than him. He had a horrible feeling that he'd gaped at her dress, which was down to here and up to there, but that was the reaction she wanted anyway.

His date was surrounded by people, half of whom came with them. All men. He discovered that one was her manager, one her personal trainer, one her make-up man, and the rest were her bodyguards. He and Larry and Larry's wife were consigned to the limousine jump seats. One bodyguard sat up front with the chauffeur, the other staff surrounded Amanda. She had greeted Josh sweetly with a kiss on each cheek in the European style, but other than that had not paid him any attention. Before they arrived at the Royal Lancaster the bodyguards gave him and Larry and Larry's wife orders as to how they would all exit the car, cross the pavement where the photographers would be waiting, and enter the building. The crowd of screaming teenagers who gathered wherever Amanda Chela was due to appear, was contained behind barricades.

Posing for photographs, Josh discovered, was not just standing there while flashbulbs popped. As soon as they were free of the car Amanda wrapped herself around him, pulling him this way and that in a tight embrace, lying her head on his shoulder, gazing up at him with a loving look, and even reaching up and kissing him. Her gown was by Donatella Versace, she called out in answer to a question from a reporter. The three minutes allocated to pictures seemed like three hours to Josh, and he uttered an audible sigh of relief when they were at last inside the hotel. Amanda still clung to him, looking about with a possessive air, acknowledging the adulation of the crowd gathered in the ballroom, all of whom had seen on the news or read in the papers that Amanda Chela would be at the Wimbledon Ball, and were waiting in anticipation of seeing this fabulous entertainer in person.

For Josh it was some kind of dream. If a magic carpet had come down and transported him to the minarets of a Sultan's Palace, he could not have been more overwhelmed. In a few short hours he'd been transformed from an unknown professional tennis player to the escort of a huge celebrity, at her instigation.

"Why me?" he asked Larry, in genuine puzzlement, when it was all over.

"Publicity. You're famous now, and the famous prefer to associate with their own kind in their exclusive world."

Josh knew that from watching Entertainment Tonight, and the other tabloid television shows. He was aware that he lived in a celebrity driven culture, but never in his wildest dreams had he ever believed that he himself would be included in that elitist group.

When they returned to the States there was a crowd of young women awaiting him at the airport. How had they known which flight he was arriving on? Someone said they'd been there all night. It took him forever to get to the car Larry had waiting for them. His wrist ached from signing his name over and over. His ears buzzed from the noise; the shouting, the questions, the shrieking. When he was finally able to get into the car Larry said, "Now you know why celebrities have all those bodyguards."

"But I'm only a tennis player," Josh protested.

Larry's wife smiled at him. "It was only tennis players who captured the attention of Barbra Streisand, and married Brooke Shields, and Tatum O'Neill, and sundry other t.v. actors remember?"

A small crowd waited outside the Armstrong home in Westchester County, but these weren't screaming teens, well, mostly not. These were neighbours who were loitering around the drive to congratulate the young man who had grown up in their midst and was now famous all over the world. He was the Gentleman Champion of Wimbledon, the most prestigious tennis tournament in the universe. Arguably.

"You're going to need a manager, Josh," Larry said, including his parents and siblings in the comment. Josh was an adult, but he still lived at home in a tight family unit, which was about to find itself profoundly affected by his sudden fame. "You've got the U.S. Open coming up. The Canadian Open and Cincinnati before that. Someone will have to take care of your business. I can't do that and coach as well. You need someone to deal with the marketers and promoters who are going to be on the doorstep any minute."

"Can't you put them off?" Josh's mother, Greta, asked naively.

Larry shook his head. "No way, and I'm not sure it would be wise. Promotion means endorsements, and endorsements mean financial security."

"Suppose he doesn't win any more major tournaments?" Josh's father, Hugh, asked.

Larry grinned. "That isn't a possibility which enters into the equation."

True to Larry's prediction, the phone began ringing that first day. Justin, Josh's older brother answered, and kept on answering; tabloids, newspapers, magazines, the tennis association, television stations, friends, strangers, a sports clothing manufacturer.

"See what I mean," Larry said. "There's no way you can deal with this. As it is, you'll have to change your telephone number and go ex-directory. No, you can't fight it." He shook his head as both Armstrongs tried to say they wouldn't do that. "Josh is a celebrity already. He took Amanda Chela to the Wimbledon Ball."

"Is that what all this is about, because he took that pop star to a dance?"

"I didn't take her, she took me," Josh corrected.

"What's she like?" his sister Julia asked eagerly.

"I dunno. She didn't speak to me."

"She didn't speak to you? So why did she ask to go to the dance with you?"

"The celebrity syndrome," Larry answered. "Expect a lot of it."

"Only if he wins the U.S. Open," Justin snorted deprecatingly.

Among the telephone calls Josh took that day was one from Eastbrooke Management Services, one of the most important agencies on the east coast with branches from Toronto to Florida. The next day Josh and Larry visited their offices in New York. Within a very short time the burden of handling the affairs of the young man who was to become a superstar was lifted from Larry's shoulders. Dan Banks was assigned to Josh as his business manager and agent. Dan was a fantastically energetic individual whose forte was forging, cultivating and nurturing relationships for his clients. His belief in Josh Armstrong was profound. As was Larry's.

Josh won the Canadian Open.

The Canadian Open was a nice tournament for the players. It was close to home, meaning the United States, relatively stress free and considered a warm-up for the U.S. Open which followed a short time later. Of course it had its groupies, every tournament did, but the sponsors had never before seen anything like that year. Josh Armstrong was mobbed by teenagers wherever he went, they were at the airport when he arrived, and at the airport when he left. Josh was completely bewildered. How did they know where he would be and when? And what exactly did they want of him? His male admirers were relatively easy to understand. They were preteen boys who had aspirations to become the next Pete Sampras. They clamoured around Josh at every opportunity, asking how they could achieve their ambition. How had he done it? He was at a loss. How had he done it? Well, it wasn't him, it was his parents. Being told by the coach at their local tennis club where he was taking lessons that he had a special talent which should be encouraged, his parents had responded by paying the not inconsiderable fees at the recommended tennis camp, and from there he had been accepted to train at the Kissimmee Tennis Academy in Florida.

As a junior Josh won titles and when, by the new rules, he was old enough, he was put on the ATP tour, winning consistently on the minor circuit, impressing only, it has to be said, the most discerning of observers. Until he won Wimbledon.

The win at the Canadian Open, and his appearance in the final at Cincinnati did not attract worldwide attention but the groupies knew exactly where to find their hero, and to Greta Armstrong's dismay they began to gather outside her house like Alfred Hitchcock's 'Birds'. Thankfully not as many, but it was unnerving to look out of any window to see young people camping out around the suburban property. At first, Greta didn't believe that the unwelcome visitors were in any way malicious or dangerous but they were *there*, watching and waiting, and because of it she felt unable to leave the house unattended and so became tied to it. The academic year was over, her classes were finished, but her husband was teaching a summer course which kept him away all day. Justin and Julia were not there either as they were working summer jobs with staggered hours. Julia had named the groupies the aliens. The aliens watched the house. Greta watched the aliens.

As time passed Greta became increasingly spooked. The daily walks of Monty the dog were suspended. Greta even deprived him of being in the garden, afraid – afraid of what? That he might attack the aliens? Monty wouldn't attack a mouse if it was sitting in his food dish. Did she believe that the aliens would steal Monty? Surely not, Monty was the sort of dog whose appearance only a mother could love. For heaven's sake, those silly kids weren't interested in her dog. What then? Greta couldn't explain.

Justin confronted the groupies. He asked them why they were there. To see Josh, of course, and they would stay until they did see him! Justin shook his head in disbelief. Josh was his nineteen year old kid brother. Just a kid brother, like any other kid brother on the street. What did these weird hangers-on see when they looked at him? Justin didn't understand. The senior Armstrongs didn't see either, and it rattled them. The whole experience rattled them. What if not all of those individuals out there were friendly? The family began to feel vulnerable.

Whenever Josh left the house, or arrived home, his fans ran at him, surrounded him, screamed at him. Cried! Going to or from the car they attached themselves to him. Touched him. Tried to hug and kiss him. Pulling and pushing. Working themselves up into a frenzy. Perhaps the number was no more than a dozen out there at a time but it seemed like a mob to Greta when she watched her son struggling to break free of them. On one occasion when he'd stepped out of his car and was making for the front door she went to meet him, to pull the girls aside. Josh was laughing but she could see the tension in his face. They clung to him right up to the front door. A couple of the girls wrested his sport bag away from him. Greta dived at them and took it from them. What did they want from him, these aliens? Autographs. Photographs. He stood on the doorstep and patiently signed. He stood first with one girl, then another, while they were photographed together. He did all that, but it wasn't enough. Every day he had to tear himself out of their grasp, out of their reach, and when he got inside and the door closed on them, they had worked themselves up into such a state that they rang the bell and shouted out, and ran wildly around the house looking in the windows. What did they want of him? Only to worship. That's all. Only to worship.

The family home was declared just too accessible.

A security guard was put on the payroll.

The siege did not abate.

Every morning and every evening for ten days Josh ran the gamut. In the beginning he had taken it in good part, but the novelty soon wore off, and he began arriving on the practice court tense and irritable, only to find another team of groupies awaiting him. The stress began to work its evil magic. He was not only bemused by but totally unprepared for this sudden and intense scrutiny. All the time he had been on the tour no-one had paid him the least attention. He was exactly the same person now as he had been then and to find himself regarded so differently, always at the centre of a seething mob was bizarre - and exhausting. He couldn't relax. There was too much going on. His life was suddenly out of control, and out of his hands. He had no privacy. There was no respite.

Dan Banks called a meeting of Josh's growing staff. Time was short until the U.S. Open. Every minute of practice and training counted. Security was a huge issue. Josh could not be protected while he lived in the suburbs. Something had to be done.

A personal bodyguard was put on the payroll.

It wasn't enough.

Josh was moved in with Dan and his wife. It was a temporary arrangement until after the U.S. Open. The Banks' lived in Forest Hills, totally convenient to Flushing Meadows Park.

With some of the pressure off - but with his bodyguard always present - Josh was able, and Larry thanked the stars for it, to focus on his training. The groupies were always there, of course, gathering at whatever venue he would be. Don't they have any homes? Josh grumbled. Like every coach of every professional tennis player Larry had seen it all. He'd been in the business for fifteen years. From experience he knew the reaction of star players to the adulation of their young fans. It was a progression from appreciation to impatience, and then to annoyance and anger at the interference which their unrelenting presence caused in a player's private life. Josh had not yet reached that point but it was going to come so now was the time to begin wrapping him in the cocoon which would separate and protect him from the intrusions of the public.

EMS's address was given out as Josh's. All correspondence was directed to them. His fan mail began to fill sacks. Head shots were taken by a famous firm. Josh's signature was stamped on a few dozen of them and they were sent out from Dan's office in response to requests from fans. A young woman sent her photograph in to the office, one of many trying to attract Josh's attention, but this one was somewhat different. Her name was Nikki Miller. She was the president of the newly formed Josh Armstrong Fan Club. He was a wonderful ambassador, she said, and she would be working to promote his image around the country. In the meantime, 'his' club invited Josh to be their guest of honour at an event they were planning.

The sponsorships came pouring in. Dan dealt with it all. All Josh had to do was approve the decisions Dan proposed. Easy. No, not so easy. Well, Josh, you may prefer product one to product two but the contract for product two is better.

The requests came pouring in. Sports Day Magazine wanted a spread for the Summer issue. On the court, and some interiors with his girlfriend.

"Dan, I don't have a girlfriend."

"No problem, they'll provide one. On Friday you have American Morning." Dan would drive him to the studio at first light. Josh was not a morning person. He groaned.

"What do I have to do on American Morning?"

"Just be yourself."

Josh was uncomfortable. He spoke to Larry. "I'm really uncomfortable with all this publicity business, Larry."

"You'll get used to it."

"Why do they want it?"

"To feed the rapacious appetite of the media. Gotta fill up all that air time. Gotta fill up all those tabloid pages."

"I'm just a guy who won Wimbledon."

"An American guy who won Wimbledon. Remember what it did for Andre and Pete."

"Yeah, but they're different. I'll probably never win another Grand Slam in my life."

Larry was mad. "I never want to hear you say anything like

that ever again, you hear me?"

A sports psychologist was put on the payroll.

Dr. Mark Damer. At Larry's instigation Dan arranged bi-weekly sessions to wipe out any negativity, to bolster Josh's ego, to mold him mentally into a champion, as Larry was molding him physically. Larry developed a new physical regime. Weight training at the Queen's Club; running in Corona Park; relaxation at the exclusive Raymont Spa. "Can I afford all this?" Josh asked worriedly. Dan and Larry laughed.

A personal trainer was put on the payroll.

It seemed there was to be no respite from the growing glare of the spotlight. Josh began to have some idea of how Princess Diana had felt. Whenever he appeared his adoring fans materialized from the shadows like ghosts in a haunted house, but unlike ghosts these were very vocal admirers; calling, questioning, photographing, touching, if they could get close enough. Not harassing. Not exactly harassing. They loved Josh. Not harassing, but getting bolder, sometimes breaking through the security. When one young girl rushed him with what seemed to be an icepick in her hand – but which turned out to be a joke pen, Josh was shaken. For the first time he believed what Dan was telling him. He was vulnerable. Remember Monica Seles?

A second bodyguard was put on the payroll.

The hype going into the U.S. Open was almost more than Josh could bear. It was arranged that Dr. Damer would attend the tournament, on hand, as was the trainer, as were the bodyguards, in the background, to be called upon at a moment's notice to cater to his need. It helped. Yes, it definitely helped. His people provided a cushion. They provided a barrier. They dealt with his problems. They took away the stress. They did everything except hit the ball, and he could hit the ball.

The Sports Day photographer was at the Open. As Josh felled each opponent, the man became more visible, taking dozens of action photos. It was decided to do the interior shots for the spread at the end of the first week. One of the Kennedy relatives had offered their Fifth Avenue condo as the setting. It would be done on Sunday so as not to interfere with Josh's matches, and wouldn't do too much damage to his practice. He was afraid it might affect his concentration. Both Mark and Larry advised him that he would have to get used to multi-tasking. Mark did a bit of work with him on that, leading up to the photo shoot.

When Josh and Dan arrived at the condo the crew was already there, along with a rack of outfits which someone had picked out for Josh to wear. Under the watchful eye of a wardrobe stylist he tried on the elegant garments. They came from various fashion houses. In consultation with the photographer, the stylist told Josh which outfit to wear when, after which he was directed into the massive spa-like bathroom given over for their use where his hair was washed and styled. A make-up artist joined them and actually made up Josh's face. He couldn't believe it. When he was dressed in the Ralph Lauren jeans and shirt which the stylist unbuttoned halfway to the waist, embarrassing him, and saw himself in the glass he didn't know who it was. Certainly not the Josh Armstrong who usually looked back at him.

Only when the stage was set and Josh was completely ready did the young woman appear who would be identified in the hugely successful series of photographs as Josh's girlfriend. She was introduced as Bo Stannard, an already famous name in the modeling world, but quite unknown to Josh. She was a young, beautiful, and oh such a typical American beauty. A face, as someone once said of a celebrated glamour girl, unclouded by thought. Josh, it was discovered was extremely photogenic.

Like Amanda Chela, Bo Stannard hardly spoke to Josh. In a totally professional way she moved herself into position on and around him as if he were a piece of furniture. She related only to the photographer, who gave her directions in funky terms Josh didn't understand. Oh, it was English, but the words were used in such a way to make their meaning incomprehensible to him.

A different world. Maybe even a different planet! He felt like an idiot but when there was a break to change clothes Larry and Dan told him he was doing brilliantly.

On Monday Josh was back on the practice court, and he won his match on Tuesday against the Englishman who was not expected to advance beyond the round of sixteen but put up a stiff fight, desperately wanting to teach a lesson to the young American who had taken the Wimbledon crown. On Wednesday Josh was astonished to see Bo Stannard sitting on the bench alongside his practice court. The groupies were gathered, of course. A certain number of spectators were permitted to watch the practices but tough security on the site made him feel that there was some measure of protection. Bo stood up when he and Larry appeared. Gorgeous face. Brilliant smile. Sparkling teeth. Shining blonde hair falling straight over her tanned shoulders. "Hi."

"Hi."

"You don't mind if I watch, do you?"

They went for coffee after the practice. The next day, his quarter final against the Aussie, she was in the friends' box with Larry, and the trainer, and Dr. Damer. Josh won. Not easily, but he won. That's good. A fight is good. It makes you tournament tough. It sharpens your reflexes. It gives you an edge. Bo went along for a bite to eat with them after the match. Larry said Josh must get an early night. He was closing in on the title. He needed to focus 100% on the tournament. Bo said she understood, and kissing Josh on both cheeks, light kisses like the brush of butterfly wings, she drove off in her Porche.

At home Josh sat with Dan and his wife to watch the replay of his match on television. He was stunned by how many times the camera turned on the friends' box to frame Bo's beautiful, model-girl face, identifying her as Josh's girlfriend. Each time the commentators rapturously extolled her loveliness.

"She isn't my girlfriend," Josh protested when his mother

called, complaining that he hadn't told her about Bo Stannard.

"So why are they saying she is?"

"I dunno."

"She's sitting in the friends' box, Josh."

"Larry said she could."

"Let me speak to Larry."

"No."

"What's she like?"

"I dunno."

"Josh!"

"I don't know her, Mom!"

After the semi-final in which he beat a popular Spaniard, the whole world knew everything there was to know about Bo Stannard, the beautiful, glamorous young model, aspiring actress, Josh Armstrong's girlfriend.

Josh had a day off before the final. He took the opportunity to go to see his parents, and was pounced on by all the relatives who had gathered there. "Isn't Bo with you?" The disappointment was palpable.

"I don't even know her," Josh insisted.

"We'll see her Saturday," Julia said gleefully. "She'll be in the friends' box with us."

The whole family would be at the match, watching Josh tackle the Argentine leftie with the big serve, Guillermo Barrantes, whom he had beaten at Wimbledon. Guillermo was out for revenge.

"Have you ever noticed," Julian said. "How the women of all these top tennis players look alike? Luscious young, mostly blonde, beautiful faces, fabulous bodies, actresses, models, singers. How do you account for that, Josh?"

Josh shrugged. "I dunno. Their agents called the players' agents, I guess. That's how it was in my case."

"Oh, so the stars' 'people' arrange these things," Julia smirked. "All part of the great marketing machine. Okay, I'll buy that."

"But I don't understand," Greta Armstrong began. "why all the attention is on the wives and girlfriends of the male players. The camera goes to them over and over again, and rarely to the husbands and boyfriends of the woman players."

There was a burst of laughter. "What do you expect when the directors and camera crew are men?"

It wasn't only the director and camera crew who were giving Bo Stannard rapt attention at the final of the U.S. Open. Josh's own family sat adoringly at her Jimmy Choo-clad feet, unable to drag their eyes away from her perfect face and figure. When Josh finally got to view the tape of the match with Dan and Larry he was miffed to see that every time the camera was on his box, his family were chatting animatedly to his so-called girlfriend with nary a glance at him, battling like a gladiator against the Argentinian lion, Guillermo Barrantes. It was the final of the U.S. Open for God's sake. And he won!

With Josh Armstrong's second Grand Slam victory the promotional and publicity machine went into overdrive, and the security net tightened.

Two more bodyguards were added to the payroll.

Following the U.S. Open Josh bought a condo in a gated community in Florida where many of the current tennis stars made their home, and which was suited to their security needs, as well as being only minutes from the Academy grounds. His father and brother planned to help him move but Dan said it wasn't necessary. EMS would take care of it. EMS would take care of everything. Josh should not be distracted from his training. The Davis Cup captain had been in touch with them. Josh had agreed to play. Training had to begin immediately. Larry and his wife would move to Florida, at least temporarily. Larry knew, as did all coaches, that their prodigies very often outgrew them; wanted to divest themselves of the men and women who'd been their mentors in their budding years. They didn't want to be treated like children any more, they wanted to graduate into adulthood with someone new who would let them develop in their own way. Sometimes it worked. Sometimes it did not. If it didn't the player might return to his old wise and loyal counselor. Or might not.

The great marketing machine gathered momentum. Dan's deputy in Florida, Paul Harrison, would be Josh's local contact, but Dan would continue to handle all Josh's business from New York. A terrifying landslide of requests to lend his name to everything from sports equipment to condoms threatened to bury them all. Josh drew the line at condoms.

"Do they want to print your picture on them, Josh?" Justin asked satirically. "Look, it's not my fault," Josh exclaimed.

He told his brother that if he agreed to a fraction of the public appearances he would never play another tournament, but that was only part of it. To Paul and Larry he complained that he just wasn't competent to give speeches at society charity functions or stand in front of roomsful of schoolchildren and lecture them on the dangers of smoking, and snorting cocaine. Surely they had sense enough to know that without him telling them. Young people need role models, Paul exhorted him, and Josh, through no fault of his own, was the epitome of Mr. Clean Young American Manhood. Young men and women like him had to be held up as an example to the kids whose values, if they'd ever been taught any, were lost in the sad mire of modern drug and sex-obsessed life.

"I can't do this," Josh cried. "I just want to play tennis."

"Sure, yes, we understand," Paul exclaimed. "And that's exactly what's so brilliant about you, Josh. You have the character and personality to move beyond the game of tennis. Look, a product has a limited lifespan, so it's important that the individual associated with that label be a likeable, charismatic personality who promoters would want for their next product. You must start to view tennis as a conduit to a greater career. You can make a difference. There are plenty of tennis champions around, but very few have touched the hearts of the public as you are doing."

Paul jumped in, "And you will. Nothing will stop you from playing tennis for as long as you want to, only now you're going to be a rich tennis player instead of a poor one. The envy of all your contemporaries."

Not only his contemporaries.

Begging letters. Hundreds of them. Thousands of them, and not all from charities and organizations. From individuals, young and old.

Dan and EMS's accountants made the decisions as to which organizations to support, and how much to give them. They told Josh it all had to do with tax planning and complicated tax laws such as loss carry backs and loss carry forwards and planning loans so that interest expense could be projected against future income and shifting capital losses into non capital allowable losses, that kinda stuff, Josh. Don't worry about it. We'll deal with this. You play tennis.

The individuals who wrote wanted money for dental work, or for a child's operation, or to travel to New Zealand to see a grandmother who was dying, or to mend the roof on their house which leaked on the children's bed, or to pay for a daughter's university education to guarantee her a better life than the writer. 50% of them were no doubt valid, but Dan said no to them all. Where would it end? Don't worry about it. We'll deal with it. You play tennis.

"Josh," his mother said on a visit to stay with him Florida. "I've brought these for you." She opened one of her small bags which he'd carried into the guest bedroom of his new condo. It was full of envelopes.

"What's this?"

"For you."

He stared into the bag without touching it. "All correspondence is supposed to go to EMS. Haven't you been passing it on? Aren't you sending the mail collect to Dan via courier?"

"Yes, but this isn't the same."

"How come?"

"This is from the neighbourhood."

Josh was bewildered. "What?"

Greta touched his arm. "Josh, can we have some coffee?"

"Oh sure, I'm sorry. Come on through to the kitchen." He led the way into the sunny room which overlooked the pool. "Carla has made it fresh."

"Carla?" Greta looked around. "Is she a new girl in your life?"

Josh laughed. "She's the maid, Mom."

The maid!

"The maid?"

"Well, you didn't expect I could look after this place myself, did you?"

Greta sat at the counter and Josh poured their coffee. He brought out a frosted coffee cake, a knife, two plates and two forks. Greta said, "This looks homemade."

"It is. Carla made it."

"Where is this Carla?" Greta looked around as if expecting her to materialize out of the woodwork.

"Probably gone to the market."

The cake was delicious. Greta was intimidated. Her nineteen year-old son's maid was a better baker than she. His newly purchased condo was not only more elegant than her house, it was a darned sight cleaner. She suddenly felt way out of her depth. "Josh, those letters I brought with me, they're from people around where we live."

"Yes, you said. It's okay, I'll get them to Dan."

"But they aren't *for* Dan, Honey, they're for you."

"Dan takes care of all my business, you know that."

"These aren't business. They're personal."

Josh laughed. "They say you don't know how many friends

you have until you get famous."

Greta gave him a hard stare. "Is that what you think you are, famous?"

Josh flinched at her critical tone. "Mom!"

"I wouldn't like to think that you're getting a big head."

Josh shrugged. "It's just a fact, that's all. Mark says - "

"Mark says. Dan says. Larry says. What about what your parents say?"

Josh froze. His face pinched up. He understood what she was saying but the fact is, *she* didn't understand. He was no longer the kid who was fighting his way up through the ranks of the tennis world, the kid who lived at home with his parents, the kid who went to Grandma's house every Sunday. Well, deep down inside he was, of course, but the reality was that in a few short weeks he'd moved into a fast-paced world where he had been packaged as quickly and efficiently as if he were a product on an assembly line. A package on which the livelihood of other people depended. It had happened so smoothly that he wasn't even aware of how far he'd come. Each step had seemed logical and, well, inevitable. If his parents disapproved on moral or ethical grounds, or even because they didn't want to relinquish control over him, what did they expect him to do to please them? Walk away? If he walked away from all the hoopla, he would have to walk away from tennis, as another budding star had done, Michael Evans, and that Josh could not even contemplate. Where was Michael Evans now? No-one even remembered his name.

His mother's voice came to him. "Those letters, Josh. I know what's in them."

"You mean you've opened them?"

"No, I didn't need to."

"What do you mean then?"

"They're from people we know."

"EMS deals with fan letters."

"These aren't fans, they are people in the neighbourhood who want help, Josh."

"Help? What sort of help?"

"You'd better read them and find out."

Josh didn't want to read them. He didn't read any of his mail. Dan or Mark or Paul dealt with all of that, but his mother insisted, and in complying Josh was horrified. They were begging letters from the neighbours, and not only the neighbours, from his own relatives! Distant relatives and closer cousins. The letters ran the gamut from obsequious to the audacious. Some were openly hostile, telling him that he didn't deserve all the money he was being paid, that people of much more worth; surgeons and nuns working in disease ridden countries, teachers of disabled children, and others of that ilk, were struggling to make ends meet, while he, doing nothing of merit, was an instant millionaire, living in luxury, mixing with movie stars, and traveling the world.

Greta read some of the letters along with him. "It might be a good thing if also do something for your brother and sister," she advised in an admonishing tone.

Josh was perplexed. "In what way do something for them?"

"Give them money, of course."

"Oh." Josh was totally nonplussed. Such a thing had never occurred to him. Of course he would give them money if that is what they wanted, but, well, is that what they wanted? "Okay," he muttered awkwardly. "I'll speak to Dan."

"Josh!" Greta was furious. "You don't have to speak to Dan. You can write a cheque to Justin and to Julia for a couple of hundred thousand each to get them started. It's your money! Not Dan's! Considering that your father and I gave you every opportunity to get started in your career, the least you can do, now that you have the means, is the same for your brother and sister."

"You know I've always been grateful for what you did for

me," he protested.

"Then show us."

Josh was deeply hurt.

Dan and Paul were sympathetic. "You're going to get a lot of this, Josh. We'll deal with it."

"What about the money for my brother and sister?"

"Sure. You can make them each a gift, if that's what you want, but as for the rest of these." Paul indicated the letters Greta had brought. "Best leave them with me. I'll take care of it. And Josh, don't open any more letters unless you know the senders are people you wish to hear from. Do what other celebrities do, give your friends a little rubber stamp with some kind of symbol on it. I'll get some made for you. When they send you material through the mail have them stamp the envelopes with it and you'll know it's something you should open. Josh, you're really uptight. You need to talk this out. I think you should have a talk with Mark. Can I get him on the phone for you?"

Josh nodded.

The interest in Bo Stannard did not abate. Whatever match of Josh's was televised there she was, adorably pretty, in the friends' box, applauding or frowning, depending on how the game was going. The commentators would remark upon her beauty, upon her budding film career, and speculate on when she and Josh would get married. It seemed to Josh as he watched this that he was as much a spectator to his own so-called romance as were the other individuals who seemed so interested in it. Even when Bo asked him to accompany her to events in her life, like different benefits, like the Fashion Award ceremony, and movie premieres - he even went to the Daytime Emmy's as her guest - he never felt that he was actually a part of those occasions, but Dan said they were good publicity, that the sponsors would be happy to see him out and about so much. It was good for business. Tennis stars were only in the public eye for a short time each year, mostly during the Grand Slams which were televised throughout the world on the networks, so, Dan said, it was important to keep his name front and centre for the rest of the season. Yes, he was totally involved in tennis, with Davis Cup and the ATP Tour, but only avid sports fans would be aware of that. The sponsors wanted to see him out there promoting their products just by his presence. And the teens loved him. Larry arranged for him to visit tennis training camps to work with the kids. Bo was encouraged to go along with him for that extra added touch of glamour. They were seen everywhere together, and when Josh went home to visit his family, occasions which were becoming rarer because of time and security constraints, Bo began to go along. Their pictures appeared in the tabloids on a regular basis. Two beautiful young people living the high life, and Josh's ranking ever increasing. He wasn't number one in the world yet, but it was only a matter of time, and everyone knew it.

That year there was an incident at the Masters which shook the tennis world as much as when Monica had been stabbed while she was on the court in the middle of a tournament in Germany. Josh was not involved but he could just as easily have been the victim as Tyler Boucher. Tyler was attacked and hurt. When a death threat against Josh arrived in the mail, similar to the one received by Tyler Boucher, Dan and Larry boosted the security around him even more. That did not stop someone from breaking into the condo in September when Josh and Bo were at the China Open, and leaving what seemed to be an explosive device, found by Carla who hysterically cried that she couldn't work for Josh anymore. When the bomb squad arrived they discovered the device was a fake with a ticking clock inside. A note said that the next time the bomb would be real. Obviously Josh was no longer safe in that complex. Dan began looking for a house for him which could be properly guarded.

At about the same time the Armstrongs had organized a 60th wedding anniversary barbeque for Greta's parents and were furious with Josh because Dan had advised him not to go. Or if he did, it had to be with his bodyguards. The whole family was so up in arms that Dan drove to Westchester to see them. He had to try to make them understand that Josh was now a public figure.

"Damned nonsense," Hugh Armstrong snorted. "If you people would just leave him be and let him live his life like a normal person there wouldn't be any need for all this security rubbish."

"We did have a bit of a problem, Hugh," Greta reminded him. "Remember when the aliens were camped out around the house. That was scary."

"They would have got tired of hanging about here in the end, and if they didn't the police could have handled it."

"I don't think you would have wanted the riot squad in your street, Mr. Armstrong," Dan said.

"Riot squad! You're crazy!"

Getting nowhere Dan had to bring out the big guns. "Josh's life has been threatened."

Greta screamed. "What? When?"

"And a bomb, a fake bomb as it turns out, was planted in his condo."

Hugh Armstrong didn't believe it. Later he told Greta he didn't trust the sycophants who were all around Josh. It was all a ploy by Dan and his crowd to get Josh away from his family, to get control of the boy because of all the contracts they had signed which required him to promote dozens of different products, and a line of clothing, and sports equipment. "He's their money in the bank!" Hugh shouted angrily.

Dan chose a selection of houses for Josh to look at. They were large, elegant; all had high walls around them and state of the art security systems. One had a gatehouse suitable for a live-in bodyguard. That was the one Bo chose. It seemed to be taken for granted that Bo would move in with Josh even though he didn't actually ask her to do so. Up until then they hadn't slept together. Josh had never regarded her as his girl, and sex was something she didn't push. Shortly after they moved into the house they did begin sharing a bedroom and she took him to meet her family in South Carolina. They were nice people. Josh liked them, and they were certainly a whole lot more understanding about his position as a public figure than his own family. Bo's mother, Katrina Stannard had been a 1980's supermodel, and was still a gorgeous looking woman. She and her banker husband had homes all over the world, so if Josh had the thought in the back of his mind that Bo was more interested in his money than in him it was swiftly banished. What was undoubtedly true was that Katrina Stannard's modeling and movie connections had provided Bo with her entrée into those worlds, but money this family did not need. Perhaps, after all, Bo actually did like him for himself. Well, whether she did or not, as soon as she moved in with him she began conducting herself as the lady of the house.

When, on a talk show, Josh was questioned about when exactly he and Bo would be married, he was at a loss to say anything other than, 'you'll have to ask Dan.' Like everything else that had happened to him since he had won a Grand Slam, this issue was out of his hands. Josh played tennis. Dan took care of everything else.

It was the Tennis Masters' Cup in Houston in November. The rumour went around the courts like wildfire. Guillermo Barrantes was in the quarter-finals, as was Josh. It looked as though they might play one another in the semis. While Josh was on the court, and winning, he became aware of something going on in his friends' box. With one eye on the ball and the other on the box, Josh saw one of the tournament officials in conversation with Larry. Larry had risen and the two men seemed disturbed. Bo was looking up at them. Listening. She wasn't watching the match. Her attention was on the men. When the official left

Larry resumed his seat next to Bo. Her head dipped towards him and still they did not look towards the court. Josh took from that, that whatever had occurred, it had nothing to do with him personally. With that thought in his head he won his match. Not easily, but he pulled it off, and thankfully shook the hand of his opponent, and of the umpire, then grabbed his things and with a quick wave to the crowd moved swiftly to the exit. On this occasion to the disappointment of his fans, he did not stop to sign autographs.

Larry was waiting for him in the locker room.

"What's happened?" Josh demanded.

"It's okay, your family is fine."

Josh hadn't thought he was all that tense but when he heard those words he felt his muscles relax. "What then?"

"It's Guillermo."

Guillermo was playing on the stadium court.

"What? Is he injured?"

"No, his match has been stopped."

"Why? Larry! What's going on?"

"His parents have been kidnapped from Cordoba. They're being held for ransom."

A chill went through Josh. "What? His parents? Why?"

"He comes from a poverty-stricken nation, Josh."

"Sure, I know that. I've spoken to Guillermo about it."

"Guillermo is a millionaire. A high-profile millionaire. The criminals want money, a lot of money, in exchange for his parents."

"What will happen?" Josh began shaking, showing signs of shock. And no wonder. It was dreadful news. What would Guillermo do? He would pay, of course, but what guarantee was there that his parents would be returned? Suppose they had already been murdered? Those bandits were ruthless. They had no consciences. His mind flew. Were his family members at risk because of his wealth and acclaim? Larry read the wild speculation in his protégée's face. "It won't happen here, Josh." He gave him a gentle nudge. "Into a hot shower before you catch cold."

Josh didn't have the opportunity to speak to Guillermo. He would have liked to extend his sympathy and support, but Guillermo was being rushed to the airport, surrounded by his entourage.

Josh needed to talk to his mother. When he got back to the hotel he excused himself from the others as they were walking into the restaurant, and went up to his room to call her.

"I've been watching you on ESPN," Greta said. "Congratulations on today's match."

"Thanks, Mom."

"Playing like that you'll win the tournament."

"I take one match at a time."

"Well, it's nice to hear an element of modesty."

A surge of resentment went through Josh. What was it with his family? Once they used to rejoice in his success. Nowadays they took every opportunity to snipe. What did they want from him? He'd complied with his mother's wish and given Justin and Julia a large gift of money each. Somehow he'd thought they would be pleased, but if they were he saw no evidence of it. Both thanked him, of course, but without joy. He found himself disappointed. He had nursed a vision of Julia dancing up and down with glee, knowing that now she could train to be a veterinarian without having to work three jobs, and take eight years to do it. She could pay for her studies and all her expenses without taking out loans or asking their parents for help. Hurrah! But it didn't happen. She wrote Josh a short, solemn note of thanks, and never mentioned the money again. Justin was equally restrained, and polite.

Greta said, "I just read in the National Enquirer that you and Bo are already married."

"You know that isn't true."

"There's a picture of you both and she's in a wedding gown."

"Photoshop, Mom."

"So when *are* you getting married?"

"Mom, I'm not even twenty years old. I'm not getting married. Okay?"

"Just checking. We know so little about your life these days."

"You know everything that's important."

"Which is?"

"Tennis, Mom, Just tennis!"

"Funny, you didn't used to need a company of paid employees around you in order to play tennis. Your father and I managed to look after you pretty well."

"You know things are different now, Mom."

"They're different because you've made them different."

"Not me, the circumstances! I'm winning Grand Slam tournaments, that changes everything."

"And you are loving the changes."

"No, Mom, I'm not."

"Be honest, Josh! At least be honest!"

"Of course I like to win. Who wouldn't? But what you don't understand is what it feels like to have everyone in the western world know who you are, where you live and what you do every day. It's a fishbowl existence. That makes you a target, Mom. It's really scary."

Greta was not sympathetic. "And haven't we got, oh so, dramatic. It must come from living with a movie star!"

"Mom, Guillermo's parents have been kidnapped."

There was silence from the other end of the line.

"Mom."

"I heard you." There was no softening in her tone.

"It's terrible," he cried.

"Yes, it is, but what can you expect? The money you top

sports people make is crazy enough in prosperous countries but where most of the population lives in poverty, well, it doesn't take much brainpower to figure out the likely consequences of that, and there'll be more of it, mark my words!"

Josh's maternal grandfather died in November. Bo's father put his Leah jet at Josh's disposal to fly him and Bo to Connecticut for the funeral. Dan advised Josh against going, but when Josh put this to his parents they were incensed. Of course he would attend his grandfather's funeral. If he didn't they would never speak to him again.

Josh complied full of foreboding.

Unbeknownst to anyone at EMS Nikki Miller had rallied the fan club. When the solemn procession, following the gleaming hearse, pulled through the gates of the Garden of Eden cemetery for the interment, it was straight into an excited mob of groupies who were tramping heedlessly over the graves, sitting and standing on the headstones, working themselves up into a frenzy of anticipation at the prospect of seeing Josh close up and in person.

When the procession drew to a halt and the door of the limousine carrying Josh and Bo opened, and the couple alighted, Bo charmingly dressed in black Armani, there was a swell of noise such as that peaceful place had never heard, and the mob descended.

The family was appalled.

Julian began yelling at the horde to go away.

Within minutes Greta Armstrong and her mother, the wife of the deceased, had dissolved into tears.

Hugh Armstrong and Julian struggled through the heaving mass to Josh's bodyguards and shouted at them to do something. The only thing security could think of to do was to push Josh and Bo back into the limousine, scramble in after them and charge the driver to get the hell out of there! That wasn't so easy. The vehicles ahead and behind had to make room for the limousine to maneuver out of the line while trying not to run down the fans who were trying to cling to it, to open the doors, to climb onto the hood and the trunk. Slowly, slowly the driver eased his way clear, and as soon as he could he gunned the accelerator to carry them away.

Josh twisted in his seat and looked back at the melee. His fans were rushing in and out of the line of cars holding up mourners who had yet to alight. Some were trying to run after his car. They were furious, uncontrolled. His grandfather's coffin had come to halt as the crowd milled around. Justin had his arms around their grandmother, his fury palpable even at a distance. Josh could see his mother stretching her arms out towards his father in distress. It was a scene of total chaos and Josh's heart sank in the realization that he would never be forgiven for being the cause of destroying the calm dignity of his grandfather's funeral. He felt Bo's hand in his. Without changing his position he glanced at her. Not speaking, but with a small, understanding smile, she urged him to turn and face forward.

After a moment's hesitation, he did.

THE BRAIDING MAN

In the year 2003 James and Emily Sinclair had been married fifty years. They had lived in New Hampshire for the last forty of them. They had moved to the village of Hemmingford in Rockingham County after their nine-year old son was run down and killed in their home town of Boston. He was their only child.

Jim joined the staff of the Hemmingford Hardware Store and worked his way up through the ranks, eventually buying the business. Emily was a homemaker. For many years she volunteered twice a week at the local pensioners' association, and she started a village horticultural club which was a great success. Most of her time, however, had been spent tending her home and garden. Jim worked until he was seventy. In 1998 he retired and let the staff take over.

When they first moved to Hemmingford the Sinclairs bought an old farmhouse with the money from the sale of their Boston house which had increased in value a thousandfold since their parents, jointly, had bought it for them as a wedding gift in 1953. In the early years at Hemmingford they renovated the old building into a modern home without disturbing its historic exterior, but it was not until after he retired that Jim set about restoring the old red barn which had fallen into disrepair. This was so successful he undertook the henhouse which he improved with new nesting boxes, perches, roosts, and fresh paint. When it was finished friends and neighbours proclaimed that it would do credit to Martha Stewart. In fact, it was deemed far to exquisite to house common Rhode Island Reds or Leghorns, so Jim and Emily went off to the County Fair and bought Silkies, Frizzles, and old English Game hens, any breed which would lay dainty eggs in tints of blue, green and grey.

The old farmhouse, not far from West Rye, stood on ten acres of meadowland with a fair-sized brook slashing through the back two. Weeping willows added a romantic touch along the stream's banks. Emily's formal garden, close to the house, was daintily fenced. Its lawns, herbaceous borders, and rose beds were laid out in pleasing symmetry, to be joined by trellises, arbours and pergolas as time went by.

Jim had his own little garden plot alongside the barn featuring a picnic table at which he could entertain his men friends to a pint of ale on a summer afternoon without disturbing his wife's perfect landscaping.

The spare acreage was rented to a local man who operated a riding school and stables and needed pasture for his horses, so when Emily was working at her kitchen sink she had the pleasure of looking at a rustic scene of grazing horses charming enough to grace a calendar.

Nothing would ever compensate the Sinclairs for the loss of their child, but they made a life for themselves in that bucolic place with the help of a supportive community and they led, within the limitation of their grief, a happy life, and were as devoted a couple on their golden wedding anniversary as they had been on the day they exchanged their vows.

There was just the one small problem.

It began to reveal itself just after Jim's seventy-fifth birthday. He was bored. Time had begun to weigh heavily on his hands. While he was working at the hardware story he had never been able to fit hobbies into his life. During his early retirement his days had been filled with restoring and revitalizing the property, but everything had now been done. The old farmhouse, the barn, the garden, the acreage, were picture postcard perfect. In fact, tourists driving through the village would stop and take photographs of the Sinclair homestead, as Jim whimsically called it.

In the early spring of 2003, on a cold, blustery night, Emily and Jim were sitting by the fire watching the news on television. Emily was knitting, and Jim was just sitting. When the news came to an end there was nothing else on television Jim wanted to see. He sat for a while twiddling his thumbs and watching his wife's busy fingers. All of a sudden he startled Emily by asking her if she would teach him to knit.

Emily grimaced. No, she wouldn't.

"Why not?" Jim demanded. "I suppose you think it's woossy for a man to knit."

Emily was silent for a minute and then she said, "No, it isn't that, love."

"What then?"

"I don't think I'll be knitting much longer."

Jim was puzzled. "What do you mean? Is it hurting you? You've never complained of arthritis."

Emily let her knitting rest in her lap. "No, it isn't arthritis. It's - " She stopped, perplexed, as if groping for words.

"What then?" Jim persisted.

Still Emily hesitated. "The truth is, Jim, I don't seem to be able to remember how to do the patterns anymore." She lifted the piece of knitting she was working on and stared at it. "Do you see? It's all wrong."

Two weeks later Jim was leaning over the garden fence watching a couple of young women who worked at the stables braiding the manes of two horses before taking them off to a riding lesson. The women had hitched the horses to a fence post and were painstakingly transforming the flowing manes into dozens of long, narrow braids. Jim was fascinated. He asked the women to show him how to do it. They thought his request funny but they were happy to demonstrate how the braids were made. They let him try one for himself. The hair of the mane was coarse, and when the braids were made they felt like string. Jim could see at once that his braid was not anywhere nearly as nice and neat as those done by the women. Theirs were straight and each loop was the same size and very even. His braid was twisted and lumpy.

The women laughed at his dismay. "It's only practice, Mr. Sinclair," they consoled him.

Having nothing better with which to occupy himself Jim decided to find some string and practice making braids. He went into the barn where he kept all the necessities for minor repairs around the house, and found several balls of string. He chose a hairy one because it was most like the manes of the horses. He cut himself three lengths and tried to start making the braid, but of course the string wouldn't co-operate because it wasn't attached to anything, whereas the manes had been attached to the horses. After some experimentation he found that he needed to knot the three pieces of string together and secure them to something so that he could keep them taut while he worked. He hooked the knot over a nail in the barn wall and began working the string as he had seen the women do with the horses' hair. To his delight a braid began to form, but in a very few seconds he was at the end of the string and had only a short braid to show for his pains. Clearly if one wanted a braid of a particular length one had to allow several times the length of unbraided string to achieve it. Also Jim discovered that if he left the ends of the braided string loose they would unravel, from which he concluded that he would have to secure them in some way. He recalled that the women had finished the ends of the horses' braids with coloured ribbons. He didn't have a mind to do that so he simply put a knot in the end of the braid.

Jim eyed his first braid critically. It wasn't very good. He didn't like it. It was as lumpy as the horse's braid the women had let him make. Still, it was a start. He stood for a while in contemplation. Being a methodical man he took from a shelf a large plastic pail. It was clean, as was everything in the barn, clean and tidy. He took all the string he had out of the bag hanging on a peg which is where he kept it, and tipped it into the pail. He then went outside to the picnic table and sorted out every ball and piece of string. First he grouped it into type and weight, then sorted it all into sub-groups of length. He discarded the very short pieces having learned that they braided up even shorter, then put all the right lengths in small hanks and tied them neatly together. Sitting at the picnic table he selected three lengths with which to work and left them ready. He decided not to begin braiding until after lunch.

Jim went into the house to prepare something Emily and himself. After Emily's confession that she couldn't remember how to follow her knitting patterns, it dawned on him that it had been a while since she'd been able to keep up with the domestic chores. He didn't know why. She just seemed to be forgetful. She would start a task, like vacuuming or indeed, preparing a meal, and it would not be completed. Jim would find her wandering around the house, or outside, or standing in the middle of a room looking confused. He put it down to age. Emily was a little older than he, seventy-nine, soon to be eighty. It was only natural that she was slowing down, whereas Jim was as active as ever. He had always been a physically strong man, and while he admitted that he wasn't able to lift and carry the way he used to, he was generally acknowledged in the village to be a wonder for his age.

Emily's creeping disability was emotionally stressful for Jim but in all other ways he was able to fill in the gaps. He could cook, and he could clean, and he was happy to undertake these duties. On that day, that is, the day that he started braiding, he made a lunch of ham and cheese sandwiches on whole-wheat bread with Branston pickle. Emily's favourite. He brewed a pot of good Indian tea, and they each ate a slice of the lemon cake he had bought from the village baker. Dishes done and the kitchen tidied, Jim settled Emily in her chair on the porch where she could see her pretty chickens pecking and scratching in their spacious run, and he went off to teach himself how to braid.

When he first started braiding Jim had to have the knotted end of his three strands of string attached to a peg of some kind to keep the string taut. If he didn't do this his braid turned out lumpy and twisted, but as he grew more adept he needed only to braid a few inches while the string was attached to something firm, and from then on he was able to keep the braid smooth and tight just by the manipulation of his hands. When the braids were finished he hung them up in the barn. It was not many days before he had used up all the string he had.

On the evening of the day he came to the end of his reserves of string, Jim was sitting in the comfortable parlour of the old farmhouse restlessly watching television while Emily was in her armchair knitting. The trouble was, Jim was still bored. It was all right for Emily, she had her knitting, although he had to confess that some of the articles which now fell from her needles looked very odd indeed. That evening Emily was working with some very soft yarn in a rich shade of blue, cobalt blue, he thought it might be. It came in large skeins. While he watched, the ball Emily was using came to an end, and reaching down she picked up one of the skeins from the basket at her feet. She asked Jim if he would hold the skein in his hands so that she could roll the yarn into a ball. Before they had got very far into this exercise it became clear that the ball was never going to work. Emily was winding it so badly that it was already falling apart. Jim put down the skein and took the ball out of her hands. While she sat frowning he untangled the ball she had started and rewound it very carefully, then he hooked the skein over Emily's hands and wound the wool himself. When it was finished it was a beautifully round, very even, tightly formed sphere. That was when the idea of what to do with his long strings of braiding came to Jim.

The next morning he prepared their breakfast, washed the dishes and fetched the Monitor from their box at the end of the drive. Leaving Emily to read it, he went off to the barn and took all his braids of string out to the picnic table. Carefully and intently he began winding one into a ball. He was amazed at how small a ball each braid formed. That was obviously no good. He wanted to make a statement with his braids, and little tiny balls no bigger than a hen's egg was a very small statement indeed. He wondered how large a ball of braided string had to be in order to make an impression. He unrolled all but one of the balls and began winding all the braids around the one he left intact. He found that if he wove the ends of each new strand in, the ball did not make any attempt to unravel. When he had used up all the braids he found that he had a ball somewhat larger than a melon.

Jim put his braided ball on the table and stared at it long and hard. The look of it was exceedingly pleasing to him, and he was filled with the urge to make more. The only problem was, he didn't have any more string. With sudden resolution he heaved himself up and went in search of Emily. He found her upstairs sitting on the bed staring at the chest of drawers in bewilderment. "I can't remember what I came up here for," she told him.

"Doesn't matter, love," he said. "Come on, we're going to the shops."

Sometimes they walked into the village which was only half a mile, but recently Emily had been a bit shaky on her pins, as Jim put it. He helped her find her handbag and took her out to the car. Their first stop was Hemmingford Hardware. The staff was always pleased to see Mr. Sinclair who, since his retirement, had never interfered in the day to day running of the business. So long as the store turned a profit he was content to let the Manager do her job. He kept an account there and always paid for the goods he took home.

"How much string to you have in stock, Brent?" he asked the young man who came forward to serve him.

Brent laughed. "How much do you want, Mr. Sinclair?"

Jim walked out with a shopping bag full of twine. He had contemplated buying the white but reflected that it could easily get dirty which wouldn't be nice, so he settled on the brown. He had already reached the car when a thought struck him. He turned around and went back. This time he asked for Karen, the manager. Brent eyed him nervously, hoping that he'd not done something to upset Mr. Sinclair.

"What do you do with your old string, Karen?" Jim asked her.

"Our old string, Mr.Sinclair?" she questioned, not understanding him.

"Yes, the used stuff that comes around the deliveries."

"Oh, I see what you mean. Well, we don't get a lot of string these days. Most suppliers use tape, the same way we do when we send stuff out."

Karen could see that Jim was disappointed and asked him if it was important.

"I'm doing a project," he told her. "It requires a lot of string. I thought that rather than you throwing used string away you could put it aside for me."

"Of course, we'd be happy to do that." She gave a satirical smile. "This company believes in recycling! I'll send out a notice to the staff. Will any kind of string do?"

He nodded. "Any kind at all." In time Jim would be more particular about the sort of string he used but at this point in his new interest he was just grateful for the promise of anything he could use.

Before they left the village Jim took Emily for a little walk along the High Street. They called in at the Mayflower Tea Room which was a great favourite with the tourists, and ordered an English tea for their lunch. The owner, Dorcas Campbell, came over to have a word with them, and Jim asked her if she would save her old string for him. She was quite amused and teased him about being on a recycling campaign.

"Yes, you might say I am," Jim nodded, and extracted a promise from her that she would indeed put aside her string for him.

When Dorcas had gone off to serve other customers Emily leaned across the table. "Jim, what – what is her name?"

"Whose name, dear?"

"That woman who was just here talking to us."

"You mean Dorcas?"

"Dorcas, yes. Who is she?"

The light left Jim's face. "She owns this teashop, Emily," he reminded her gently.

Before they left the village Jim did some grocery shopping. He bought lamb chops for dinner, and, at the bakery, a cheesecake for dessert. Emily was intrigued by the bakery, admiring the elaborate cakes, and exclaiming over the varieties of bread, acting as though she had never been there before in her life.

It took Jim but three days to braid all the string he had bought at the hardware store. It would have taken him less but Emily was requiring more of his attention. Sometimes he could find things for her to do which would keep her happy and occupied but at other times he had to watch over her. One day he couldn't find her in the house, or the barn, or the chicken coop. A telephone call to their closest neighbour on the next farm revealed that she was there. The tone of Joan Bishop's voice gave Jim some concern so he took the car rather than walking along the lane to the white clapboard house, which was at the end of a long drive. Joan let him in and he found Emily sitting in an armchair for all the world as if she were in their own home. In fact, she was dozing. Leaving her be, Joan ushered Jim into the kitchen. There she sliced up some of her homemade pound cake for which she was justifiably famous, and poured them both steaming mugs of coffee.

"Jim," she began. "I have to be honest with you. I'm worried about Emily. You know I'm always pleased to see her, to see you both, and you're welcome any time, but today when Emily came over she didn't know where she was."

Jim took a sip of his coffee. "She's getting on in years, Joan."

"Granted, but I don't think that accounts for what I'm seeing."

"She's a bit forgetful, I know."

Joan Bishop laid a hand on Jim's arm. "I think it is more than that. Has she seen a doctor?"

"Not for a while."

"You must conduct your business however you see fit, Jim, but I think you should consider that Emily may be in need of medical attention."

Of course Jim already knew that. Emily was not herself, and as time passed she was not improving. She became not only more forgetful but more disoriented. On two occasions she was brought back from the village where she had wandered without his knowledge. Once Karen had found her in the yard at the back of Hemmingford Hardware, apparently lost, and had driven her home, and on another occasion the mailman brought her back, having discovered her sitting on the doorstep of a residence in Pickhurst Lane. Jim's solution to this problem was to keep Emily as close to him as possible. If he had to leave her in the house alone he locked the doors, but that didn't happen very often.

As September advanced and the evenings grew shorter and cooler Jim moved his string indoors and sat at the kitchen table braiding and rolling. He bought himself one of those little red carts that children pull. This he kept in the house, and as the ever larger balls of braided string accumulated he piled it up with them. When the cart was full he hauled it out to the barn and unloaded it there. Emily thought this was good fun and asked if she could pull the cart. Of course he said she could but when it was fully loaded she couldn't manage it. Tightly wound balls of braided string, some as large as pumpkins are weighty. Put a dozen of those together and the load was really heavy.

Inevitably Jim's ongoing quest for string became known in the village, until eventually everyone who knew him was saving it for him. He would go out and collect it from businesses. Individuals would deliver it to the house. He hung a plastic bag on the fence at the end of the drive and those who didn't have time to stop and visit dropped their offerings into it.

As Jim's hoard of string grew so did his ambition. Those friends and neighbours who had seen his different-sized braided spheres were so impressed with their strange, alien beauty that they told him he should sell them. Jim thought that was hilarious. Who would want to buy such useless objects?

"Gift shops would love to have them," Dorcas Campbell exclaimed positively. "And interior decorators. They are beautiful, Jim. So perfect. Would you sell me one?"

"No, but I'll give you one," Jim offered, and he did.

Of course the men in the village had quite a different idea of what Jim should do with his newfound hobby. He should make the biggest ball of braided string that he was able, and submit its dimensions to the Guinness Book of World Records. If they accepted it as a record he would be famous!

Once that idea had been implanted in Jim's mind nothing

else would do. He was not only much taken with being included in the Guinness Book but equally by being the inventor and constructor of the world's largest ball of braided string. He wondered how big it would have to be, but as someone pointed out, if no-one else had conceived and accomplished the making of a large ball of braided string, any size would do!

Jim sat in contemplation for two days, working out in his mind how best he could accomplish his newest project. The first consideration was the potential weight of such a ball and how, when it got to an unmanageable size, he would be able to deal with it. Obviously at some point it would be too large to work on in the house and would have to be transferred to the barn. As soon as that thought entered his head Jim didn't like it. Such a huge ball would take up much more room in the barn than he wanted to allot it. The barn was a useful space for parking the car, and storing the ride-along mower and the snowblower, and the Bobcat. Not to mention all the assorted domestic paraphernalia of a house and garden. The idea of dumping his record-breaking ball of string in with such mundane detritus just wouldn't do. His monumental achievement, such as he anticipated it to be, required a specialized space of its own, a place of honour; a place where it could be viewed by an admiring audience. He had a vision of it reposing in the centre of a purpose-built room like the Hope Diamond in the Smithsonian Institution.

Among the outbuildings on the property were two adjoining sheds which he thought might serve his purpose. Jim took Emily along on an inspection tour although she didn't understand why they would want to look in the empty sheds. Jim tried to explain but to no avail. He contemplated the space. The two sheds shared the same roof but inside were separated by a wall. He thought that the structure must once have been a single space but had been divided by a previous owner. There was nothing in the sheds now and hadn't been in the thirty years Jim and Emily had lived at the old farmhouse. In fact it had been years since

Jim had opened the door of either, and when he did all there was to be seen were octogenarian spiders in their ancient webs, and a liberal tonnage of dust.

Jim called in a local contractor he knew, an irascible old man named Pete Saunders, to inspect the shed he had selected, and to make the changes he wanted for storage and display. Pete said that the wooden floor was so worn it probably wouldn't support a lot of weight because it was built over what might once have been a root cellar. Sure enough, a search revealed a space which ran under both sheds. It was a simple dirt cellar, and with the aid of a flashlight they saw that part of it had fallen in. Pete's advice to Jim was to take up the planks, fill in the cellar, and install a concrete floor, or find somewhere else to store his handiwork.

The next week work started on the conversion of the shed, and Jim began braiding for the largest ball of braided string in the world. Word about these two enterprises soon got around the village. People began to drop by to see how things were progressing; to wish him luck, and Jim was always pleased to see them, but one of these visitors was not so welcome. Jim didn't know the woman, so supposed that she had come to see how he was doing but alas, Miss Alison Fairweather was not interested in string, braided or unbraided. Miss Fairweather was from Social Services.

With all the activity engendered by Jim's new pastime it had got to the ears of Social Services that Emily Sinclair was suffering from dementia and that she had no family but a very elderly, eccentric husband to look after her. There were some, acting with the best intentions, who said that Jim himself needed looking after and was not fit to be her guardian. Miss Fairweather had come to make an evaluation.

Jim was puzzled but not unduly concerned. He and Emily were managing perfectly well. He was able to take care of her, the domestic chores, and his hobby without any problem. He thought it a little presumptuous of Miss Fairweather to ask to see over the house, and to poke into the kitchen cupboards, and the fridge and the pantry, but he allowed her to do so. She checked the bathroom as well. There were three bathrooms in the house but Jim had decided that they would use only one to save on cleaning chores. Miss Fairweather also sat down with Emily, talking to her and taking notes. She stayed for over an hour, and left without giving Jim any notion of what assessment she had made. He was so unconcerned by this development that he did not mention it to anyone.

Government wheels move slowly and as the days passed Jim forgot about Miss Fairweather in the excitement of the conversion of the shed into what he now referred to as his gallery. The concrete floor was poured. Electricity was hooked up. He got rid of the window because he didn't want thieves breaking in to steal his treasures, so it was boarded up and concealed behind the refinished walls. Shelves were built to accommodate his smaller braided balls. Because he was convinced that burglars from around the world would be drawn to Hemmingford by the lure of his treasures he secured the door with a strong lock. When the gallery was ready Emily helped him move all the finished braided balls into it and got a great deal of pleasure from arranging them.

Jim changed his *modus operandi* for the production of the largest braided ball in the world. Until then whenever he had a length of braided string finished he would wind it onto the ball which was under construction. When that ball reached the size he liked he would add it to the collection. He handled the new project differently. Realizing that at a certain point the ball would become so heavy that he would not be able to move it, he resolved to wind it to a certain size, then remove it to the gallery and finish it there.

Half the string needed for Jim's record-breaking ball was already braided when Miss Fairweather returned with the documentation which would transfer Emily from his care to that of the Social Services. Sitting in the dining room with the official papers spread out on the table in front of her, Miss Fairweather briskly explained the procedures which would ensue. Jim hadn't, at first, understood why Miss Fairweather was there but as soon as she began talking about removing Emily to some facility in Manchester, Jim said he was taking Emily up to her room to rest. That wouldn't be possible, Miss Fair-weather informed him officiously, it was necessary that Emily be a party to her fate. No protest from Jim would stop Miss Fairweather's stream of official jargon. She was so concise and assertive about what was going to happen it began to dawn on Emily herself, and as Jim looked on in horror, tears began to roll down his wife's cheeks. In a fury he abruptly ended the interview and showed Miss Fairweather the door. She did not go quietly. She was affronted and aggressive, informing Jim as he hustled her out, that he could expect her back – with support!

There was no need for her to come back with or without support because the next day Emily was found dead in the gurgling stream which ran through the Sinclair property. The coroner for the district, who had a law practice in Portsmouth, and who was an enthusiastic supporter of Jim's braided ball aspirations, returned a verdict of accidental death, even though both he and Jim guessed otherwise.

The whole community gathered to support Jim in his tragic loss. After the funeral string poured in, and Jim continued to work diligently, keeping his goal firmly in mind. Not long after Emily's funeral Jim estimated that he had enough string braided to make a sphere the size of a demolition ball. He began rolling and it wasn't very long before he had to heave the ball onto his little red wagon and drag it over to his gallery before continuing. He wrestled it into the middle of the new concrete floor from where he would be able to move it this way and that as he wound it to its allotted size. Then he was struck by a shattering thought. He called Peter Saunders.

The old man was amazed. "Have you finished that gigantic ball all ready?"

Jim said no, he'd barely started, but he now realized that he could end up like the man who built a boat in his basement, then couldn't get it out. If he managed to make the ball as large as he hoped he would never get it out of his gallery. He wanted Pete to fix up the adjoining shed but without the shelves, and install double doors. This new space would be only for the winding and display of his unique braided ball. All the rest of his work would remain in Gallery One.

Pete shook his head in puzzlement. He didn't understand Jim's obsession with braiding string. Villagers had told him that what Jim was able to do with the braided string was quite extraordinary, and besides, he needed something with which to occupy himself now that Emily was gone. So Pete got busy with renovating the second shed, and Jim awaited the moment when he could transfer his potentially record-breaking ball into it.

The second shed, now known as Gallery Two was as successful as Gallery One. Jim had decided to keep the window in this space. No thief could lift the braided ball which would repose in that room, so there would be no point in breaking in through the window. The double-doors, however, were fitted with a hefty lock. Jim made quite a little ceremony of the opening of his new gallery. He invited friends and neighbours over for a drink, and to show off the refurbished sheds, and the progress of his newest ball.

As Joan said to her husband when they returned home, thank God for Jim's absorption in his hobby, eccentric though it may seem, for without it he would surely never have been able to deal with Emily's death.

Once settled in Gallery Two Jim charged ahead with winding his championship ball. The question very soon became just how far should he go with it? When it got to the size of a demolition ball he called in those of his friends who had urged him to go for a place in the Guinness Book of World Records. Was the ball, in their estimation, large enough? The consensus was yes, the ball was large enough, and it was resolved that it should be exhibited at the Hillsborough County Fair which was coming up the following week. The next question was how was this ball, whose weight could not be estimated by the gathered group, to be moved. As in everything, the villagers rallied around. Joan's husband offered the use of his heavy-duty pick-up to transport it if someone could come up with a means of getting the ball into it. Well, that was easy enough. Hemmingford Hardware used forklifts.

Jim's huge braided sphere was the conversational piece of the fair, far outranking Big Boris, a three thousand five hundred pound Brown Swiss bull, the usual main attraction. Awesome was the adjective most used to describe the sphere, not only for its curiosity value and size, but for its beauty. Every braid was mathematically even and lump free, and the ball itself was a perfect sphere. Jim had developed a mastery and skill which could be duplicated by very few. And nobody at the Fair asked what the braided ball was for.

An outcome of the exhibition at the Hillsborough County Fair was a request from Merrimack County to borrow the ball to put on display at their Fair, and following that Coos County wanted it, and so for the next few weeks it was circulating around the State. It was still away when Jim's doorbell rang one late October morning, crisp enough to suggest that snow was on the way.

"Mr. Sinclair?"

"Yes," Jim agreed with an air of suspicion. The last time a stranger had appeared on his doorstep it had presaged trouble of major dimensions, and he didn't know this man.

"My name is Lloyd Bennett. I wonder if I might have a word?"

A thought struck Jim and his mood lifted. "Have you come

about the ball?"

Lloyd Bennett frowned. "The what?"

"About entering it into the Guinness Book of World Records."

The other man's confusion deepened. "I'm sorry, I don't know what you mean. I'm from Social Services."

In the blink of an eyelid Jim's demeanor changed. His face darkened and every muscle in his body tensed. "What do you want?"

"I'd like to ask you a couple of questions."

"Is that so? Well, I have nothing to say to you." Jim began to close the door.

Lloyd Bennett thrust out an arm to stay its progress. "Mr. Sinclair, do you remember Miss Fairweather?"

"I'm not likely to forget her, am I?"

"Can you tell me the last time you saw her?"

Jim eased his pressure on the door. "What?"

"She's missing."

"Missing?" Jim echoed, then shrugged. "So what?"

"We are checking on when she was last seen, and it seems that around about that time she was due to come here to discuss the disposition of your wife."

"My wife is dead."

"Yes. We – er – received notification. I'm sorry."

"Are you?"

"Mr. Sinclair, can you confirm that Miss Fairweather came here on - " He consulted the clipboard he had in his hand and read out a date.

"No, I can't," Jim snapped. "And I'll thank you to leave me alone." And with that he pushed the door shut.

The next day Joan Bishop came around. Mr. Bennett, it seemed, had made his way over to see her after being given short shrift by Jim.

"Damned nerve coming around here after what they did to

Emily," Jim exclaimed wrathfully. He banged the teapot fiercely on the table.

Joan had brought some shortbread she had baked so they ate that with their tea.

Joan was surprised. She hadn't known that Social Services had even been to see Jim about Emily. "Mr. Bennett claims," she ventured. "That this Miss Fairweather has not been seen since the last time she was scheduled to come here about Emily."

"Well, that's not my fault, is it? I'm not her keeper."

"When was that, do you remember?"

"No."

"The date he mentioned to me would have been a few days after Emily died."

"She wouldn't have come here then, there was no need for her to, was there? Not with Emily gone."

"That's what I told him."

The next person who arrived on Jim's doorstep in search of Miss Fairweather was not so easily put off. This was a state trooper answering a complaint by Social Services.

Miss Fairweather was missing. Her whereabouts were unknown. Her family in New Mexico had been contacted and were unaware of where she was or where she might have gone. They hadn't heard from her for a few weeks but that was not unusual. She had lived and worked in the East for a number of years. She telephoned home quite frequently but not in any regular way. The family was, of course, very worried now that she seemed to have disappeared.

Jim was churlish with the trooper. "I told the other guy who came here, I don't know anything about her."

The towering law officer was not aggressive but he wasn't going away either. "I think you'd better let me in so we can have a talk, Mr. Sinclair."

Once in the hall the officer introduced himself, "My name is Molloy. Trooper Molloy."

Jim led the way into the kitchen. "You want some coffee? It's fresh."

The trooper sat at the kitchen table and accepted coffee, sugar and cream. "Now, Mr. Sinclair, Miss Fairweather was an evaluator for Social Services."

"You don't have to tell me that."

Molloy ignored Jim's attitude. "And as such she kept notes. According to these notes she was coming here on the day she disappeared."

Jim stirred his coffee. "That doesn't mean she did."

"We found her car in Manchester."

"So why aren't you looking for her there?"

"It's impounded there. It was found abandoned in Exeter."

Jim looked wise. "Probably stolen by one of those students at the Academy."

"That's always a possibility. The fact remains, Mr. Sinclair, she was supposed to see you that day."

"Well, she didn't get here."

Molloy gave him a long, hard look. "According to her notes you were very much opposed to Social Services stepping in to take care of your wife."

"Damn right! There was no need for them to interfere. I was looking after Emily."

"It was reported that Mrs. Sinclair had wandered away on her own more than once."

"I was taking care of that."

"Didn't she wander away to her death, Mr. Sinclair?"

Jim's face paled and tears welled in his eyes. "Have you come here to torment me?"

"I've come to see if you can help me find Miss Fairweather."

"Then you're doomed to disappointment."

"You'll understand the concern, Mr. Sinclair. She came here that day and hasn't been seen since."

"If she came here that day I didn't see her."

"Were you away from home?"

"I was in and out, back and forth, like always."

Molloy became firmer. "We are considering the possibility of foul play."

"And you're looking at me?" Jim eyed the trooper disdainfully. "I'm seventy-five years old and Social Services seemed to think I am too frail to care for my wife. Does it appear to you as if I could kill someone and dispose of the body?"

The trooper conceded that the old man had a point, but he also had the only motive anyone could come up with for murdering Miss Fairweather, who was definitely due to be in Hemmingford the last day she was seen, and whose car had been abandoned in Exeter which was only a few miles away. If the car had been reported stolen they would have got to it sooner but only the later investigation into Miss Fairweather's disappearance turned it up in the impound lot in Manchester where it had been towed.

"Mr. Sinclair, I'm going to have to ask you to allow me to search your property."

Jim didn't reply immediately, then gave a deep sigh and nodded. "Go ahead."

"Thank you."

Of course Molloy found nothing. He was very intrigued by the braided balls, and he stopped off outside the village for coffee at Dunkin' Donuts on his way back to Concord to see what scraps of gossip he could pick up about Jim Sinclair. There he heard all about the construction of the gigantic ball which was more than likely going to be included in the Guinness Book of World Records.

"Where is that ball now?" Molloy asked.

Someone hazarded a guess, "Must still be in Dover if Jim don't have it back home."

"And how big is it?"

"Oh, they reckon about the size of a demolition ball, eh, Al?"

Another man nodded wisely. "Must be all of that."

Trooper Molloy and his partner Rick Beatty strolled around the Dover County Winter Fair garnering somewhat puzzled looks from the patrons who were not used to a police presence at this rural event. When the officers came to the specially built platform on which Jim Sinclair's gargantuan braided ball was displayed they stood as much in awe of it as everyone else. It seemed unbelievable that one man had braided all that string much less actually rolled it into that perfect sphere.

The printed legend, giving information about the ball, stated that Jim Sinclair, at the age of seventy-five had constructed the ball alone, and that it was to be submitted to the Guinness Book of World Records as the largest braided ball in the world.

Beatty gave a snorting laugh. "Probably the only one."

"Alone," Molloy pondered. "He rolled that ball all by himself." And he speculated silently that Jim had to be stronger than he looked.

"Curious sort of hobby," Beatty mused.

"Very," Molloy responded grimly.

The organizers of the Fair were not happy when Molloy informed them that the braided ball was to be taken into police custody. It was proving to be a huge attraction. Those locals who had no interest in agriculture and normally wouldn't attend the Fair poured into the hockey arena to have a look at this unusual object, mainly so that they could later boast that they had a connection with something featured in the Guinness Book of World Records. Hundreds of snapshots were taken in front of it. A story and a photograph had appeared in the local papers. The television station had asked for an interview with Jim. Then suddenly the ball was gone, ignominiously hauled off by the police in a truck to the detachment at Concord.

It took much less time to unwind the braided ball than it took Jim to roll it up, but all the while the officers assigned to dismantle it marveled that Jim had managed to construct it in the first place. As the pile of braided string grew and the size of the ball diminished, tension in the detachment heightened. Hardened police officers they may have been but the expectation of what Molloy believed they would find in the centre of the ball was not doing their digestion any good.

News that his giant braided ball was no more was eventually reported to Jim by Officers Molloy and Beatty in person. They had the braided string from the unraveled ball with them. It filled the entire back of the cruiser and also the trunk. Jim stared at in dismay. "Not a lot going on in your barracks, I reckon."

"We were looking for something, Mr. Sinclair."

"What did you expect to find in my braided ball?"

"There's a woman missing."

Jim let out a burst of derisive laughter. "And you thought she was in the middle of my braided ball? If I'd been able to accomplish that I would certainly deserve to be in the Guinness Book. I don't reckon anyone would have ever broken that record!"

The law officers were not amused. "Where would you like us to put the braided string, Mr. Sinclair?"

"Well, seeing as how I've got to start rolling it up again you'd better put it where I'll be working on it." He pointed across the property. "Over there, in my gallery alongside the fence. The one with the double doors. It's locked so you'll have to wait till I get there."

Molloy drove the vehicle slowly towards the sheds. Jim followed behind. He unlocked the doors of Gallery Two and watched while the troopers heaved the massive tangle of braided string out of their vehicle and piled it onto the smooth new concrete floor which had been poured not so long ago. It was Jim who had prepared this shed for its new floor himself much as Pete's men had prepared the other shed. It was Jim who had taken up the broken floorboards and filled in the old root cellar with sand and gravel transported there in the shovel of his Bobcat from another part of the property. When it was finished and tamped down firmly it made a wonderfully solid foundation for the new sub-floor and the thick layer of concrete he allowed Pete's men to lay on top of it. They did a fine job.

Jim stood in the doorway watching the prowl car disappearing down the drive, and he smiled.

FRESH BLOOD

Kent made it a practice never to open the door without knowing who was there, and only certain people were admitted to the house after nightfall — people in whom he had a special interest and who had a special interest in him. He wasn't expecting anyone, but sometimes they came without calling ahead.

He was a portly man, no, he was, well, fat. He'd been fat all his fifty-five years. He had a large, round, moon face and bulging, pale-blue eyes. What was left of his light hair lay like duck down on his pink pate. That night he was dressed in a blue cashmere sweater, and his cords were from Ralph Lauren. His house was also Ralph Lauren. Kent was rich. He'd started life as a window dresser, now he was a successful Broadway set designer and a professional interior decorator.

When the ring came again, he puffed his way to the front door. The bell shrilled again as he looked through the peephole. *My God!* He recoiled. *My God!* Moving cautiously forward he looked again, and what he saw took his breath away.

Strangers! Strangers on my doorstep. He shuddered. *Don't let them in!* But the more he looked at her the less resolute he became. How could anyone resist opening the door to such beauty?

"I'm so sorry." Ashley's breathy voice conjured up soft nights under a southern moon, even to a man who was old enough to be her father. "We seem to be lost." She was shivering in her knee-length wolf fur coat. Long legs in alluring pale stockings were lengthened even more by her high-heeled flesh-toned Manolo Blahniks. "Do you think we could use the phone?"

The man beside her, also strikingly good-looking, in a trench coat with the collar turned up against the bleak weather gave Kent a look as beseeching as hers. Kent felt a strange, irresistible pull to allow them in, mixed with a sense of caution. But when he looked past them and saw the sleek outline of their gleaming BMW, he needed no more reassurance.

Ashley practically collapsed into the hall, thanking him profusely. Immediately Kent experienced a *frisson* – a faint stirring, a sense of recognition, no, not from the fair curls tumbling about her heart-shaped face or from her porcelain-pale complexion or the cornflower eyes ringed in dark lashes... nothing to do with her looks.....it was not so much a sense of recognition as a feeling of *déjà vu*, a lingering remnant of..."Do I know you?"

"Everyone thinks she's Nicole Kidman," her companion informed him amiably. "She isn't Nicole, but she is an actress."

"Actor," Ashley corrected.

The man winked at Kent and introduced himself. "Bruce Spence."

"Kent Radcliffe," Kent returned.

Ashley leaned forward and held out her hand, "Ashley Woodbridge. We're sorry to disturb you, but ..." She shrugged her pretty shoulders.

"Could we use your phone?" Bruce appealed fetchingly. "We're late for a party, and we seem to be out of our cell phone range."

"Are you? I wouldn't know. I hate the things." Kent pointed across the foyer. "There's a phone right there or in the kitchen, if you prefer," he offered, then saying in response to Ashley's shivering. "It's warmer in the kitchen."

"I'll use this one," Bruce said.

"And you'll come into the kitchen," Kent ordered the young woman, with self-conscious gallantry. He gestured ahead, indicating the way. "These old houses tend to be draughty."

"Is it old?" she asked, allowing herself to be led along. "It seems quite modern to me."

Kent nodded, proudly, "It's been totally renovated, to my specs."

"Old cellars and Priest's Holes dispensed with?" she laughed.

He ushered her into the comfortable Provencal-style kitchen. "I retained the cellars. Thought they might come in handy one day. Can I offer you some refreshment? Wine, perhaps?"

"That would be nice."

He went to the wine rack and pulled out a bottle of Medoc. "Is Bruce an actor, too?"

"He directs." She slipped out of her fur coat.

Kent's eyes started out of his head at what she was wearing, or nearly wearing, beneath the coat; a knee-length sheath of mother-of-pearl sequins on nude soufflé, giving the false impression that the only things covering her flesh were the spangles. *Marilyn Monroe singing happy birthday Mr. President.* Seeing his look Ashley's eyelashes fluttered coyly. "We're on our way to a wrap party. At least, we were, but we took a wrong turn somewhere."

Bruce tapped on the open kitchen door.

Kent started and began moving again. "Come in. Come in." He slid three stem glasses from the rack under a hanging cupboard and filled them with wine.

"Where exactly are we, Kent?" Ashley asked sweetly.

"Northwoods."

"Northwoods? Is that the name of this house or the town?"

"Village. Population five thousand. Where were you heading?"

"Richmond."

"Ah, then you're nowhere near." As he handed her the wine Kent was again seized by that unaccountable sense of familiarity. "Where are you from?"

"L.A."

L.A.? He'd never been to Los Angeles. He'd never been within five hundred miles of Los Angeles.

Bruce shrugged off his trench and tossed it aside. He accepted his wine from Kent with a warm smile and sat next to Ashley at the large pine table.

"From L.A.," Kent echoed. "How did you manage to get this far off course?"

Ashley giggled. "We haven't driven from L.A.! We shot the movie at Lake Placid."

"Ah!" Kent nodded as if this made sense then frowned. "Northwoods is not en route from Lake Placid to Richmond."

"Tell me about it!" Ashley cast a sideways glance at Bruce which was not kind. "But Bruce knew best, as always. Did you reach Al?"

"Yes. God knows how we got here. He says we're so far off track we might as well give up the idea of going there tonight."

"What? Oh, shit! I was looking forward to that party." Her face turned sulky. "I wish you'd listened to me, Bruce. I told you we were going in the wrong direction."

Bruce reached out and stroked her cheek with the back of his fingers. "Never mind, darling. We may be lost but we've found a new friend."

That notion seemed to mollify her. She turned to smile at Kent over the rim of her glass, her eyes half-closed. If Kent been asked to describe that look he would have said, smoldering, but that was ridiculous. Why would a captivating young woman in the prime of life, a movie star, make eyes at him, an old, slightly overweight nobody? He gulped some of his wine, trying to compose himself, not too successfully. He blushed and moved uncomfortably, searching for something brilliant to say. "Here I was, sitting alone, longing for some company - " he babbled untruthfully, " - willing someone special to drop by, and suddenly the night is brightened by two beautiful individuals from the land of make believe."

"So you *did* will us here." Ashley favoured him with another smoky look.

"Like a spider hoping for a fly." Bruce lifted his glass in a salute and drank.

"Bruce!" Ashley gasped. "That's not very nice." She shot Kent an uneasy look, which dissolved into a radiant smile. "Don't take any notice of him."

"What? Oh no, no!" Bruce was charmingly apologetic. "I didn't mean it like that. Not at all. I was just thinking how lonely spiders must get sitting in the middle of those webs all day."

"I can't imagine why you would be thinking of spiders at all." Ashley snapped. She turned to Kent and softened. "Do you live here alone?"

"Yes, my - " His eyes shifted away. "My wife died two months ago."

"Oh, I'm sorry. I shouldn't have pried. Was she sick?"

"I - didn't think so." He hesitated. "It was all very unexpected."

"We're so sorry to hear that, aren't we, Bruce?" Ashley prompted him.

"Of course we are." For a brief moment his handsome face registered a sort of sorrow then lit up with a sly hint of amusement. His dark eyes danced. His warmth seemed to reach out and encompass Kent who felt slightly disconcerted.

In a few short minutes these alluring visitors had drawn him to them, engaged him as a friend. Was that why he thought he knew them?

"What's the name of the film you were shooting?" Kent asked. "I must make sure to see it when it's released."

"Fresh Blood." Bruce told him with a quirky grin. "It's a thriller with a twist."

"What's the twist?"

"Ah, now that would be telling."

"And now we're missing the wrap party," Ashley pouted. "I was really looking forward to that."

"As if it's likely to be any different from every other show biz bash," Bruce murmured to Kent with a conspiratorial look, surely attempting, it struck Kent, to claim him as an ally in this little tussle with Ashley.

"Except that I'm the star, so it's my duty to be there! Isn't it Kent?" she appealed. Her beguiling eyes fastened on him willing him to side with her.

There was a sudden stillness in the air, sense of expectancy, of waiting.

Kent's mind was in a whirl. Was he to referee their dispute? No! No! It was impossible! He couldn't support one against the other. Each one had a fascinating attraction — Ashley's beauty, Bruce's charm. And anyway, these people were strangers.

Weren't they?

Bruce broke the tension with a soft laugh, "Don't mind us, Kent. We're being naughty, and we're not going to tease you anymore. Come on, Ash, we have to find our way home. Do you have a map of this area I could look at, Kent?"

"Yes, I have, but now where is it?" Dizzily, Kent rose and stood, trying to collect himself. "Things have become a bit disorganized since...since Fran...ah, in the study, I think."

It only took a minute and he was back, dropping the map on the table in front of Bruce. Ashley was over at wall telephone.

"I'm going to call Al back and get proper directions," she said and then frowned. "That's funny." She began clicking the phone cradle up and down.

"What's the matter?" Kent asked.

"The telephone isn't working."

"It isn't?" Kent went over and took the receiver from her. He also jiggled the cradle. "No, you're right. That's a bit strange." He hung up and went to the window. "Oh my God, it's started to snow. The lines must be down somewhere."

"Snow couldn't have knocked the phones out," Ashley protested.

Bruce joined Kent at the window and peered into the darkness. "Of course it could, darling, don't be so Hollywood. This snow is real, and you know what?" Bruce said with sudden resolution. "If it's going to be a stormy night, we should get going while we still can."

"No," Kent fussed. "You don't want to take off in the dark and the snow. You've already gotten lost once. It's too risky. I've plenty of room. Stay and keep me company. You can start out fresh in the morning." He caught Ashley's unconvinced look which he took to mean she thought it too much trouble for him, and continued encouragingly. "Fran and I were always ready for guests. She loved company. You can have your pick. There's even space in the wine cellar if that appeals to you," he chuckled trying to lighten the mood.

"Thank you, you're very kind, but we must go." Bruce drained his glass and put it beside the sink. "We'll be fine. I've checked the map, and the car is reliable. It ought to be - " he chirped, "-for what it cost. No problem, Kent."

But Ashley was jittery. "Kent, I need to wash my hands before we go."

"What? Oh, of course. There's a powder room just off the foyer."

She picked up her evening purse and went to the door.

Scanning the dimly lit hall she asked, "Where?"

"To the right of the front door."

Hesitating, she blinked into the gloom. "You know," she began a little breathlessly. "I have an irrational fear of closed doors. I think it comes from reading about David Niven's first wife, was her name Poppy? No, Primrose. They were at a Hollywood party in one of those Beverly Hills mansions in the nineteen-forties — I think it was the forties. Anyway, the guests were playing a game of Murder and when they were looking for places to hide, Primrose opened a door off the hall thinking it was a closet and stepped inside. It turned out to be the top of a flight of unlighted stairs to the basement. She tumbled down and died."

"Honey, I'm sure that's of no interest to Kent," Bruce reproached her.

"But is it true?" Kent asked, intrigued.

"That's what I read." She gave him a beseeching look. "So, will you please show me which door it is?"

Kent shrugged and laughed. "Right this way."

"Is this going to take long?" Bruce asked with an exaggerated sigh.

"No more than usual!" Ashley returned snippily.

"Oh God!" With a wry grin at Kent, Bruce shrugged and folding his arms leaned back against the kitchen counter.

Kent was a little surprised when Ashley pulled the kitchen door closed behind them, and once in the hall she didn't seem to need him to lead the way. She went tap-tap-tapping over the parquet in her high heels then startled him by suddenly darting through the study door.

"No," Kent said. "That's not the - "

"I know that!" Ashley hissed. "Come in here, quick!"

Perplexed, he followed her into the study and was astonished when she also closed that door behind them. "What's - " He broke off as she suddenly turned and grasped his upper arms with fingers like little steel pincers.

"Kent, you've got to help me!"

"Help you do what?" His eyes popped.

"Get away!"

"I've given you the map."

"I'm not talking about the stupid map!" She let go of him with an agitated push so hard that he almost fell. Twisting away she clasped her arms around her body and bent over as if she had a terrible stomach ache.

Kent stared at her, confused and baffled. His concern was tinged with apprehension. "What's the matter? Are you sick?"

"No! Listen, you've got to help me, please!" She straightened and looked past him at the door, apparently almost too frightened to confide in him, then hissed, "Bruce is going to kill me."

"What?" Kent's jaw dropped. "Kill you? Is that what you said?"

"For God's sake concentrate, Kent. He's going to kill me!"

"But people just don't - " He was stupefied.

"Yes, they do! People kill each other all the time, you idiot, that's why we make movies about it."

"But he's just been drinking wine with us."

"Oh God! Let me tell you what's going to happen, Kent." Her breath snagged in her throat and she pressed a hand against her breast. "Between now and midnight Bruce Spence is going to murder me for my money. OK?"

"Your money?"

"We're in the middle of a divorce, and he doesn't want to split our assets. He wants it all."

"Is that what he says?"

"No, of course not!" She looked at him as though he were an imbecile. "But I can read him like a book, and there's no way we are lost. He planned this!" She jumped at Kent, clutching his shoulders and shaking him. "He's going to kill us both! He'll set it up to look as though I drove out here because we're having an affair."

"What?"

"He'll make it look as though we had an assignation and he followed me here and found us in a compromising situation! He will say you attacked him and he killed you in self-defense, and that I - "

Kent blundered towards the desk. "I'm going to call the police!"

"You can't. You know you can't! The phone is dead! He must have done that when he asked to use it. He wasn't calling Al, he was disabling the phone."

"No!" Kent snatched up the receiver not wanting to believe her, but she was right, the phone was still dead. Wildly he hit the cradle again and again, gripped by a sudden terror.

She grabbed his arm. "Do you have a gun?"

What? He screeched to himself. "No, of course I don't have a fucking gun!"

"But you have knives in the kitchen!"

Knives in the kitchen — Bruce is in the kitchen!

"Don't you!" she exhorted.

"Yes, there are knives!" Kent broke down. He began to shake. Tears welled. He was not a violent man. He was not a wicked man. He was just a lonely man whose beloved wife had died and left him alone. *Why did I let these people in?* He didn't understand anything, anything at all. They had come to his house in what seemed like a dream and now it was a nightmare!

Suddenly, the study door swung open, and Kent nearly jumped out of his skin, uttering a shriek of alarm.

"What's going on?" Bruce exclaimed, staring from one to the other of them.

"Just checking the phone again," Ashley told him, her expression carefully guarded.

But Bruce was staring at Kent. "Are you all right? You look like you're having a heart attack."

"I'm - fine, really. It's nothing, thanks," Kent panted.

"Okay, well, I know where we took a wrong turn. I've got it all worked out now. Come on, darling, let's go. We don't want to get stuck in the snow." As he moved towards Ashley both she and Kent cowered away from him.

"Maybe Kent was right," she said nervously. "We should stay the night. We could get in a terrible accident."

Bruce smiled glancing at Kent drawing him into the conspiracy again, these women! He moved to Ashley and put an arm around her shoulder. "It'll be fine." He squeezed her to him.

She tried to pull away. "I'm not ready to go yet."

"Darling?" Bruce dipped his head to look into her face. "Are you okay?"

"I'm...I'm not feeling well."

"All the more reason for us to leave now."

"But Kent wants us to stay."

Bruce regarded Kent, an oblique look from under half-closed lids, which made Kent's flesh creep. "He was just being polite." Bruce returned his attention to Ashley, his tone charming and persuasive. "Come on, darling, get your coat."

Still Ashley resisted. "We could get stuck in the snow miles from nowhere and freeze to death."

"Don't be silly. Kent will give us his map."

"Oh, yes, take it! Take it! Oh, yes, please take it," Kent exclaimed with unflattering eagerness, now as anxious to get rid of them as he had been to have them stay. "No problem."

Still Ashley did not want to give in. "It's not safe for us to go, Bruce. The cell phone doesn't work. What would we do if something happened? And Kent wants us to stay, don't you, Kent?"

No! No! Please go! Kent stood there willing them away.

"Darling, we really need to get home." As Bruce urged her past Kent, she mouthed 'help me,' but he turned the other way.

Kent followed them into the hall, and when Bruce asked for their coats, he skittered into the kitchen and fetched them. Unable to control his impatience Kent stood fidgeting while Bruce first shrugged into his trench and then helped Ashley on with her fur. At last they were ready.

"Thanks so much for your hospitality, Kent." Bruce held out a hand, his smile disarming. "Don't forget to see 'Fresh Blood'."

"No, I won't," Kent muttered, avoiding Ashley's entreating expression.

When the door closed behind them, Kent thrust the bolts, leaned back against it and let out a long sigh of relief.

Deliverance!

The experience had exhausted him, but now he felt safe, though a little uncertain about Ashley. She was just being melodramatic, wasn't she? She wasn't really in any danger? No, of course not. He brushed any doubt away elated to be on his own, and made sure he would remain so by going around checking every lock on both the doors and windows. He closed all the curtains, banishing the night and any further danger. In the kitchen there was still a lingering of the woman's elusive essence, which as it assailed him, evoked in him that same twinge of recognition as when he had first seen the couple. But he didn't know them. They had never met before. Anyway! They were gone now and no-one would ever know they had ever been there. Thinking of that Kent hurried to wash the glasses, then polished and hung them back on the rack. There. All evidence gone. He poured himself another glass of wine and flushed his visitors out of his mind.

Now what? Had Fran been there they would have sat and companionably read together or maybe watched something on television. He could do that now on his own, but, well, it wasn't the same without her. He was restless and at the same time drained of emotional energy, but not tired. For a while he prowled about shaking off the lingering misgivings, until finally gathering up his book and a few magazines to take upstairs with him.

He was reading in bed when the house rang with the shrill sound of the doorbell. His heart lurched. He lay there for the longest time, gasping for breath, riveted to the bed, but the ringing persisted. Eventually he got up and went to the window, carefully moving the heavy drape, just a smidgen. Snow was still coming down in large heavy flakes and settling.

Oh Christ! The BMW was in the drive!

He started to shiver convulsively. As he stood looking down from the darkened window, a figure moved out from under the porch. He watched it bend down to pick up some pebbles from the drive and then look up. His relief was palpable when he saw that it was Ashley. Still alive! But a second later that relief was followed by apprehension.

What were they doing back again?

He watched as Ashley tossed the stones up towards his window. They didn't hit but spattered down again. Then her sweet voice rose to him.

"It's Ashley, Kent! Kent! Open the door!"

His mind was a wild tangle. He didn't want to respond, but she was out there in the snow in her little strappy shoes. And she looked so helpless, so heavenly.

"Don't worry, Bruce isn't here!" she cried.

He opened the window a crack. "What? Where is he? What are you doing here?"

"Please! Come down and open the door."

He didn't move. "Where's Bruce?" He squinted into the darkness.

"For God's sake, Kent, please come down and let me in, I'll freeze to death!"

Yes, she would. He left the window and went to his dumb valet. He slipped his pants on over his pajama bottoms and went down stairs. As soon as he opened the door, Ashley fell breathlessly into his arms in a swirl of snow.

"What's happened?" He looked past her into the night. "Where's Bruce?"

She pulled him inside and slammed the door. "He had to stop the car and get out to check a fork in the road so I seized the opportunity."

Icy tentacles crept down Kent's spine. "What do you mean?" he whispered.

"Well, I couldn't wait for him to murder me, could I?" She suddenly lunged at him and buried her head in his chest.

"For chrissake, what have you done to Bruce?" He pushed her away from him. He hated the feel of her wet fur coat. He hated the smell of her perfume.

"You've got to come with me, Kent."

"No," he managed to stutter as he backed away from her.

"You have to help me move him."

"Move him? I don't know what you mean."

"We have to make it look like an accident. I couldn't do it alone even if I were dressed for the snow. He's much too heavy." She inched closer. "And afterwards we'll come back here...and..." Her bewitching smile glowed up at him. "You aren't going to let me go back there by myself?" She gave him the sweetest little kiss. "C'mon now, where's your coat? Do you have a parka, some gum boots and warm socks? Where are your keys?"

He told her as if he were in a dream. She helped him on with his clothes. He was suddenly outside. Somewhere in the night a dog howled. "Oh listen," Ashley cooed. "I love that sound."

With her arm through his she hustled him to the car. He marveled at how strong she seemed to be as she pushed him into the passenger seat. The door slammed. In a fraction of a second she was behind the wheel, and they were tearing down the snow covered drive.

Kent clung to the door handle. "Maybe we should just call the police. You could tell them he had a heart attack - "

"What?" She cut him off, her tone withering. "I hit him over the head with a tire wrench!" She gave a short laugh and shook her head.

Ashley drove maniacally fast for several miles then cut the speed and began edging her way slowly along, searching the road ahead as the wipers swished back and forth. The headlights illuminated very little else but the falling snow. "Wouldn't it be hysterical if I couldn't find him again," she giggled.

Kent sat still as a stone, terrified.

She suddenly pointed as a huge maple came into view. "There! It happened by that tree. Right there," she exclaimed.

Kent leaned forward peering into the darkness trying to spot Bruce, but the snowfall was too dense. "I can't see a thing."

"He's somewhere over there," Ashley said, stopping the car.

Taking the flashlight she got out and left Kent in the passenger seat, hugging himself, trying to still the shaking of his stressed body. For one moment, he thought about driving off and leaving her there, but even self-preservation did not totally banish his instinct to protect a fragile woman. So he forced himself to watch her as she searched for Bruce in the snow. Where they had stopped was hardly more than a lane, very narrow, with deep ditches on either side. As he watched she half-slid into one of the ditches and began scrabbling around in the undergrowth and accumulating snow.

How could she do that in her thin dress and those shoes — her coat wasn't big enough to be use, it barely covered her. Why wasn't she freezing?

"He's here," she called out. "Come on, Kent! This will only take a minute."

Oh so reluctantly, Kent climbed out of the car. He made to go forward but something stopped him. He stood hesitating, sure that he could sense something beyond the horror of the dead man in the ditch, something more like - a chilling presence in the eerie blackness of the night.

Just get it over with! He hugged his parka around himself. *Help her to do this thing and let her go.* "Why are you waiting? Come here," Ashley was ordering him

He dragged himself to the edge of the road where she was brushing the snow off a still form in the bottom of the ditch.

"Down here. Come down here. We've got to move him."

"Why can't we just leave him where he is? It looks just like an accident. It looks just like he was hit by a car and thrown into the ditch."

"And how was he supposed to have sustained that head wound! Don't let's go through all that again, we have to get him onto the road."

Kent stumbled and slithered into the ditch. In the beam of her flashlight he saw the body lying there, a small stiff mound, hardly distinguishable from the fresh snow. Reluctantly he scrambled towards it and crouched down to lift it.

Kent's scream was terrible to hear. He staggered backwards and fell down. Frenzied, he scrabbled about trying to save himself from the body - the body who wasn't Bruce! "Fran?!" He screamed out her name.

Two months ago he'd buried beloved wife, so how could she be lying in that snowy ditch? Then an awful possibility filled him with dread. Had Bruce and Ashley taken Fran out of her grave and brought her here to torment him? Shaking with fear, forcing himself not to throw up, he willed himself to look back at the corpse in the snow.

"Aren't you pleased to see her, Kent?"

He stared at Ashley, riveted. She had that look in her eyes, that 'come hither' look which had earlier enchanted him but now repelled him. "It is her, isn't it, Kent?"

He didn't want to look back at Fran but as Ashley's voice encouraged him he couldn't prevent himself, and as he watched, transfixed, Fran's lids began to flicker and her eyes slowly opened.

"Kent!" she smiled. "I knew you would come."

He heard a cry which was his own stricken voice. His heart was thudding so hard against his ribs he thought they would crack. Cold perspiration ran under his collar. He was desperate to run but he could not move.

"Won't you help me up, darling?" the woman in the ditch appealed.

No!

Heaving, clawing at the snow, pressing himself back, gasping for breath he was too shocked and horrified to speak. He was drenched in sweat. Feverish but icy cold. He tried to get away but all he could do was slide about in the snow, his feet catching in the hidden tangle of wild plants and rushes. It wasn't Fran. It couldn't be Fran be because he had seen her in her casket and had stood by her grave as it was lowered into the earth. That nightmare of sickness before her death came flooding back — the sudden change in her demeanor, the falling away of weight until she became a shadow of her self, so pale, resting in a darkened room, flinching away from the doctor, refusing medication until she was suddenly dead at the age of forty.

"Shall I ask Bruce?" Fran wheedled. "He'll help me up. He's a real gentleman."

"Bruce — where's Bruce?" Kent managed to mutter through lips that were literally frozen.

"Right here," a voice said from behind him.

Kent turned so violently he lost his footing and almost crashed down on Fran. He spun away from her, and staring up he saw a figure on the road at the edge of the ditch with his arm around Ashley. He looked ten feet tall. Kent began to whimper. Sensing a movement behind him he fearfully looked over his shoulder. Now Fran was on her feet and moving towards him, shaking off the snow. He backed away but was not fast enough. He was suddenly wrapped in her arms. He struggled but could not free himself from her. Then, he didn't know how, for he had no sensation of his feet moving, she eased him out of the ditch, as though it was the easiest thing in the world and he found himself on the road where he stood moaning and trembling.

Fran was murmuring in his ear, "I thought you would be pleased to see me, darling." Had her voice always been like that? He didn't remember it like that, so low and seductive, vibrating like a cat's throat. And that perfume? Wasn't it the same scent that had lingered in his kitchen after Ashley left? Fran was making strange soothing noises. Purring. Purring. She laid her hands on his cheeks. Hot hands on his cold cheeks.

"I - I am," he said weakly. "I am."

Strange how the moon distorts everything. Black against white — like her eyes, glittering black in the cold, white light.

Kent began to cry.

"Hush, darling. Everything will be all right."

"Do you know these people?" he asked her, piteously.

"Ashley and Bruce? Oh yes, of course. I've known them for… oh, a little over two months. They came to the house looking for directions when you were in town one day." She snuggled her face into his neck, and he was immediately overcome by the most unimaginable terror which he couldn't define. All he knew with absolute certainty was that this woman, this creature, whatever it was, was not Fran, and he had to get away from it! Terrified, sobbing with emotion and exhaustion, he pushed and shoved her, trying to tear himself away, but she did not let go. She had superhuman strength! And then she pressed her face into his neck. Only after she had left a seductive kiss close to his throat did she relax her grip. He jumped away and clapped his hand over the place her mouth had sucked on him, and when he withdrew it, saw the blood. *And, My God there was more dripping from her lips!*

He let out a violent cry and ran, ready to fight off a further attack by Ashley or Bruce, for surely they would try to stop him, but they did nothing, and she, that woman who pretended to be Fran, she didn't follow him either. They all three stood as if turned to stone. Looking at them instead of where he was going, he crashed into the side of the car. The impact shook him to his senses. He scrambled inside. The keys were there! He had to get away from them. They were evil! Evil — whoever they were!

With a great sob of despair he jammed the car into reverse and shot backwards up the narrow lane before swinging recklessly into a u-turn and gunning the engine. How he got home he didn't know and thanked God they had not tried to block the road, forcing him to stop.

Why hadn't they?

He left the car in the driveway and ran to the door. Where were his keys? Did she have his keys? But the door wasn't locked.

Inside! Safe! Safe!

For the second time that night he bolted his door and lay against it panting and crying.

The next day the snow had cleared out leaving a crystal blue sky, and Kent could have taken his usual walk, but he didn't want to step outside the house. He was terrified of showing himself or seeing if the BMW was still there. He thought he still had no telephone service until the phone rang and nearly gave him a heart attack. It was a recorded message from the library to tell him a book he had requested was in. So there probably had been a downed line which was now fixed. Agonized, bewildered, trying to make sense of what he had experienced, his day was spent nervously pacing, jumping at every sound. Possible explanations for his experience of the night flitted around in the disorganization of his mind. Emotionally exhausted, he finally settled on the whole frightening episode being a nightmare, a waking nightmare brought about by the stress he had suffered through Fran's horrible illness and death. It had been a mistake to stay in the house they had loved, and he made up his mind to sell and move into town, closer to his friends. Then totally drained, he fell asleep in an armchair in the study.

The doorbell rang.

But Kent made it a practice never to open the door without knowing who was there, and only certain people were admitted to the house after nightfall — people in whom he had a special interest and who had a special interest in him. He wasn't expecting anyone, but sometimes they came without calling ahead.

When the ring came again, he puffed his way to the front door. The bell shrilled again as he looked through the peephole. *My God!* He recoiled. *My God!* Moving cautiously forward he looked again, and what he saw took his breath away.

Strangers! Strangers on my doorstep. He shuddered. *Don't let them in!* But the more he looked at her the less resolute he became. He couldn't resist opening the door to such beauty.

GRIEVANCE

Sheridan Kelly Hallowell settled herself contentedly in her seat and stared out of the window at the other passengers hurrying to board the train. It was due to leave New Haven's Somerset station in three minutes, and while she waited, Sheridan savored the pleasurable feeling of having once more done her duty. Now she could turn her thoughts to the more desirable activities of her very comfortable life without the hovering specter of guilt. It wasn't that she really minded visiting poor old Eric – rich old Eric – in his nursing home, but the fortnightly visits did seem to shadow her like a slight headache which never quite went away. Most people would say she was an absolute angel to bother to see him at all, never mind with such conscientious regularity. Certainly his two sisters had never shown such loyalty. But then, why would they? He had, under the provisions of their father's will been able to enslave them, to control and manipulate their lives to the point of eventually driving them mad. So it wasn't to be expected that when he, through illness, had become as wretchedly helpless as they had been under his tyranny, they would have a scintilla of sympathy for him.

Though she had never remarried and still lived in the home she had shared with Eric junior, Sheridan did not see her aunts–in–law. Having never, as a result of the machinations of their despotic elder brother, been able to marry, they lived together on a small estate at Martha's Vineyard. By all accounts the place was like some nightmare of a fright movie, rundown and overgrown; although, someone who knew them told Sheridan that the place did, in fact, have a sort of wild beauty. The eccentric ladies had no need to live in such neglect. Indeed, the inside of the rambling stone villa, while dirty and untidy and full of strange looking cats, still revealed evidence of family wealth in the Bellange chairs, the Daniel Pabst sideboards and magnificent Meissen and Sevres – not to mention the Venetian glass and the vermeil which in moments of weakness Sheridan found herself coveting, without, she knew, any hope of success.

Although she knew her father-in-law was a martinet, Sheridan had never personally experienced his wrath. He had been a particularly indulgent parent to his only child, her late husband. This forbearance had understandably not endeared Sheridan and Eric to the two maligned aunts. She recalled that those ladies had been positively gleeful when they learned that Eric junior had been on board Flight 90 out of Washington, D.C. in 1982 and had perished in the crash of that unfortunate airliner when it hit a bridge over the Potomac and sank beneath the river's icy waters.

The shock of that disaster had played on her mother–in–law's mind until that meek lady had swallowed strychnine and writhed to death on the Carrera marble floor of her bathroom. Eric senior, for all his ghastliness, was shattered. He closed the Manhattan triplex and took up reclusive residence in his isolated Newport 'cottage' which during his marriage had stood empty for all but two months of the year. It was there, alone and despised, that he eventually suffered a massive stroke and was subsequently removed to Laurel Park.

Finding herself in charge of the old man and his affairs, Sheridan Hallowell was the one who had made arrangements for him to be accommodated in the luxury nursing home. He needed constant care, which he could certainly have afforded at home, but what was the point of that? He had no family who wished to live with him. At Laurel Park he would be as physically comfortable as at home, with the added benefit of the company of others, and some mental stimulation. Until he died and his last Will and Testament was made public, nothing could be done with his two abandoned luxury homes. Hallowell Enterprises looked after them with not much enthusiasm and ran everything else for him. The company took care of all his financial affairs and made sure that there was always money for his sundries in the nursing home comfort fund. This suited Sheridan very well. Her only responsibility was to go and see him.

As to who would be the beneficiary of Eric Hallowell's money and property, Sheridan was as much in the dark as the executives of Hallowell Enterprises whose future would depend upon whatever whim had overtaken the old man after the loss of his son. Despite past conflicts, he could have left the lot to his two dopey sisters, and they, in turn, would doubtless bequeath the fortune to a home for Manx cats.

As the train pulled out of the station, Sheridan took up her book. She read for a while then, following her usual routine, for she was a creature of habit, she put the book aside and went to the snack car for a coffee. This she took back to her seat where she overheard someone mention Laurel Park. With no intention of eavesdropping she allowed the woman's voice to come to her and was amazed by what she heard.

"Yes, I go to Laurel Park every two weeks," the woman was saying. "I used to take the car from Hyannis, but it was such a hassle. I'd get into frightful traffic gridlock and sit for hours.

Then when I got to New Haven, I could never find anywhere to park; and if I did, it cost a fortune. You know, they won't let you take your vehicle inside the compound at the nursing home. I mean, they want you to leave it in their car park which is half a mile away from the residence, and I refuse to do that, on principle. It's a damned nuisance when one is going there to visit a patient. Anyway, I finally discovered that I could leave my car at the train station in Hyannis for nothing and ride the train to New Haven for half of what it cost me to drive and park. The nursing home is only about five miles from Somerset station, and there's a shuttle bus from there which drops you right outside the gates."

Very carefully Sheridan stretched around to see who was speaking. It was not that the woman had said anything momentous, only that she had described exactly the routine which Sheridan herself followed for the same reason. It was an extraordinary coincidence because Laurel Park was an elite and stupendously expensive institution, catering to only a small number of men and women who needed extended care and who, despite their wealth, had no family to look after them – or who wanted to. It was privately funded and built to reflect a high standard of luxury and exclusivity. The elegant clutch of buildings stood, as the name was meant to invoke, in a private park of sweeping lawns, exotic shrubs and colorful flowerbeds, all superbly maintained. The main gates were watched night and day by a uniformed guard, while the service entrances, discreetly hidden, could only be opened with plastic cards held by authorized staff.

When the woman moved on to another topic, Sheridan pretended to look down the train car for some imaginary acquaintance. However, her surreptitious observation of the speaker, could only be maintained for a few seconds. It was only after they both left the train at Hyannis that Sheridan got a good look at her. Walking behind the woman as they made their way to the car park, Sheridan noted that she was about her age, mid–fifties. She had short brown hair, not too well cut but not bad. She wore a plain grey suit and black kid pumps. Over her shoulder was a black leather bag of quite good quality. The car she drove was a small hatchback – a very ordinary car for a very ordinary woman. She was someone no-one would ever look at twice.

Sheridan, on the other hand, drove a Porche. Her neutral hued suit and pastel silk shell were from Armani. Her shoes were from Ferragamo, her leather purse from Gucci, and her fairish hair was colored and dressed at Elizabeth Arden. Still, despite being a little better presented, she too was an ordinary woman, as easily forgettable as the other. And by the time Sheridan had driven to her white clapboard villa on the sea, she had, indeed, all but forgotten the other woman whose trips to Laurel Park paralleled her own.

It was not until the next time Sheridan visited Eric that the other woman was again brought to mind, and only then because when Sheridan got on the bus outside the Somerset station, she was already on it. They both alighted at Laurel Park, and Sheridan immediately approached the front gates which were set back some distance from the wide sidewalk. Out of the corner of her eye she saw that the other woman was not headed in the same direction. Curiosity got the better of manners and turning to look Sheridan saw the woman cross the avenue to where half a dozen elegant little shops had opened up shortly after the nursing home was built, and pass through the door of the florist.

The guard on the gate glanced out of his glass–sided booth to greet Sheridan with a friendly salute. He might not have been able to put a name to her, but her face was familiar, which it should have been considering that she had been visiting for, well, years. Passing by the booth Sheridan walked up the drive and entered the spacious lobby where a white clad nurse was busy behind a high curved counter which was more like the reception desk of a grand hotel than a nursing home. Sheridan waved. She did not know all the nurses, but she knew this one and called out a soft greeting.

Eric Hallowell was in his room as usual. In all the time she had been visiting she had never known him to be anywhere else. He was hunched in his wheelchair near the window where an attendant had put him earlier. It would not have mattered, however, if he had been put in a corner facing the wall, because Eric was no longer concerned with looking at anything. He was completely paralyzed down one side, had lost sight in one eye, and could utter only one or two words – at least, that is what was believed to be the case. With his helplessness had come a lack of interest in everything including communication.

"Hello father," Sheridan chirped brightly and was answered with a phlegmy gurgle.

She bent and kissed the top of his head. The stretched skin was unnaturally shiny. One or two silky white hairs had been combed over the bald dome. He smelled faintly of English Leather cologne. He looked smaller than ever. He had never been a big man, which amateur psychologists would no doubt claim accounted for a lifetime of insufferable behavior, but now he looked like a withered little gnome, no, not a gnome exactly, because gnomes were stocky, colorful creatures and Eric Hallowell was nothing but ivory skin and bones.

Sheridan sat beside him in a cream brocade armchair and waved a hand towards the manicured landscape beyond the window. "Aren't the spring flowers lovely, father? It's so heart–warming to see them, don't you agree?"

The old man grunted. By now Sheridan pretty much knew what each grunt indicated. This one meant 'No'. He was telling her that there was nothing in the world that would do his heart good, and he would not indulge Sheridan in her pitiful efforts to cheer him up. She was fully aware that he was not at all appreciative of her concern for him or thankful for her visits. In the past he had tolerated her for his son's sake, but he had been a disagreeable old man when he was well and continued to be just as disagreeable in his sickness. It did Sheridan great credit, applauded her friends, that she was able to endure that hour or two hours in his company every two weeks.

When she left that day, Sheridan looked for the other woman and didn't catch a glimpse of her until they were both on the station platform. This time they did not sit in the same railcar, and by the time Sheridan had left the platform at the other end, the hatchback had already pulled out of the car park.

On the next visit it was the same. They climbed onto the same bus at New Haven, and the other woman went to the flower shop across the street before going into Laurel Park. She was not on the same bus going back as Sheridan, but she was on the same train. On this occasion she was a little behind Sheridan going into the car park at Hyannis, and she left by a different exit.

Two weeks after that Sheridan noticed with interest that the other woman was carrying a bunch of flowers with her, early summer flowers which could only have come from her own garden. So this time when they alighted at the Laurel Park bus stop, she had no need to cross the road to the florist. As a result the two women were walking practically side by side approaching the gates of the institution. Sheridan felt it was only polite to speak but was having difficulty thinking of something more original than 'good afternoon' or 'what lovely flowers' when she was saved the trouble.

"I hope you don't mind -" the other woman said, drawing closer to Sheridan, " -but I can't help having a word with you since we both appear to be regular visitors here. And it seems so extraordinary that we both ride the train from Hyannis." The woman was blessed with a beautifully modulated voice bearing the slightest trace of a foreign accent – European, Sheridan decided, and in that brief moment Sheridan had a fleeting sense of something familiar about her companion – some time or place where they may have met, but she quickly dismissed the idea. She had probably seen someone on television who bore a passing resemblance or shared a mannerism with this woman.

"I must admit I have noticed it too." Sheridan indicated the flowers the woman was carrying, "That's a beautiful bouquet."

"Yes." The woman held it up slightly. "Flowers from my garden."

"I thought perhaps they might be. You live in Hyannis, I take it?"

"Yes." The woman suddenly thrust out her hand. "Marie Graham."

"And I'm Sheridan Hallowell."

"So pleased to meet you, Mrs. Hallowell."

As they drew close to the gates, Marie chatted on about how sad it was that so many elderly persons were forced into nursing homes at the end of their lives. Sheridan said she supposed nature hadn't intended humans to live beyond the age of thirty, and Marie thought that a very grim notion. They were thus engaged when they passed through the gates, and Sheridan waved to the guard who gave his paramilitary salute in keeping with his smart paramilitary uniform.

"The security is so marvelous here, isn't it?" Marie observed, giving the man a wave. "Now, I mustn't delay you." She veered off at a junction in the path, calling out, "I'm sure I will see you on the way home. Goodbye for now!"

The two women did indeed travel back together, during which Sheridan learned that Marie was visiting an elderly second cousin at Laurel Park, a Miss James.

"Oh yes, I think I've seen her, well, at least, I've heard her name," Sheridan nodded. "I don't actually get about the facility much since my father-in-law refuses to leave his little domain. He won't even let me take him for a walk in his wheelchair, so my visits are confined strictly to his room."

"What a pity. The lounge and the conservatory are so lovely. My cousin just loves being wheeled among the tropical plants. Poor dear, I don't think she's got much longer." Marie gave a rather sweet, conspiratorial grin. "I shouldn't admit this, but I rather hope she has remembered me in her will."

When they reached Hyannis they walked to the car park together. "It has been very pleasant, Mrs. Hallowell." Marie extended her hand. "For me, at any rate, the tedium of the journey was alleviated. I hope we will see each other again."

They did, two weeks later, and once again they entered Laurel Park together. This time they were on a first name basis. On the way in Marie had suggested that she might wheel her Miss James over to see Mr. Hallowell. Sheridan didn't like to refuse, but she felt it incumbent upon her to point out that her father-in-law was a cantankerous old buzzard who saw no–one and might make an awful fuss if someone he didn't know appeared in his room. Marie did not take offense. She said she quite understood and arranged to meet Sheridan at the bus stop.

On her way out that day Sheridan observed that the security guard was outside the gates. Someone was trying to park their Cadillac right in front of the entrance, and the guard was waving them along. At Laurel Park the ownership of a Cadillac did not guarantee the privilege of parking illegally. Marie caught up with Sheridan as the limousine moved away, and the guard turned back to the gates. He grinned, shrugged his shoulders, and both women murmured something appropriate which he answered.

The women traveled together to Hyannis, finding plenty of uncontroversial topics to discuss as the train clacked its way through the suburbs and the countryside.

In the course of visiting Laurel Park, Marie had discovered that the security guards worked a four day shift. So when she returned to the nursing home two days later it was the same guard on the gate, the one who had moved the Cadillac. She

called out a cheerful 'good afternoon' to him and he responded
with a friendly acknowledgement. In the lobby she checked the
reception desk for a nurse, having noted in previous visits that
the area was often left unattended. There was really no need
to have anyone there at all, the visitors knew the routine and
rarely had to approach the front desk for help or information.
However, when patients were to be removed from the residence
for a day or even for an hour, they had to be checked out at
reception. It was not an arduous process, simply a matter of
signing the ledger which was kept open on the counter. And
as Marie's intention was to do just that, she walked over and
signed the book, then continued along to the room.

There were one or two residents about. Some patients were
able to slowly wheel themselves along the halls, propelling
themselves with one foot. Laurel Park discouraged the use of
electrically driven wheelchairs. The governing Board believed
that they were too difficult to control, both from the viewpoint
of elderly disabled drivers injuring themselves or others, and
from keeping track of where such a mobile resident might be.
There was, for instance, a large ornamental pond on the grounds
whose cream and pink water lilies were a source of great
attraction. An appreciative flower enthusiast might unwitting
drive himself into the pond and drown. Laurel Park couldn't
afford that sort of scandal.

Marie walked confidently along the hall and entered the
large, bright room. The wheelchair was by the window, the little
figure collapsed down in it. It happened that the occupant was
asleep but it would not have, in any case, mattered. Marie took a
thick wool blanket from the foot of the bed and tucked it around
the slumped form in the wheelchair. It was a warm, sunny day
but old sick people always felt cold. She touched nothing else in
the room. Releasing the brakes of the wheelchair she turned it
and pushed it gently before her. She had been in the room such
a short time that the same residents were still perambulating

slowly and aimlessly about in the hall when she pushed the chair out. Nobody was at the reception counter; but since she'd already signed her patient out, Marie did not have to stop there. She passed an orderly pushing a utility cart through the lobby towards the lounge. And in the distance she saw a brisk nurse disappear around a corner. Outside Marie noted a gardener so engrossed in a border that he didn't look up.

"Just going for a little spin," Marie sang out to the security guard as she passed through the gates.

"Lovely day for it," he called back.

Unhurriedly Marie steered the wheelchair along the sidewalk under the branches of chestnut trees in their summer greenery. Freshly mown grass verges spread out on either side of the path. The broad avenue was kept as neat and clean as if it were all a private estate. Large homes set well back from the road in their own lush grounds attested to the impressive per annum income of the local residents. It really was a very charming part of town.

Marie walked slowly to the end of the long block then turned right following the perimeter of Laurel Park to the gates of the car park – a paved area somewhat further on, concealed behind hedges of Leyland cypress. A few vehicles were dotted about, one of them her hatchback. She pushed the wheelchair up to the passenger door and opened it. She locked the wheelchair brakes. Then calmly and smoothly she pulled the blanket away from the figure in the chair.

It was when she was undoing the safety strap with which all wheelchair patients were secured in their seats that the old man woke up. Like an animal operating strictly on instinct he began to twist and struggle, at the same time uttering cries and growls of protest. Marie took no notice. With a skill she had learned in a recent first aid course, she planted her feet firmly, thrust her hands under the old man's arms and employing an almost acrobatic movement swung him out of the chair and into the passenger seat of the car. He was, of course, as fragile and light as a moth and quite as undesirable. She reached down and thrust his limp feet unceremoniously in, then fastened the seat belt around him and covered him up to his chin with the blanket. Ignoring his feeble thrusts, she slammed the car door.

Marie opened the hatchback, folded the wheelchair and lifted it inside next to several suitcases – a matched set of navy blue canvas and leather, and an odd one, dark brown and rather the worse for wear. She went around to the driver's side and got in, but before she drove on Marie lifted her hand and removed the wig she was wearing. It was a rather nice wig of real hair, a blondish colour, not garish or brassy, very natural–looking. She leaned past the old man and tucked it into the glove compartment in front of him. Using the rearview mirror she straightened her own brown hair and checked her make–up. A moment later she drove out of the parking lot and began to speak in a soft and pleasant tone.

"I've noticed Mr. Hallowell that your daughter–in–law never takes you out; so I thought it would be rather nice for you to have a little run in the car. Are you pleased? I'm sure you will be because I'm going to show you a lovely house, a beautiful house. It is empty now, but once upon a time it was home to a very, very rich man. This man is old now and not really dead, but he might as well be. I always think it so sad, don't you, when a rich man finds that his money suddenly cannot buy him back his health and strength? Still, he had a good run, this one, a much better run than many others I could mention, but we'll talk about that later, shall we, Mr. Hallowell? Oh, isn't it a lovely day for a drive?"

All the while she was speaking the old man beside her stormed like an ineffectual baby, squeezing up his face and clenching his one good fist which he had managed to wrestle free from the confining blanket. Restricted though he was he managed to make it perfectly clear that he did not wish to be taken for a ride in the car. Marie seemed to find his frustration and anger amusing. "I think we'll take I–84 up," she murmured. "It isn't the prettiest route, but it is the quickest way to Route 24. Your daughter–in–law, Mrs. Hallowell, Sheridan, she said I may call her Sheridan, doesn't much care for driving but I enjoy it. I wonder if you can guess where we are going, Mr. Hallowell? No? I daresay you will when we get to Newport. Yes, Newport! That rings a bell, doesn't it? It should, of course. Bellevue Avenue. Bailey's Beach."

It was lunch time when they crossed into Rhode Island and drove down the short length to the town which had once been the most fashionable enclave of millionaires in the late 19th and early 20th centuries. But before reaching Newport itself, Marie veered off the highway onto a quiet lane and drew up against an open field which afforded a broad view of the bucolic landscape. Here she turned off the ignition and unbuckled her seat belt. With a contented sigh she took out the sandwiches she had packed for herself. She did not offer food to her companion. She doubted if he would have eaten anything even if she had wanted to provide it for him. She had also brought a flask of coffee, and as she drank she gazed out at the familiar countryside. Time had passed since she had lived here and true to any strictly rural area controlled by governances to protect its beauty for its privileged taxpayers, nothing seemed to have changed.

The old man was asleep when she pulled out and continued their journey. A short distance along she again turned off the major road onto a discreetly identified narrow, paved lane called Mayflower Way. This was not a private road to Mara Vista, but it might as well have been for it gave access to only two of the Newport country estates. She brought the car to a halt in front of tall wrought iron gates which were closed and secured by a rusting chain wrapped around the metal scrolls and padlocked. This was no deterrent for she had a small but strong axe in the hatchback toolbox. Within minutes the car was inside the property, and she had pushed the gates closed again just in case there happened to be some errant local nosing around.

Some one hundred yards ahead, through sadly neglected grounds, was an impressive mansion, one of the famous oceanfront 'summer cottages' built by the Vanderbilts and their ilk. This one was a forty-eight room edifice in the style of a Norman manor house set in two hundred acres of meadow and woodland. There was a time when a visitor's carriage or car would have circled the elaborate fountain court with its now empty pool and been brought to a halt under the *porte–cochere*, where it would have been met by a butler or a groom but that time had long since passed.

Marie did not stop at the front of the house but chose instead to orbit the great mansion in the car. Since the magnificent flowerbeds and rare shrubs had long since gone she destroyed nothing by driving along a path meant for walking – bumping over cracked paving and coarse grass under the silent walls. She circled the glass conservatory with its high dome, and gained the rear lawns or what had once been lawns and were now no more than an uneven pasture, rolling down to the ocean. A long, covered terrace ran the length of the main floor at the back of the house which, in the old days, had served many glamorous purposes of the leisured class. Marie brought the car to a halt at the bottom of the terrace steps with its echoes of cocktail parties and summer cotillions. When she turned to look at the old man and saw the expression on his face, there was no doubt that he knew exactly where he was, and the knowledge made him seem to wither even more.

"Well, what do you think?" Marie asked cheerfully. "It's not quite up to the mark, is it, but they aren't doing too bad a job keeping the old place standing until you decide to die."

Eric Hallowell gathered all his strength. With blazing eyes and murderous intensity he spat out one word. "No!"

Marie gave a little laugh and reaching out patted that part of the blanket which covered his knee. "Oh yes, you are eventually going to die, Mr. Hallowell. We all are. Sad, isn't it? It makes one wonder why we are here at all, especially someone like me. I mean, people like you may not have any better reason for being born than a person like me, but at least while you're here you are able to enjoy life." She paused to contemplate the house. "Just look at this place. It was built by Humbolt Milner in 1889. Do you remember when you bought it? It was in 1964. You would have been about fifty-two years old then. You'd just made your thirtieth million or was it your fortieth? Well, I suppose anything after the first ten is immaterial. People do say that they would be happy with one million but I've always felt that I wouldn't be really secure unless I had at least ten." She let her eyes drift over the neglected grounds, still beautiful in their own natural way. "Of course, I wasn't around in 1964. Well, I was around but not here. No, I was married to my late husband then. When he very inconsiderately died, I was shocked to discover that there was no money, nor any insurance, and I was forced to go out to work. That wasn't such a great tragedy, except that I wasn't trained to do anything. All I knew was how to run a house. That's how I ended up as a domestic servant. I daresay you aren't much interested in my history, Mr. Hallowell. You were never concerned about anyone other than yourself. That's part of the problem, do you see? Are you too warm? Why don't I open your window for you? The sea breeze is so refreshing. Better still, why don't I open the door?" She climbed out of the car, walked around it and opened the passenger door as wide as it would go. Immediately the brisk wind blowing off the Sound lifted the threads of the old man's hair. He muttered petulantly and tried to get his good hand, so white it was almost transparent, under the blanket.

"There, that is much more comfortable, isn't it?" Marie returned to her seat, leaving her door open so that the wind blew straight through the vehicle, chilling even her veins. Very soon the old man's teeth were chattering, and his nose began to run. But there was nothing he could do about it.

As her glance strayed to the high walls of the deserted house, Marie's voice was as distant as the times she recalled. "Do you remember when I came here? It was after your wife committed suicide. In your grief you'd secluded yourself here at Mara Vista. You hired me as your housekeeper when your New York staff rebelled against spending all year up here at Newport away from the bright, city life. It wasn't terribly convenient for me to isolate myself either, but I had little choice since you were offering a few cents more than anyone else. Well, you had to, didn't you, to get anyone to stay."

The old man groaned and writhed as he grew colder and colder.

"Are you trying to say something, Mr. Hallowell. Um?" She made a pretence of trying to understand his garbled sounds. "Cold, did you say? Well, there's no fire in your blood to sustain you now, is there?" She banged her door shut and leaned over him to close the passenger door, then settling herself, slowly drove on.

The car bumped uncomfortably over the coarse, uneven terrain. Yes, now the landscaped gardens were simply terrain. She drew up under the shadow of the East wing and turned off the engine. In the quiet that followed it was possible to hear the birdsong in the woodland glade at the edge of the clearing.

"No, you no longer have the sort of pep that drove you in the days you kept everyone under your thumb; your wife, your son, your poor mad sisters, and your overworked employees." Marie spoke gently in her pleasant, flowing voice with its tiny hint of an accent. "Oh yes, I've heard all about the family. I didn't know any of them, of course, by the time I came here to skivvy for you, you refused to see what friends or family were left. Not that they really wanted to see you, I'm certain, but some people do put others' needs before their own it might surprise you to learn. I do remember Sheridan appearing a couple of times when I first came here, but you were so rude to her that she soon gave up. At first, when I traveled to Laurel Park with her I thought she might recognize me. If she had, I would have been forced to alter my plan to take you on this sentimental journey, but she didn't. It's understandable. The times she came to visit, poor old Burton opened the door and took in the tea so she had only a glimpse of me. Besides, no one ever remembers servants, have you noticed that, Mr. Hallowell?"

Marie leaned forward in her seat and peering up through the windshield, pointed. "That was your bedroom up there. I don't suppose you remember that you were there alone when you had your stroke. Old Burton found you unconscious in bed. Poor man he was so shocked. How he sobbed. He should have saved his tears for himself. So long as you were accommodated in the way you ordered, you spared no thought for those serving you. Do you ever wonder what happened to Old Burton? He was with you for years, wasn't he? In case you are interested, in case there is the remotest possibility that you are curious, he's in a shelter now, poor devil. It would have been better for him if you'd died. That way he would have got a bit of a pension from your estate. Sheridan would have made sure of that if you hadn't made provision for him. Old Burton devoted his entire life to you. He was a good and faithful employee. He trusted you to see him right and you discarded him like an old dog you'd grown tired of. It's ironic that with you hanging on to every last thread of existence, he'll be gone before you are. Sheridan told me that Laurel Park's consulting physician says that you have the constitution of an ox." Marie turned in the car seat to give him a searching look. "I must say, you don't look much like it, but the consultant must know what he is talking about, he certainly gets paid enough." Her expression softened, a smile, almost affectionate, curved her lips. "But that's good, isn't it, Mr. Hallowell? No one wants you to die yet, do they? Not until you've had your reward. I've been giving this considerable thought over the last few weeks, planning a nice trip for you, just so that you know there is still someone who often thinks about you and wants you to have an experience unlike any other that has come your way."

As she was speaking the old man managed to dislodge his blanket and began a futile attack on the seatbelt restraining him, all the while making pitiful spitting noises in his mouth so that the saliva ran down his chin. Marie watched him dispassionately, then reached out, pulled up the blanket and once again wrapped it closely around him. "Oh, I've been rather foolish. I don't want you to be cold. It could induce you to pop off too fast with pneumonia. That would spoil my plan to put a little excitement into your boring Laurel Park life." Her voice became kind. "Poor old man, it's so sad, even if you could get out of the car where would you go?"

She turned the ignition and began driving again. Off to the right were a series of outbuildings; stables, garages, and storehouses. Once bustling with life and energy they were now silent and deserted. An air of desolation hung over everything. It was a place without life and without hope.

"It's depressing, isn't it?" Marie said, braking. "Oh but, you probably can't see just how awful it is. They tell me you've lost the sight of one eye – is this the one? The left eye? So you probably haven't had a good look at me. I'm sure that if you could see me well you would recognize me, Mr. Hallowell. Or didn't you look at me at all in the six years I ran this mansion of yours? That would be no surprise. But the name, well, you couldn't be expected to recollect that. I had to use an assumed name in case Sheridan had talked to anyone about me. I couldn't risk being connected in any way with you. That would have ruined it all. And Sheridan, naturally, would have remembered my real name if not my real face." She laughed at her little joke. "Does Genevieve Marie Beilman mean anything to you? Ah, I see it does. Genevieve Beilman, your Mara Vista housekeeper. There now, don't you feel better? I'm not a stranger anymore, right?"

With a supreme effort the old man raised his good hand, pointed a shaking finger at her and screamed, "No!"

"That has always been a favorite word of yours, hasn't it, old man?" She turned slightly in her seat and indicated the huge pile of the great house behind them. "So strange to think that we lived under that very roof together for six years, you and I, Mr. Hallowell, and you know, it was the worst six years of my life. You looked upon me as a different species from yourself. You followed the Victorian dictum that servants are there to be inconvenienced. I daresay it was the same way the colonial masters viewed their slaves in the old days – creatures who felt no pain, had no needs, no emotions, no human feelings. That's how you treated me, Mr. Hallowell, with derision, with contempt. There was no courtesy, no consideration, no grace whatsoever." She frowned. "I think I could have borne it all, and when the time came could have forgotten it all, because hate is so bad for one it eats at the body and destroys the soul, if it had not been for mother. Yes, I really think I could have put it all out of my mind if it had not been for mother. You wouldn't remember my mother, Mr. Hallowell, you never met her. Just after I came here to Mara Vista to work for you she suffered a terrible stroke, just as you did later. Like you she did not recover the use of her limbs. Like you she became as helpless as a babe, totally dependent on others. Only unlike you she didn't have the money to enter a fabulous nursing home to be waited on hand and foot by well-paid professionals. She had only me, Mr. Hallowell, a widowed daughter."

Marie moved the car slightly again, this time turning it to face the grey stone walls and blank windows. She pointed to a row of windows level with the ground. "That was my bedroom." Barely suppressed anger appeared on her face at the memory.

"Second from the left. Old Burton was on the corner. I shared a bathroom and a little sitting area with Burton, the daily women, the handyman and the gardeners. It was ludicrous considering how many unused rooms there were in this house. Still, I could endure my small discomforts, my concern was for my mother, my old mother who'd never done a mean thing in her life." She smiled sadly as her thoughts dwelt briefly on her mother. "I asked you if I could bring her here so that I could care for her myself, so I could nurse her, but do you know what you said, Mr. Hallowell? You said – no."

The old man squirmed and sniveled. "No!" he snarled.

"Right," she nodded. "You said no. Out of the question. I had to put that poor dear lady in a home, a dismal place but the most I could afford." She paused, her pain evident, but when she spoke again it was just as softly and agreeably as before. "Those who knew my sad story, people like Old Burton and the daily women asked me why I stayed on. The truth was I had no choice. I had no prospects nor a cent to bless myself with, as my Granny used to say, and you paid me more than I could hope to earn for the same work anywhere else. In addition I had room and board. Because of this I could just keep up my mother's medical insurance premiums. You had me trapped, Mr. Hallowell, just as your helpless sisters and heaven knows how many more were trapped by your malevolence. Well, all that is in the past. My mother died shortly after you had your stroke. I had just enough money to bury her. It was a pitiful effort but what does it matter when one has gone? The dead they know not anything, didn't someone say? Your burial would have been very different if it were not for this little outing, Mr. Hallowell. Oh, you would have been sent off in great style like an Egyptian pharaoh. Well, enough of this." She snapped her seat belt on. "We'd better be on our way. We have a bit of a drive. Not too tired, are you, old man?"

By the time they were back on Route 24 and had crossed

the bridge, Eric Hallowell's head had fallen forward and small snores emitted from his paper thin nostrils.

Marie glanced at him and almost laughed aloud. How long she had waited for this moment! She could hardly believe that she had pulled it off! Everything had gone as planned. Joy filled her heart as she thought over the steps she had taken. Then a moment of regret. "I do feel a little sorry about poor Miss James," she murmured aloud. "Of course, she had no idea who I was, and as she couldn't speak she couldn't tell anyone that she didn't know me when I began following Sheridan to find out where you were, and it was easy to discover which patients rarely had visitors. It's a sad truth that many old people are effectively forgotten by their family members once they have been in care for year or two, and Miss James had never married. When I told the staff that I was a distant relative of hers visiting America for a few months they accepted that. After a while Miss James was delighted to see me. She's going to miss me. I wish I could have said goodbye to her, but that was out of the question."

Eric jerked awake as the horn of an eighteen-wheeler blasted out. The traffic across Boston was heavy but moved steadily on the multilane highway. Marie had heard it was called the Fitzgerald Expressway and supposed that was something to do with President Kennedy's grandfather. She had no problem maneuvering off the Expressway into the congested city traffic because she'd found out how to leave the Central Artery when she went to Markham Street to make the arrangements for the old man's stay. "I expect Laurel Park will have missed you by now," she speculated musingly. "They will have called your daughter-in-law to find out why she hasn't taken you back. I signed you out in her name, you see. When they investigate your disappearance they'll find her signature is forged. They don't know my handwriting, but I disguised it anyway. Of course, they may think Sheridan was trying to disguise hers. She'll have a difficult time proving it wasn't she who took you out, unless she has a really good alibi for the time the security guard will say she left with you. He'll think I was her because of the fair wig and this cream suit I'm wearing. Did you notice it? It doesn't matter anyhow. It was only a way of getting in and out of Laurel Park without causing suspicion."

Chatting away as if to a trusted friend Marie hadn't noticed that the old man had again fallen asleep. "The full force of Hallowell Enterprises will move into action," she went on. "But they'll never find you. I can guarantee that, so the assumption will be that you are dead. I thought about killing you myself but violence of that sort isn't in my nature."

She drove in silence until an unhappy groan signaled that Eric Hallowell was again awake. Marie glanced at her watch. "How are we doing for time? You know what it is like these days, one has to be at the airport hours before the plane is due to leave. I expect you saw the luggage in the back of the car. It's very odd, you know. Now that the time has come to return to Switzerland I'm quite excited. Have you been to Switzerland, Mr. Hallowell? You must have. A man in your position has traveled the world. It's a beautiful place, isn't it? Serene. Far away from the world's troubles. Perfect for a person in his old age. Would you like to know the arrangements I've made? Well, they're quite exciting, and as you can guess, a complicated trip like this took a lot of planning. For instance, this is a rental car which I'll leave at Logan. It was expensive, but it was the safest way. No, I don't mind you knowing the details. We shouldn't have any secrets between us now; so I'm going to tell you what I have not told another living soul, starting with your new identity. You know, it's really astonishing how easy it is to obtain a false social security card if you have the money. Of course, you know all about what money can buy, but it was quite a revelation to me. I can see how one would become addicted to such power! So I bought you a whole new identity with all the correct papers."

Not taking her eyes from the road she leaned sideways

towards him. "How did I get the money to do it, you are probably wondering. Well, getting the money was the simple part. When they took you off to hospital after you had your stroke, Burton and I had to wait awhile until we knew how serious it was. As soon as we were told you would not be coming back and the house was to be closed up, I made plans to secure my future. I got your keys, the ones you always kept in your bedside table at night, and went into your safe, Mr. Hallowell. Yes, I lifted some cash from it. Oh, I knew all about your safe and what was in it, and I guessed that no one besides you and me would know just how much loose cash you kept in there. I took half of it, fifteen thousand dollars to be exact. If I had taken it all no one would have known the difference, but I'm not a greedy person. All I wanted was enough to expiate my grievances however long that might take. The irony is that most of it is coming back to you anyway because it cost so much to buy you an identity and to pay for a year's residence in your new home. The only thing I acquired solely for myself was my airline ticket to Geneva." The thought of her imminent journey to her homeland occupied Marie's thoughts while the old man slept again. He was jerked awake by a sudden swerve Marie had to take to avoid a collision.

"Sorry about that." Marie didn't sound exactly sorry. Her voice was light with happiness. "We've done well. It can take hours to cross Boston if you hit the rush hour. You knew Boston quite well, didn't you, Mr. Hallowell, friends on Beacon Hill, that sort of thing? You wouldn't have had occasion to spend much time in the North End. That's where we are now. Ah, I think this is the cross street with Markham right here. Oh, I almost forgot, from now on you are known as Philip Bellamy."

No amount of early evening sunshine was capable of making Markham Street look anything other than a dingy backwater. It formed one side of a small square which once, in the distant past, might even have been relatively desirable. In the middle of the squalid quadrangle was a patch of scrubby ground used by the neighborhood dogs to do their business. Markham was the only street of the four facing the square where some residential premises still stood. Though never elegant, for this in all its history had never been a fashionable part of town, these houses were considerably better than tenements. On the other three sides of the square disused warehouses with white-washed windows had, in the 1940's, taken the place of private residences. Now abandoned themselves, they were slowly crumbling into the ground. The aspect was dreary indeed.

The old man became distraught.

"What?" she asked, as if puzzled. "What are we doing here? Did you...oh dear.....did you think you were coming to Switzerland with me, Mr. Hallowell? Did I give you the impression that I was taking you with me? Oh, I am so sorry! No, no....that would be far too good a resolution for you. I hope you are not too disappointed, but I am going, and you are staying. This will be your new home from now on. I don't want you to worry about your health. Just remember your strong constitution. Chances are you will live for many long years here on Markham Street. You'll like the place, I'm sure. The Hoopers, the couple who run this home for elderly gentlemen, respect a person's privacy. They don't ask questions, if you know what I mean, and you never liked people prying into your business, did you? And they won't so it should suit you very well."

Marie drove slowly along the seedy street and pulled up before one of the tall, narrow shabby houses in front of which the only tree in sight desperately clung to life. Leaving the old man where he was she got out of the car, opened the hatchback and hauled out the brown leather suitcase. It was quite heavy. It contained a whole new Sally Ann wardrobe for him, also bought out of the money she had taken from his safe. Once she got a good grip on the case, however, she was able to carry it quite easily up the steps to the peeling front door. She was not kept waiting very long after her ring.

"Mr. Hooper?" She smiled warmly at the man who opened the door. "I'm Doris Unger."

"Ah yes, you've brought Mr. Bellamy along."

"I have indeed. He's out in the car."

Mr. Hooper took the suitcase from her and placed it in the dark hall. "I'll come down and get him."

Together they went down the steps and crossed the grimy sidewalk.

"His wheelchair is in the back," Marie said. She watched silently as the man took the wheelchair out of the car and opened it up. "Nice," he remarked, impressed.

"Yes, the family thought it was the least they could do for poor old Uncle Phil."

"Lucky guy."

"Yes, and don't think he doesn't appreciate it, poor old boy."

Eric Hallowell fought and spat as Mr. Hooper extracted him from the car. Mr. Hooper took no notice. He was used to dealing with cantankerous old men. He handled them as he would ferrets, holding them behind the head and keeping clear of their claws. He wrestled Eric Hallowell into the wheelchair, strapped him in and pushed him towards the house. At the bottom of the cracked steps he bellowed, "Victor." A face appeared at the dirty front window, weasel eyes peering over dingy lace café curtains, but they belonged to a woman.

A burly, youngish man came to the front door and stared morosely down the steps.

"Need a hand here," Mr. Hooper snapped. As the younger man heaved himself slowly down the steps Mr. Hooper introduced him, "My son, Victor."

"Hello." Marie was cordial, not letting her distaste show.

"Hi," said Victor. He glanced furtively up and down the empty street before leaning down and taking hold of one side of the wheelchair. Mr. Hooper took the other and together they easily carried it up to the door. All the time the old man protested, shrieking out, "No!" and clenched his good hand into a powerless fist. As soon as the wheelchair was dumped in the front hall Victor faded away into the shabby interior of the house.

Mr. Hooper called down, "Come on up, Miss Unger."

Marie closed the car doors and locked them before she mounted the steps and entered the house. Looking about she supposed it was clean, all things considered, but there was no mistaking the sinister odour of death and decay.

To the right was the room overlooking the street. As murky as a stagnant pond it contained no other furniture but a mishmash of chairs in a circle around the walls. Each was occupied by a failing old man. Some slept, others had their glazed eyes fixed on the floor, one or two stared forlornly towards the flurry of activity in the hall. Now that her eyes were becoming accustomed to the dimness Marie could see that the hall stretched back quite a distance and that two more rooms opened off it to the right. A steep flight of stairs rose to the left. There was a gate at the top, presumably to stop the residents from flinging themselves down either by accident or design. Judging by the smell of frying bacon coming from the rear of the house the kitchen was beyond the turn in the hall behind the staircase.

The woman whose face she had seen at the window of the front room now fully materialized. She was wearing a wraparound apron over garments it was better not to ask about, and dirty slippers.

"This is my wife," Mr. Hooper said without enthusiasm.

"Hi." Marie greeted her.

"I expect you'll be wanting to see his room," Mrs. Hooper suggested uneasily.

"Yes, I would. Very much."

"This way, then. I guess we might as well put him in there now. We like to get the wheelchair guests in bed about five.

It's less trouble that way." She led the way down the hall, her slippers slapping depressingly on the uncovered linoleum. Mr. Hooper pushed the wheelchair and Marie followed.

Eric Hallowell had been given the rear room on that floor. It had a single un-curtained window overlooking a grim cemented yard enclosed by the high walls of surrounding commercial structures. The room, barely twelve feet square was sparsely furnished with an old hospital bed, a nightstand with a book under one leg to keep it level, a dresser and a sagging armchair. Over a disused fireplace hung a clay crucifix which had once been bright with paint and gilt, both worn off except for a few shreds here and there. A single light bulb in a paper shade hung from the centre of the room. A fly or two circled it listlessly. In his wheelchair in the middle of the grim room Eric Hallowell grunted and babbled, exhausting his small stock of energy so that he was left crumpled and gasping. No one took any notice of him.

"He's got his own closet." Mrs. Hooper opened a door in the wall to reveal a dusty cupboard with a half dozen wire coat hangers on a rail.

"Yes, well," Marie looked about with an air of supreme satisfaction, "I think this will do very well, very well indeed. It isn't a lavish environment, but it's enough to sustain life and plenty of poor souls live on less. He has the room to himself, does he?"

"Unless there's a big demand," Mrs. Hooper responded defensively. "Then we'd have to move another bed in. Social Services have authorized it if necessary. The number to a room is based on square footage."

"Yes, I understand."

"Of course, we'd reduce the monthly rate if that happened," Mrs. Hooper added reluctantly.

"Let us not worry about that at this stage," Marie said obligingly.

Mr. Hooper had left the room and now returned with the suitcase Marie had prepared for Eric Hallowell. He also had some forms in his hand. "I just need you to sign these, Miss Unger." He took the papers over to the shaky bureau and spread them out. He offered her a pen, but Marie preferred to use her own. She was taking no chances with fingerprints. She signed the forms 'Doris Unger', niece, and filled in a non-existent address and telephone number. Where a form asked what medication the patient took, if any, she marked: Not applicable.

"As I mentioned when we spoke before -" Marie said with a charming smile,

"- because of other commitments I shall be traveling for the rest of the summer, so to avoid any misunderstanding I intend to pay for one year's residence for Mr. Unger in advance."

The Hoopers exchanged delighted glances.

"Also to avoid any difficulty you might have in cashing so large a check I hope you will accept the payment in cash." She reached into her purse and took out a brown manila envelope. "I trust one hundred dollars bills are acceptable?"

Broad smiles had now broken out on the faces of the Hoopers.

"The wife's in charge of finances," Mr. Hooper said as Mrs. Hooper stepped forward to take the envelope. She carried it to the bed, sat down and took the notes out. Very methodically she counted them, then looked up and nodded.

Marie now produced another envelope. "Here are his papers, including his Social Security card."

Mr. Hooper took it, screwing up his mouth. He had something on his mind. "Now – er – you say you will be traveling quite a lot in the next few months."

"Yes."

He scratched his face. "Mr. Unger don't look too well." That was an understatement if ever there was one, the old man looked positively battered. "What happens if he dies and we can't get in touch with you?"

"I've arranged for the Memorial Society to deal with that. The necessary forms are in that envelope. All you have to do is telephone the number given and they will take care of everything. He has paid for a very simple disposal with no ceremony whatsoever." She walked over and stood in front of Eric Hallowell. She squatted down so that he was able to see her clearly from his one good eye. "It's what he wants, isn't it, Uncle Phil?" She found it difficult not to laugh out loud at his expression of the most vitriolic hatred. His fist was raised to her face, his babbling a combination of invective and frustration. Marie straightened and moved away from him. She took one last look around the joyless room and left with a radiant smile. As she walked towards the front door she heard his scream. "No!"

MATTERS OF TRUST

I have been rich, and I have been poor and rich is better.

When I was growing up, my mother was very comfortably off. She was widowed when I was five years old and left with heaps of money. Life was very sweet. We lived in an Edwardian villa in Wimbledon, not far from the tennis courts. Mother led a busy social life and even as a child, so did I. Like hers, my life was an endless whirl of outings and parties. Mother promoted me relentlessly as a guest at the parties of her friends' children, where gorgeous gifts and elaborate cakes were presented as monuments to family wealth. I didn't understand for many years that the birthday cakes of small children were usually modest, pink-iced Victoria sponges in a frill for girls and renditions of toy trains or some other masculine icon for boys. In such offerings as these, modest candles were plopped into the icing, lit and blown out, and the cake sliced up on the tea table just as any ordinary day. The cakes at the parties where I was a kiddy guest reposed upon pedestals in some prominent part of the house, perhaps an antechamber to the dining room or a conservatory. Once, even an impressive front hall was utilized. This offering would be as commanding as a wedding cake with dazzling white icing and extravagant decorations, topped by fresh flowers with the birthday message scrolled as brilliantly as the illuminations of a medieval bible. The cutting and serving of these cakes was as formally ritualistic as if, indeed, a wedding were in progress. Paper plates had no place in such households. Minton or Crown Derby were not too good for junior hands, and the silver cake slice would preside alongside tiny, pearl-handled dessert forks, which elite children utilized rather than their fingers.

My parties were like that. My mother, a wonderfully glamorous belle, would not be outdone by members of our privileged set. And since I had no siblings, I was the happy recipient of all the bounty. As I grew up the bounty increased, as did the size of the parties. When I was seventeen, it was decided that my two closest friends and I would have a coming-out dance. We were definitely not debs, and indeed, the ritual of debdom in England had long since drawn its last breath. And, no doubt the effort our three mothers had made eight years before to present us to the world in a sort of *faux* coming-out, reeked of pretension, but we really enjoyed it.

I had one year of prancing about London in beautiful clothes, eating wonderful food, dancing in fabulously expensive clubs and generally aping what the old-time genuine debs did in order to catch a husband. At that time, however, men were in short supply — well, men with whom one would want to tie the knot. I made a big mistake there. I should have picked the one who was the least offensive, and taken my place at the head of his table which could seat eighty upon some stately acreage. But then, I was far too busy having a good time to sort that out or pay attention to the affairs of my mother. So it came as a horrible shock to me when she announced her engagement to an Australian something or other, telling me that as soon as she had sold the house and liquidated her British assets, they would be off to Queensland. I was not invited.

She suggested I take a Secretarial Course and find myself a bedsit somewhere in London.

I was aghast and scared, of course. I had not been brought up to make a living. Mother and I were alone in the world, and I had made the assumption that we would be together until I married, at which point I would be transferred from her home to my husband's, the illusionary estate in the country with a supplementary condominium in Knightsbridge. The idea of having to fend for myself sent me into a total fizz. In fact, I had a nervous breakdown. Luckily that impressed my mother enough for her to pay a year's rent on a small flat in Chelsea and guarantee me an even smaller monthly allowance until I married or could support myself. She did not give me the option of going to Australia with her and my stepfather because he did not exactly acknowledge me as being a part of his future. Frankly, he struck me as nothing but a gold-digger, and everyone except my mother thought the same. Some of her friends warned her but I didn't dare say anything. She was besotted with him, and as much as I was scared for her I didn't dare jeopardize the small stipend she allotted me by criticizing him. Besides, he would've told her I was just being vicious because I could not longer count on her fortune to support me in the style to which I had become accustomed. But in truth, I didn't see why he should be supported in the style to which he expected to be accustomed on mother's bank account. After all, he hadn't made the money any more than I had.

So off mother went to the southern hemisphere, leaving no forwarding address, but with the assurance that she would phone when they had bought a house and settled in. There was no one but me at Heathrow to bid her farewell. The few relatives we had started out with were dead, and no one on my father's side of the family had kept up with us following his untimely death many years before. I felt lost and abandoned

— a motherless child.

I took up residence in Chelsea, where my lifestyle gradually declined. I simply didn't have the funds to keep up with my friends, and after a while it became humiliating trying to do so. I started making excuses. Eventually they left me to my own devices. Then one day I sat down and made a list of my options. It was a very short list. I could take that secretarial course — there was just enough money to cover that, though the thought appalled me. Quite aside from the horrors of shorthand and typing, I'd been told what top-flight secretaries had to do if they really wanted to get on, and I was not the girl for that! Or I could inhabit a cardboard box under Blackfriars Bridge, and if I was lucky, occasionally receive a sympathetic wave from Charles and Camilla from the flatteringly lit interior of their Rolls-Bentley.

And then I met Ursula.

I had been on my own for three months and had worked out a routine which involved a London Transport pass and a lot of coffee. On that May morning I was sitting in Starbuck's on the Kensington High Street, sharing a table with a woman of about my age when a bloke came up and asked if he could sit with us since there was no other free table in the place. It was all the same to me. I was looking through an old copy of the Tatler where I'd found a small photo of mother and me, and barely glanced up. He sat down, and after a minute or two the vibes started reaching out. He was itching to make conversation with one or both of us. I looked up, glanced at him and then at her. She glanced at him and then at me. Neither she nor I spoke.

"My name is Larry," he said. "Are you twins? No? Just sisters?"

The woman and I looked at one another more closely. Yes, there were enough similarities for us to be taken for siblings. We were sitting down, but we appeared to be about the same height, five foot five, and similar weight, between seven and eight stone. She was blonde with blue eyes, and I was mousy with irises of an indeterminate hazel. We both possessed rather nondescript faces, the sort of English faces about which it is said, once seen never remembered.

Larry tried to make conversation with us, but I didn't respond and neither did she; so he finished his coffee and left. Then she held out her hand, "Ursula Pixley."

"Susan Kennedy."

"I suppose we were pretty mean to him," she said. "He seemed inoffensive enough, but I've had a pig of a day, and the last thing I need to deal with is a berk on the make."

I murmured something supportive, and she went on to complain bitterly at her lot in life. This was something with which I empathized; so we chatted pleasantly for a considerable time. That night I ruminated long and hard on what she had confided in me. In brief, she was a companion to her grandmother, a very rich old lady who lived in one of those pockets of countryside still to be found in the heart of London, the type of demesne which had been occupied by the same family for five hundred years or had become the sanctuary of some multi-millionaire pop star. Anyway, the way Ursula described her grandmother's estate was so appealing I felt compelled to see it the very next day.

Number Twelve Kew Gardens Lane was located behind discreet wrought iron gates supported by brick pillars with a pedestrian gate on one side. The name of the estate, *Mon Repos,* was announced in wrought-iron script. The pedestrian gate was closed but not locked. I passed through, closing it behind me, and was a distance up the curved drive when I heard a car coming down. I stood back in the bushes and watched as the Mercedes moved slowly over the gravel towards the gates. Ursula was behind the wheel, with her grandmother in the passenger seat. I waited until the sound of the engine died away and then continued up to the mansion.

I knew little about architecture but enough to recognize Greek revival. The serene symmetry of the white structure with its pilasters and fine moldings certainly deserved the name it had been given. I had seen other relics like *Mon Repos* dotted around English parks, brave survivors of more optimistic times, usually now small museums or the headquarters of some wealth charity patronized by a royal personage. It was amazing to think that this was still a private house. If it had been half the size and slightly more Edwardian, it could have been my mother's home. It was the sort of house which I considered my birthright.

I did a complete circle of the residence without seeing a soul or hearing the bark of a dog. Ursula had not mentioned guard dogs. I would have considered it prudent to keep a few about, but apparently she and her grandmother did not. Because of what I had learned from Ursula, I didn't expect to be challenged and I wasn't. I even managed to have a good look through the downstairs windows. I saw just what I expected, the trappings of a rich home, beautiful furniture, tasteful interior decorating and elegant bric-a-brac. But even without being inside the rooms, I could detect the neglect.

I don't have many virtues, but I do possess patience. *Patience on a rock*, my mother said when I was growing up. In her book it was unnatural, but I've always found it useful. Having formulated my plan, I sat on my rock in a milk bar across the road from Starbuck's for three days. On the fourth Ursula showed up. It was raining. The weather was cold, miserable for that time of year. As soon as I could get across the congested street, I entered the café and walked up to the counter at the same time as Ursula was placing her order. She seemed distracted and didn't notice me; so I quietly bided my time behind her until she was settled at a table. Then, I casually walked past her apparently oblivious to her presence. She, on the other hand, called out, "Oh, hello!"

I acted out a little charade of shaking myself from deep thought. I frowned, then allowed my face to clear as I mimicked recognition and pleasure. "Well, hello. It's Ursula, isn't it? How are you?"

"Could be better. Why don't you join me?" She indicated her table.

There were a number of empty tables that afternoon; so for her benefit, I checked around as if making an earth-shattering assessment of where I might sit, then looked back and smiled at her. "Well, if you're sure you don't mind. There are other tables free."

"No, sit here, please. I need a victim."

Ursula was frustrated. She was twenty-three years old (two years younger than me) and straining at the bit. Her life with her grandmother was simply too restrictive. She was tied to the house six days a week, putting in hours a union would never allow. She was at the old girl's beck and call twenty-four hours a day. Even on her one day off, she had to be available, depending on her grandmother's whim.

"I've got a boyfriend," she whined, "Raphael. He'll give me up if things don't improve soon."

"Why do you stay?" I asked, affecting a sympathetic look.

"Because we're each other's only living relatives and I'm her heiress. There is -" she confided with an arch look, "- rather a lot of lolly, an inheritance not to be taken lightly, and the trouble is we're a very long-lived family."

"Then it's surprising there aren't any more of you," I ventured.

"Plane crash," she stated shortly. "Grandad's dear little private jet went down in Kentucky on its way to a lavish party thrown for racehorse breeders. Practically the entire family was wiped out, mother, granddad, aunts and uncles, all gone. Seventeen years ago."

"How dreadful," I murmured, "What about your father?"

"He was saved by his prick."

I choked on my coffee.

"Sorry," she laughed. "He should have been on the plane but

didn't get back from Africa in time. He was there on business and got sidetracked, in the usual way. They say this one was once Miss Mountains of the Moon. No need to elaborate."

"So you do have at least one living relative in addition to your grandmother," I corrected.

"In theory, but not in practice because he only briefly came back from Jo'burg. We haven't heard from him for years. I imagine he's dead."

"He didn't keep in touch with his own mother?"

"Gran? She was his mother-in-law. My other grandparents are long dead, and Dad was an only child. Like me."

"Me too," I sighed.

Ursula grinned across the table. "Well, we'll just have to pretend that we're long lost sisters."

"That would be fun," said I, all innocence.

Over the next short while we became very chummy, and she visited me in my rooms on the top floor of the old house on Oakley Street which were said to have once belonged to Cliff Richards. Ursula proclaimed that it was the most charming little apartment she'd ever seen. She said it with the sort of longing which indicated that she would love nothing better than to have such a place of her own.

Ursula was a very unhappy young woman. Hard-done-by, she said. And because of her duties at *Mon Repos*, unable to spend enough time with her boyfriend, the captivating Raphael. Her dates with him were necessarily sporadic, which was the most titanic of her grievances. She had mentioned this to her grandmother, but the old lady was disinterested in Ursula's hormonal problems. But then, Gran, as I began to think of her, was paying Ursula well to look after her, with a huge bonus at the end!

"Why," I asked, "if your Gran is so rich, doesn't she have a companion and domestic staff to look after her?"

"Because in the same way as the rich and beautiful never

know who their true friends are or whom to trust, Gran is afraid of being exploited, as she claims the Duchess of Windsor was in her dotage. Never mind that I'm being exploited!" Ursula raged.

I nodded and commiserated with her. Was there anything worse than living in the lap of luxury and getting paid for it? Well, I could think of one situation far worse — living in a poky apartment in Chelsea with the rent coming due and the problem of how to survive in life without getting a job. And just as Ursula would have loved a charming and very private little apartment like mine, I was equally enamoured of the idea of living in a mansion like *Mon Repos*.

And so the seed of the idea was sown. Well, in my mind, anyway. The trick was to introduce it into Ursula's, and that was just a question of timing. I'd always liked puzzles, and I usually prevailed when presented with one, because of that patience I mentioned before. If something is worth having one should be prepared to wait for it, and so I waited.

In early June Ursula and I had arranged to meet in Cezar's on Temple Avenue. I was there first having taken the tube. She burst in on a wave of delight. Gran was going to spend two weeks in Biarritz visiting an old friend who had moved to France three years before. The friend's son would take Gran over on Saturday and bring her back in a fortnight. That would leave Ursula free to join Raphael who was off to Stockholm for a week on business and had invited her to go with him while his wife was in America visiting her relatives.

"His wife?"

"Well, yes," Ursula admitted.

She hadn't mentioned that he was married. I trotted out the usual platitude. "Well, there's always divorce."

"Not in this case, they're both devout Catholics." She pouted at her coffee mug. "If I had my own flat, we could at least have some kind of life together."

The perfect opening. I knew it would come. "There's always my place," I said in as casual a tone as I could summon.

"You mean we could meet there?" Ursula was startled. "Wouldn't that be a bit inconvenient?"

"Not if I was at *Mon Repos*."

"I don't get you." She stared at me, baffled.

"Why don't we try switching places for a while?"

She flushed excitedly. "Oh, you mean you'd stay over at *Mon Repos* while Gran's away, and I could use your flat when we get back from Stockholm?"

"Yes, unless of course, the two of you planned to stay at *Mon Repos*."

"No, that's not possible. We wouldn't feel comfortable there, and anyway, it's not convenient for him. But Chelsea would be just great. His office is on Ebury Street." Her eyes glittered. "Oh, Susan, it would be wonderful to have your flat for a couple of weeks, are you sure?"

"Certainly, but why only for a couple of weeks? Let's make a summer of it. I'd be happy to look after your Gran for a few weeks while you and Raphael make hay."

Ursula burst into a disbelieving laugh. "You can't be serious!"

"Why not? It would give you a break from the routine, a few weeks of freedom."

"She'd never agree to it. I told you, she's a recluse. She won't have anything to do with strangers."

"Why does she even have to know? You said she's practically blind and deaf; and remember when we first met, that bloke who shared our table asked if we were twins."

"But our colouring is different."

"So, with a little bit of adjustment, colored contact lenses and Clairol, I think I would pass muster."

Ursula gaped. "You're crazy!" But there was an expression of avidity in her eye, and I could see she was tempted.

"Well," I shrugged, acting as though it was of no importance to me at all. "It was just a thought. Shouldn't we be getting back to your car? You said you only had an hour." I put that barb in to stir up her latent resentment at being kept on such a tight domestic leash.

"Yes, I suppose so," she murmured, and came along, busy with her thoughts, as I led the way out of the coffee shop. "It will never work," she said at last.

"Perhaps you're right," I murmured.

We passed by the London Eye and the elaborate living statues along the Embankment, and by the time we had reached the car, there was a determined look in her eye. "Do you really think we can pull it off?"

I pursed my lips and tried to look wise. "We can try. If it doesn't work we can 'fess up and say it was all a joke."

"How would we do it? How would we start?" Ursula was guarded but her excitement was growing.

"Tell me everything I could possibly need to know about you, Gran, and your life, and I'll handle the rest."

The day Gran left for Biarritz, I was on the doorstep of *Mon Repos*.

Ursula let me in, giggling. "Allow me to pour you a glass of wine, madam," she invited, leading the way through the house. And when we had the drinks in hand, she took me on the grand tour. It was a mansion of large, echoing, dusty rooms, most of which had not been used for years. Ursula seemed to think that was a good enough reason to neglect them. Not that there was much difference in the amount of dust between them and the rooms which were occupied; the two bedrooms, a living room, kitchen and conservatory, about which hung the same air of neglect. Throughout was an atmosphere of gloom in direct contrast to the dwelling's light and airy design.

"The house is beautiful," I declared, when we returned to the kitchen where Ursula sorted out some uninspiring chips and dip for our lunch.

"If you like this sort of thing," she said offhandedly, in the way the wealthy have of dismissing their privileges.

"I do."

"So you haven't changed your mind about looking after the place for the summer."

My heart leapt. For the summer! She had said for the summer! "On the contrary." I responded coolly, containing my excitement. "I'm totally undaunted."

"That's one hurdle, then. The other is Gran. Do you really think she would mistake you for me?"

"You're the one to answer that." I laughed. "I don't know your Gran."

Her gaze narrowed with thought. "Well, she is over eighty. She has cataracts and can't hear a thing without hearing aids, but she's still pretty sharp. I just don't know."

"Well, I leave it up to you. You're the one who wants to get out of the situation."

If she only knew!

When it was time for me to go Ursula accompanied me down the long curved drive to the gates. The grounds were stunning. "A landscaping company takes care of them," she explained. "They come by routinely on a prearranged schedule. They have a long term contract and are paid automatically."

"Do they know you?" I asked.

"Only from a distance. I've never been friendly with them. Gran has always discouraged it. I guess she's worried about incubating a Lady Chatterley in her little kingdom. The gardeners won't come into the house. You wouldn't have to worry about them at all."

This time when we parted Ursula kissed both my cheeks. It was a fashion among the English revived by Diana of Wales. I thought it pretentious and phony, but it seemed to mark a bonding among equals so I took it that we were now true conspirators.

I heard from her the next day. She rang me to ask if she could come over. She said she couldn't speak on the phone. I invited her for lunch and gave her something a little better than chips and dip — smoked salmon and cream cheese sandwiches, cherry tomatoes stuffed with avocado and *Tartelettes au Cointreau*. She could hardly contain her excitement, oh, not because of the lunch although she seemed to appreciate that, no, Raphael was going to Japan on business, if Ursula was free, she could go with him. And she very much wanted to be free.

"Look," she said, eagerness flushing her cheeks. "Even if Gran unmasks you the minute she walks in, you can tell her what we've done and look after her until I get back."

"Of course," I smiled and nodded. "We'd better get started on the family briefing and any other matters she's likely to expect me to know about."

"That won't take long," Ursula uttered sardonically. "Since I left school I've been her caretaker. End of story."

I took out my notebook.

Over the next couple of hours Ursula told me where she went to school and all the details of her life since then. She was right, there wasn't much to tell. I jotted down information about her few friends, girls she had known at school who were now all married and absorbed in their own lives. And there was the already remarked upon dearth of boyfriends due to the restrictions of her social life.

"What about your father, didn't he ever come back from Africa?"

"Well, he came back for the memorial service and to collect Mum's life insurance, but he only stayed for a week."

"So, that's it, that's all you remember of him?"

"I was only six when the plane crashed, and I don't have any memory of that time or anything before. What I know is secondhand from Gran, except for the donkey rides. I remember them. We were at Hunstanton and every morning he took me to have a donkey ride along the sands. I've loved donkeys ever since, just the donkeys, not my father."

"Is there anything else I should know about him which Gran might bring up?"

"We don't discuss him anymore. But you can read her diaries and letters. She's never thrown a thing away, you know. She has archives the British Museum would envy. You'll find everything you need to know in the rolltop desk in the study."

She then proceeded to give me a complete picture of the practical arrangements including the household finances. In a nutshell, an accounting firm retained by Gran oversaw everything. There was, for instance, a deposit into Ursula's account every month, a very large deposit, part of which she would pay out to me. Anything that was required for the house, like the food, was charged to Gran's account. At the end of the month the utility bills were paid automatically. Ursula rarely had to sign her name to anything, but we thought it prudent that I learn how to forge her signature.

As for Ursula taking my place at the flat, that was simple. She would live there rent free. If anyone asked (and who would), she would say she was flat-sitting for me while I was away.

"Actually," Ursula said, getting up to leave, "there really isn't any reason why we shouldn't start now. It will take you a bit of time to get used to the house; so the longer you're there before Gran comes back the better. Why don't you move in tomorrow?"

I did move in the next day, but eager though Ursula was to set up home in my flat, we still had business to conduct. She came with me to pay for the colored contact lenses, two pairs, just to be safe and to have my hair lightened by a very good hairdresser on the King's Road and cut in the same style as hers. When this was done we stood side by side looking in a mirror, and I have to say that at first glance we surely did look like twins — but would it be enough to deceive Gran?

I spent the days before Gran came home taking stock of *Mon Repos*. I couldn't wait to spring clean the place but didn't even start on it as that would've immediately aroused her suspicions. I'd already thought up some strategies for explaining how Ursula had suddenly become house-proud and a more skillful cook. But my main thrust for those two weeks was to train myself to become Ursula. So I began to study the situation into whose bosom fate had projected me and spent hours with the family photograph albums. These were beautifully organized with detailed notes about each member and catalogued by occasions. Perhaps it had been a hobby of one of the family who had perished in the plane crash because there was nothing like it after the date of the accident.

I was surprised to discover how much I resembled Ursula's mother, but I couldn't claim to look at all like any of Gran's ancestors whose dour portraits hung upon the walls of the dusty library as well as two of the spare bedrooms. I put in a lot of time reading Gran's diaries and letters, and caught the whiff of a Miss Haversham since everything seemed to have stopped in her life when the family was wiped out. I moved easily around the lofty apartments examining every part of their contents. Ursula had told me that Gran never went into the kitchen so I felt completely comfortable reorganizing all the cupboards and the pantry to suit myself. It was all great fun.

By the end of the two weeks, I had familiarized myself with the family and the house. In preparation for Gran's return, I went to Sainsbury's and placed a large order which they delivered. It was charged to Gran's account.

Gran was due to arrive at two on Saturday afternoon. She was being brought home by the same relative of her friend, a Mr. Daly, who had taken her over to France. They were flying in and her escort was driving her from the airport. I was standing on the doorstep, deliberately in the shadow of the portico, having a sudden misgiving about the success of our deception, when the car drew up. Mr. Daly was a middle-aged man dressed like a London banker in a grey pinstripe suit. He hurried around the car to assist Gran out. She looked exactly like that day I'd seen her in the car — small, frail, silver-haired. She was a little stooped and used a cane. Still shaded by the portico, I bent to kiss her cheek. This, I had learned from Ursula was a required ritual, both coming and going. I was immediately aware of a delicate, expensive perfume. "Have you had a good time, Gran?" I asked.

"Yes, thank you, dear."

I turned my attention to her companion. Ursula reported that she had never met him so I was quite confident in looking at him quite openly. "Would you care to come in for tea, Mr. Daly?"

"Well I - " He glanced at his watch. "Yes, I do believe I have time. It was rather a tiring drive from Gatwick."

I helped Gran into the house and along to the sitting room. The teacart was already prepared. All I had to do was make the tea and set out the Victoria sponge I had baked earlier. It was filled with apricot jam and whipped cream. I'd sifted confectioner's sugar over the top in a lace pattern using a doily, and decorated the centre with a fresh flower. It looked gorgeous and tasted better. Mr. Daly was full of compliments. When I had seen him off with profuse thanks for looking after Gran and returned to the sitting room, she gave me an interested look. "That was a delicious cake, Ursula dear, thank you."

"It was my pleasure, Gran."

Knowing that she always napped in the afternoon, I took her suitcase and went up to her bedroom with her. While she was taking off her dress and shoes, I unpacked her case and sorted out what needed to be washed and what could be hung in the wardrobe. She put on a robe and lay down on her bed. "Don't let me sleep too long, dear. You know I always get a headache if I sleep for more than half an hour in the day."

I closed the curtains over the two windows and picked up her laundry. "I'll be up at three-thirty sharp."

That evening I cooked us a fine wild salmon with dill sauce.

I adored the kitchen. It had every appliance and gadget invented, most of which had never been used. While the salmon poached gently in its white wine sauce, I prepared the table in the little morning room which Ursula sometimes used on special occasions, with a damask cloth, matching napkins and the Royal Copenhagen. I filled a silver fluted vase with blush roses from the garden and set that in the middle. It pained me to not use the dining room, but Ursula said she had closed that up a couple of years before. It was quite large and formal, and two of them never entertained. Ursula preferred to give Gran her meals in the kitchen. I knew Gran always had a sherry before dinner; so using the Steuben glasses, I poured us both a *Fino* which I carried into the conservatory where Gran was reading the paper. The conservatory was a charming space, despite its grubbiness, with its white wicker furniture set among tropical plants and hanging baskets.

Gran looked up with a smile. "Let's go outside, shall we, dear?"

The flagstone patio was furnished with heavily upholstered *chaises-longue* and a swing chair with a canvas canopy. It was a glorious evening, and I was in heaven, sipping sherry in the peace of that lovely garden with the perfume of the flowers drifting on the breeze and the song birds filling the air with their sweet melodies.

The dinner was a great success. I knew I was taking a bit of a chance producing such a delicious meal but speculated I could cover it with the explanation that I'd become a sudden fan of Nigella Lawson and had taken a couple of lessons from the local gourmet cooking school while Gran was away.

The evening was spent very pleasantly in front of the television until we retired after the late news. When we parted at the top of the stairs, I dropped a kiss on the old lady's cheek and she patted my arm. "God bless you, my dear," she said.

And I thought, I believe He has.

It wouldn't be truthful to say that the next few days passed without worry. I was treading on eggshells; absorbing, processing and analyzing information every minute of the day all the while expecting at any moment to be unmasked. But as the hours and then the days of that first week passed with no action from Gran I began to relax and really enjoy myself.

Of course, when I say I began to relax, I do not mean to suggest that I was careless. Ursula had been right about the old lady's sensory impairments, but I also fancied myself a rather convincing impressionist. I thought before I said or did anything and was always on guard not to slide into my own personality. At the start, I kept up with Ursula's daily routine and only gradually introduced new elements into it, principal among them the cleaning of the house, a task I anticipated with great eagerness.

Gradually Gran and I began breakfasting in the bright, pretty morning room. I loved this morning ritual with the blue and white checked table cloth and thin cold toast in a silver rack. It made me feel as though I were in a Jane Austen novel. I served two kinds of shop-bought marmalade in crystal dishes, one of lemon and one of orange. Neither was as good as homemade; so I resolved to try to secure some Seville oranges and make a batch of real marmalade for us. Gran read the morning paper at the table and that precluded any discussion. I was content to look out of the window as I ate, enjoying the fine view of the pond where water lilies floated among the rich green pads. A Monet painting.

Soon I was occupied with the daily routine. However boring and restricting it may have been for Ursula I found it delightful. I was in my element in the kitchen and baked something different for tea every day. I explored all the recipe books I found on a high shelf where Ursula had hidden them and had a wonderful time creating the most divine dinners and lunches. I anticipated an increase in the grocery bills and the explanation for that was probably going to be the first practical hurdle to overcome. But I was prepared.

At the end of three weeks, it became obvious that Gran had miraculously accepted me. There were no complaints, no recriminations, no dramatic unmaskings.

"You must be quite an actress," Ursula applauded and began preparing for her trip to Japan.

With Ursula happily ensconced as Raphael's mistress and Gran apparently oblivious to any change in her household, I settled down to a summer which befitted my sensibility, no more worries about money or working or any insecurities. I loved *Mon Repos* and the Mercedes which, of course, I drove whenever I went on my forays to the supermarket. I loved being the lady of the house which, in effect, I gradually became.

Ursula was right about the lack of visitors, and the only wheels that had rolled up the drive since I moved in, were those on the landscapers' truck.

At last I felt confident enough to begin a thorough housecleaning. It was going to take a long time and I knew I would have to work my way through it slowly, so as not to bring Gran's attention to the changes too suddenly. I started on the ground floor with the most obvious chores. Gradually, I took all the crystal and china from the cabinets in the morning room and dining room and washed it. I cleaned the silver, starting with what we used then graduating to the canteens of cutlery I unearthed in the dining room. I washed all the ornaments and vases from every one of the lower rooms. I cleaned the mirrors and the glass on the portraits and paintings. I scrubbed out the conservatory whose flag-stone floor was mildewed. I laundered the sheer curtains and vacuumed the heavier draperies with a hose attachment. The result of all this was a lovely freshness about the house. It began to exude the air of a home well-loved, and it was. I loved it. Gran certainly noticed something despite the cataracts because she made a comment about how bright everything looked.

Then, one evening when we were taking coffee in the conservatory after what I have to boast was a most delicious meal of stuffed guinea fowl, she regarded me from her white wicker armchair, now gleaming, and remarked, "I just cannot get over how much your cooking has improved, Ursula. Tonight's meal was outstanding."

"Thank you, Gran," I smiled, stirring my demitasse with one of her dainty teaspoons from a set of twelve vermeil with different coloured enameled handles. I enjoyed using those teaspoons, as I enjoyed all her pretty things. Most of her possessions were intrinsically precious but that was not what gave me pleasure. I loved them for their beauty. Whoever had furnished the house and chosen the accoutrements had the most exquisite taste, something I profoundly appreciated.

"That course you took must be something rather special," she continued.

"Ah, but I don't bring my failures to the table." I murmured with what I hoped was a bashful look.

"I have to say, Ursula dear, you do seem to be very much more content since I came back. Is there anything I should know?"

I'd been expecting this moment of suspicion, or something like it, which I knew must surely come, and had already resolved to address it as if I were Ursula. In my brief association with her, I didn't think she was all that smart. I mean, all she could think about was her idiotic married lover who, in the end, would bring her nothing but grief; how clever was that? At the same time, I had begun to foster a lot of respect for Gran and I reminded myself, in that tense moment, not to underestimate her.

I kept my eyes down for a minute and fiddled with my teaspoon as though I was embarrassed. "No, nothing, I...well, there was a man, and…er…now I have my priorities straight."

"Oh, I see, I was unaware that you were involved with someone."

"I - yes, I kept it from you. Sorry, Gran."

"And now you have finished with him, is that what you're saying?"

"Yes."

"May I ask why?"

I took a chance. "He deceived me. I didn't know he was married."

"Married!" Her brows shot up. "And you say you didn't know? So the fact that he was married was not the reason you kept this relationship from me?"

My mind quickly darted ahead, hoping the interrogation would be short at best. "No, Gran, it wasn't that. I - I just didn't think you would approve of him."

"And why not?"

"You would have thought him rather like father."

There was small silence and then she said, gently and serenely, "How well you are getting to know me, my dear."

I thought that was it! That the game was up! I escaped into the kitchen to get the dessert. I stood gripping the sink, cinders in my mouth, my heart beating absurdly fast. It took me a while to compose myself and return to the conservatory, but we finished our meal without another word on that explosive subject and spent the evening as we always did. We retired for the night with the usual kiss. I didn't sleep a wink, however, and was badly stressed for the next couple of days.

At the end of that week, I asked Gran if she would like me to take her for a spin in the Mercedes. At first she seemed a little hesitant which I put down to Ursula's driving, but then, with a strange little shrug of resignation, she smiled at me and assented. I drove carefully so as not to alarm her, using back roads whenever possible. Soon I was taking her out regularly.

We picked our times and locations to avoid the worst of the traffic. Sometimes we scheduled the excursions to include a pub lunch along the Thames or in some quaint village. Once we actually went to Harrods for tea, and on that occasion I claimed the right to pay for us both instead of going dutch.

"Oh, I couldn't possibly let you do that," Gran protested. "It's enormously expensive to eat here. They even charge separately for the butter."

"But I want to, Gran," I insisted and did. I was having the most terrific time, and I wanted in some small way to show my gratitude.

We had a delicious feast of finger sandwiches, scones, strawberry jam with clotted cream, and Harrods Blend 49 tea. "We must come for crumpets in the winter," I suggested in my enthusiasm.

"Mmm, lovely thought," she agreed with such a nuance in her voice that I was sure whatever brief moments of suspicion she might have been harboring she was, for the first time in years, having a good time and would like it to continue.

It was on that occasion that the idea formed to extend this pleasant arrangement beyond the end of summer and spin it out until Gran's life ended. And this I proposed to Ursula when we next met at the flat. She thought it the most wonderful idea but before she got too excited I told her that we would have to arrive at some revised financial arrangement. At Gran's death, Ursula would become an enormously wealthy woman, and I would be back where I started on the day we met, penniless except for what I had managed to save over my weeks at *Mon Repos*. This hardly seemed an equitable arrangement if she wanted us to extend our little pretense until her Gran passed away. The new guidelines I proposed which would set me up with a percentage of her inheritance gave Ursula no problem at all. I think she would have signed away her entire fortune to enable her to continue her sordid love affair, but then, she had no concept of the value of money.

Life continued to flow so smoothly and elegantly at *Mon Repos* that I was able to take my ease and organize life to the best advantage for both Gran and me. The household began to run on oiled wheels. Slowly and methodically I finished the cleaning and I wanted to expand into other rooms. We now took all our meals in the morning room but that was not enough for me. I had managed to bring the dining room back to its former clean and polished glory without Gran being aware of it. I worked on it while she was in the garden or having her nap. Then, one evening I decided to serve dinner in there. I didn't say anything just took her to the dining room after we had drunk our sherry, and opened the door. I thought I had overstepped the mark. She came to a complete halt just inside the room and stood as if stunned. I was just behind her, riveted to the floor, unable to guess what was coming next.

"Your mother loved this room," she said at last with such a deep longing in her voice that it touched my heart — and my conscience. At that moment I was almost ready to confess our little deception, but the urge quickly passed, and I was glad it did. Gran was happy, happier I'm sure than she had been in years. Why would I deprive her of that? Her next comment gave me a moment's trouble but not enough to disturb my returning confidence. She said, softly and with what I interpreted as an element of longing, "You seem more like her every day."

Gran was so delighted with the dining room that from then on we used it for dinner every day. Thus, we moved happily into late summer, my senses lulled by ease and pleasure. We enjoyed car rides into the country to see the leaves turning to gold, and where we soon became conscious of a hint of that indefinable autumn fragrance which speaks of wood fires, snug overcoats and fur-lined boots. We would sometimes park the car and walk through the woods or alongside a river, and Gran would tuck her arm through mine, and we would trudge in companionable silence or exchange comments on some bird or a particular wildflower we'd spotted. She even began to suggest outings we might take, and I was happy to fall in with any plan of hers as I had none of my own, except for her comfort and by extension mine, of course. I think I can honestly say we were both content.

One lovely October day I went into town to Selfridge's Food Hall to buy some ingredients which weren't available locally. Gran had told me that years before, when she was in Athens on holiday, she had been served some dishes which she longed to try again. I could have bought some of what she wanted ready made but that wasn't my way. Whatever we were going to eat I wanted to prepare myself. There was no difficulty with the ingredients for the Kota Meh Bamies, but the tarama for the Taramosalta and the kefalotiri cheese for the Saganaki required a trip to a specialty delicatessen.

When I got back from grocery shopping it took me all of thirty seconds sense that something had happened in my absence. I found Gran in the conservatory and was disconcerted to see that she had one of the old photo albums on her knee and was slowly paging through it. Her whole manner was totally different from when I had left. She was pale and edgy, and her smile, brief.

"How was it in town?" she asked.

"The usual traffic nightmare." I busied myself pouring tea with one eye on her as she sat with her frail hand on the open page of the photo album. "Shall I put that aside for you?" I asked as I set the tea in front of her.

"Yes please, dear."

She handed me the album which was still open at a page with a snapshot taken at the seaside of a child on a donkey with a man alongside. My mind began to race. I felt a flush rise into my cheeks; so I kept my face averted and put the album on a side table. Gran didn't speak again until we were both seated with our tea. "Your father came to see me today," said she.

What greater shock could there have been?

I felt lucky to have sensed that something was amiss since that was the only thing that prevented me from dropping my teacup on the floor. It didn't concern me that Gran saw my reaction. It would have been very strange if Ursula had not been stunned. My thoughts were already far ahead of that, but this was one thing Ursula and I had not bargained for. I placed my cup and saucer carefully down. "I'm speechless." I kept my voice low and my words measured. "I was sure he was dead."

"We assumed that, yes, but there never was any proof. And now we know why."

"Where has he been all these years?"

"In Africa."

I was at a complete loss. My stomach was in a knot. Our plan had been based on Ursula's determination that her father was dead, and we had both supposed that we could carry on our deceit for as long as it suited us. But now our arrangement was in dire danger, and I felt a rising sense of anger that my delightful relationship with Gran was about to be shattered by this intrusive, unwanted, interfering berk!

"What did he want?" I asked through gritted teeth.

"He wanted to see you."

"That's rich! After all these years? I hope you sent him packing."

"More or less."

I was jolted. *More or less?* "What do you mean, Gran?"

"I didn't think I had the right to speak for you, my dear."

"But you do. He may be my father, but he has no place in my life. He probably just needs money, right?"

"Oh yes, he needs money."

"He didn't threaten you, did he?" I demanded anxiously.

She set her cup down in her saucer with a slight rattle, which was entirely understandable. "No, he did not threaten me. He was actually quite horribly obsequious. Of course, he always did have a sort of facile charm, something you wouldn't have been aware of. Do you have any memory of him at all, my dear?"

The look she turned on me was so searching it struck me quite forcibly that the question could have been intended as a challenge. "None at all. Well - " I hesitated, then attempted to echo what Ursula had said to me weeks ago. "Except for donkey rides on the sand at Hunstanton. I remember the donkeys," I murmured.

She did not answer for so long that I wondered with a sinking stomach if Ursula had been careless enough to give me false information. I sat as if cast in stone until Gran spoke again. "Yes." Her hand twitched in the direction of the album. "That is the only photograph of you and your father together. He asked to see it, that's why it is out."

"The sentimental fool," I sneered and immediately knew that was a mistake. It was something Ursula would never have said. Thankfully, Gran was too distracted to notice.

"He left the telephone number where he's staying and would like you to ring him," she said.

I thought about that for a moment, thinking for myself *and* for Ursula. I wasn't all that sharp, but I was fifty percent sharper than Ursula, so I knew she would be no help in this situation. For myself, I had to buy some time to work out a plan. "Do you think I should?" I asked warily.

"You may have to in order to convince him that you want nothing to do with him, if that is the case."

"It certainly is the case!" I stated adamantly. "But I don't want him coming here, Gran. If I have to meet him it will be in a public place."

"As you wish, my dear."

She gave me a look which I can only describe as quizzical, which was distinctly unnerving. My wariness increased.

I urgently needed to talk to Ursula, but I had no excuse for going out again. Instead, I went into the garden for what

I hoped would appear to be a casual stroll around the pond. Then, I slipped behind the potting shed and called Ursula on my mobile.

She went into shock. She just couldn't take it in.

"Oh my God!" she gasped. "What in the hell are we going to do?"

"I don't know yet. Can you come over to Kew?"

"To the house?" she exclaimed.

"No, The Golden Hind." This was a pub within walking distance of the gates of *Mon Repos*. "Meet me there at two when Gran goes up for her nap."

I got through the time until I met Ursula by turning out the box room. It was one of the last places in the house untouched by me. It was a small room on the upper floor where, in the old days, luggage was stored, luggage in early times mainly consisting of trunks and elegant boxes. I stood in the doorway and looked at the jumble within. Ursula had shoved everything she hadn't wanted to deal with in that room, and except for it, a photographer from *House Beautiful* could have walked into *Mon Repos* without warning and taken pictures at any time of day. I went downstairs for the vacuum cleaner.

Ursula was already sitting in the murkiest corner of the pub nursing a drink when I hurried in. "The bastard!" she burst out agitatedly. "There's no way Gran's going to give him any money. I can't imagine why he would think she would!"

I sat down with my glass of white wine. "He hasn't asked her for money."

"You said he had! You said that's what he wanted."

"Oh yes, he wants money, but he doesn't expect to get it from Gran."

"Well, he's not getting any from me. I don't have a red cent!"

"Not at the moment, but - " I gave her a wry look.

Ursula's face visibly blanched. She fell back against the wooden settle, unable to speak.

"He wants to see you, Ursula," I stated evenly.

"No! No way! I'm not having anything to do with him!"

I let her rant on for a short while until she ran out of steam. Then I said, "Okay, now let's get serious. There's no way you can refuse to see him, not while I'm living under Gran's roof. And if I'm not living there you'll have to. So you're going to have to meet him. We may have been able to fool Gran, but it's too dicey to chance that your father will accept me as his daughter." I did not tell her that I also had the beginning of a suspicion that Gran just might not have been quite so naïve as we thought. I didn't want to rattle Ursula any more than I already had. It was essential, now more than ever, that we both keep our nerve. "As long as we keep him away from *Mon Repos*, he'll never know that there are two of us," I assured her. I drank some of my wine and replaced the glass carefully on the coaster. "Okay, he's staying at the Winchester Hotel in Hampstead, room 206. Phone him and make an arrangement to meet."

"Meet him when?"

"The sooner the better. We don't want him hanging around London too long."

"Susan, he could ruin everything!"

"Eureka! So you have to get rid of him."

"How?"

I sighed. "I don't know, but it's important that you do, or we might as well give up right now. Just don't make any sudden moves," I warned. "Meet him, stay calm and let him tell you how he expects to get money from you. Don't make any promises, but don't antagonize him. Also, get as much information out of him as you can as to how he's been living and what his current circumstances are."

Ursula moved uneasily. "I wish you could do this," she quavered.

So did I, but I wasn't about to say so and shake her confidence even more. "You'll be fine if you just stay cool. And remember, we're holding all the cards."

She didn't look convinced.

"And arrange to meet him again," I added.

"What? Why?" She looked horrified.

"Because we need to keep control of him until we know how we're going to handle this. If you say you won't see him again, he will go straight back to Gran and then we'll be in even worse trouble. He's been there once. He'll go there again."

"Right, okay."

"Try to meet him tomorrow morning. If he can't, phone me on my mobile to let me know. If he's willing, and I'm sure he will be, I will tell Gran I'm meeting him and drive up to the flat and wait for you to come back. I'll have to know exactly what happens. We have to move fast, or he *will* sabotage our futures."

She nodded, reluctantly, and I understood how she felt, but I was damned if I was going to let this intruder disrupt the plans I had made for the rest of my life.

The next day when she arrived back at the flat, her first words sent a chill through me. "I think we are in trouble."

Within minutes we were heading to the Black Prince on the King's Road for a stiff drink.

"The bastard wants to make a deal," she said, tossing back her G&T.

"What kind of a deal?"

"Either I get a loan against my inheritance or he moves in with Gran and me."

Now it was my turn to choke.

"He would do it too," Ursula was blathering on. "He's that desperate. What do we do? He's got us between a rock and a hard place."

"Tell me about him. What's he doing in England? How long has he been here?"

"He's just arrived, literally checked into the hotel directly from Heathrow. He's only come for money — the bastard!"

"Is he alone in the world?"

"It would seem so," she said.

"Ursula, settle down and tell me about him. How does he look?"

"Awful. He's fifty-six but he looks seventy. He's got emphysema."

"Smokes, does he?"

"The proverbial chimney. He coughs his bloody head off. It's disgusting. And he's a dipso."

"How do you know that?"

"Besides the half dozen bottles of tequila in his carpet bag and the empties in the bin, you mean?"

"Are you kidding?"

"No. Speaking of which - " She got up to fetch herself another drink saying defiantly, "One of the few benefits of no longer having the use of a car!"

When she returned most of the pep had gone out of her. Sitting down her whole body sagged. "He's not a very salubrious character, Susan."

"How was his attitude?"

"Wheedling would probably describe it best, but that won't last once he finds out he's not going to wrestle any money out of me."

"Then you'd better stall him for now."

"And just how am I supposed to do that?" She gave me a sardonic look. "Give him an NSF cheque for a hundred thousand quid or a suitcase full of counterfeit tenners?"

"Well, we could always kill him."

"Yeah, right."

"So exactly what arrangement did you make with him?"

"I said I would talk to one of the trustees and phone him later."

"That's good. Do that, then. Phone him, I mean. This

evening."

"And tell him what?"

"Tell him that the trustee has to get back to you, and you'll call him again in the morning. We need to put him on hold for a while."

Ursula nodded. "Okay. Then what?"

"Then we figure out what to do."

Before we parted company I had Ursula describe their meeting in exact detail so that I could relate enough of it to Gran in the event she and Ursula's father had another conversation. I didn't think he would show up at *Mon Repos* again until he had had some response from Ursula, but he just might telephone.

When I got back from 'seeing my father,' as she thought, Gran was up in her room having her nap. I looked in to make sure she was all right and noticed her alarm clock was set to awaken her at two-thirty. I went down to the kitchen to bake a cake and make a *tortiere* for dinner. She never disturbed me when I was in the kitchen so I did not see her until we met for our pre-dinner sherry.

"So, what did you think of your father?" she asked.

I detected another of her disturbing little glances.

"I really don't think of him as my father at all," I replied, actually experiencing the disgust I knew Ursula felt.

"That's very clever, my dear." That remark was said so ironically that I wondered if I had made a blunder in putting it that way, it was quite unintentional. But no, she smiled. "What did you say to him?"

"I asked him to go away and leave us alone," I replied, subdued by my moment of anxiety.

"How did he take that?"

"He came up with some silly nonsense about always being my father."

"Hmm. What arrangements have you made with him?"

"In what respect, Gran?"

"About seeing him again."

"None. I don't intend seeing him again."

"And he has accepted that?"

"What choice does he have? I'm over eighteen. He has no jurisdiction over me."

"Well, I'm surprised. As I remember Keith Pixley it wasn't like him to give up so easily, not when money was a factor, and by the look of him I'd venture he is down on his luck."

"As he deserves to be."

"Well, I must say I'm relieved. I was concerned that you would take pity on him." A moment's silence, then, "If you were going to give away a part of your inheritance, I wouldn't like to think it would be to him."

My scalp tingled, but I retained my composure.

Finished with her sherry, she held out a hand for me to help her up, and we walked into the dining room. It was a lovely evening. The last rays of the sun turned the table settings into jewels. The dusky roses in the sparkling, cut glass vase glowed against the snowy damask table cloth. Gran glanced around appreciatively. "The old house is beginning to feel like a home again," she said, and I felt comforted for the moment.

But that night, for the first time since I moved into *Mon Repos*, I felt the constraint that had caused Ursula such discontent. I needed to have some time away from Gran to make plans with Ursula, and I couldn't just walk out of the door. I had hoped I could see Ursula the next day; but when I rang her from behind the potting shed as dusk was gathering, she was terribly spooked and insisted we talk right away. So, when Gran had gone up to bed I had no choice but to slip away and meet Ursula at the Golden Hind just beyond the gates of *Mon Repos*.

"I've bought you a brandy," Ursula said. "I speculated you'd need it to steady your nerves."

"You speculated right."

"I don't know why you're so worried about leaving Gran alone for half an hour," she laughed with a *frisson* of hysteria. "I'd go off for the entire night and she never knew the difference."

"You didn't!" I was appalled.

"When the wife was out of town Raphael checked into a hotel and I joined him there for the night."

"You haven't told Raphael about your father, have you?" I demanded sharply.

"Christ! No."

"Thank God for that. Where does he think you are tonight? Didn't he want to come here with you?"

"He's not at Chelsea. He's at his other home. It was his son's birthday today so he had to be there."

"Well, what was so urgent that we had to meet this minute?"

"I'm scared. Father was very aggressive this afternoon. He'd been drinking, all morning by the look of him. It was all I could do to stop him from coming back with me to see Gran."

This was serious.

"He's going to be difficult to control. Drunks are unreliable at the best of times, and he's got an agenda. He wants the money and he wants now."

"Do you have any idea what for?"

"Apparently to bugger off back to South Africa."

"Do you mean he flew to England to get the money and go directly back?"

"It sounds like it but you know how sly drinkers can be."

"Is he alone?"

"It looks like it," Ursula nodded. "I third-degreed him, but I couldn't get anything of use. His brain has been addled by the booze."

"That bad, eh?"

"Yep." She took a gulp of brandy and sat for some time staring into her snifter. Then, without looking up, she murmured. "What you said before..." Her voice tailed off.

Then, "About killing him."

I waited for a minute before responding. "Right, but are we really murderers?"

Her eyes came up slowly. "Well, we've sort of killed each other off, haven't we?"

I was surprised by her logic, but it was true, the Susan and Ursula who now sat side by side in a dark corner of a noisy pub were not the same young women who had met months earlier. We had manipulated our situations into something that suited us much better than the conditions we had been in. That took skill and planning. Still, "That wasn't a crime. This would be different."

"I know." She moved her glass around the table top in a mysterious pattern. "But the thing is, it proves we can do it. I mean, if we had the will to do this other thing, we could. I've been surfing the Net."

"What for, recipes for magic potions to make the unwanted disappear?"

"Yes. Actually."

"Witchcraft.com?"

"Chemistry.com. Have you heard of Jib?"

"You mean GHB, the rave drug?" I was stunned, positively amazed at her.

"Liquid ecstasy, yes. Apparently, a high dose mixed with alcohol can result in severe respiratory depression and… umm…coma within five minutes. It's particularly dangerous for individuals whose lungs are already compromised."

"Interesting." I couldn't help but smile. This certainly was a different Ursula.

"It's tasteless and odourless in liquid form." She chewed the inside of her mouth. "It doesn't leave any trace in blood or urine samples taken during post mortem. Some date-rape drugs turn alcohol blue, but Liquid X doesn't, and it's readily available on the street."

I fell into thought. I'd known how badly she'd wanted to maintain our comfortable situation with its promise of riches when Gran died, but I hadn't suspected the depth of her resentment against this man who had abandoned her at the age of six to go off and indulge his sybaritic lifestyle. I was all too familiar with his sort, note the Aussie who'd duped my mother, who waltzed in and out of people's lives at a selfish whim, creating chaos and misery. And now here her father was again, neither use nor ornament.

They say capital punishment is no deterrent to murder, but it might have deterred me if it had existed in England. Even the thought of a life sentence horrified me, but not enough for me to reject Ursula's proposal out of hand. We were already living day to day in circumstances where the line between reality and fantasy had become blurred so the idea of murder wasn't really such a large step. Too, we were vulnerable, and he was an intolerable threat. Humanity was not an issue here, no more than it had been for him when he dumped his daughter after her mother's death. He had no right to come into our lives and cause us any more trouble than he already had. So, it was not a matter of should we but could we take another step along a path we had proven we were competent to tread. If we did there was absolutely no question that we would do it together.

I didn't ask Ursula how or where she would get the GHB. With the money she had at her disposal she could sub-contract more than one middleman to distance herself from the actual purchase.

"What time does he start drinking?" I asked.

"Early, but with his tolerance it must take a few gallons before he slides under the table. He was pretty unsteady this afternoon, but he wasn't zonked."

"Well, if Jib works the way you say it does, he doesn't need to be totally out of it. So, are we on?"

She stared at me. I could read her thoughts. The enormity of what we were intending to do had suddenly flooded her mind, but what other choice did she have if she didn't want to give up her very satisfactory new life? "It's your call." I told her. "Why don't you sleep on it, but don't leave it too long. You're probably right about his lack of patience."

She took a breath and resolutely shook her head. "I don't need to sleep on it. It has to be done; and if I think about it too long, I'll lose my nerve."

It was Ursula's nerve which worried me the most. The plan itself was simple enough. All she had to do was meet him in his room again and dose his tequila when he went to use the bathroom. He would either die or he wouldn't. Chances are he wouldn't be discovered until late afternoon because Ursula would hang the Do Not Disturb sign on the doorknob. When he was found housekeeping would doubtless obligingly confirm that the number of empties carted out of there during his short stay had broken every known record.

Had there been anything suspicious about the death of Keith Pixley, it might have warranted a column inch in one of the tabloid papers, but there wasn't. The coroner was satisfied that under the circumstances it was a natural death within the meaning of the act and signed the release form.

It took the police a few days to track down the deceased only living relative at *Mon Repos*. I obliging paid the bills for his hotel and the funeral and donated a small sum of money to Alcoholics Anonymous in his memory. That was my idea, not Ursula's.

As the nights grew cooler Gran and I took our after dinner coffee into the cozy sitting room to drink it in front of the faux-log fire. *Mon Repos* had been well-fitted with central heating, but there was nothing as comforting as an open flame, even if it was gas rather than coal. Gran had barely remarked upon 'father's' death and hadn't even attended the funeral service, so I was a bit startled when one evening I became the target of one of her disturbing little glances.

"How fortuitous that he should drink himself to death," she observed dryly.

The tone of her voice sent the blood rushing into my face.

"Yes," I said, and as I had before when she said something equally as enigmatic I made an excuse and quickly left the room. I not only left the room, I left the house. Panicked, I ran out to the patio in an effort to catch my breath. As I stood listening to the call of a night bird, my mind raced like an out of control engine and I succumbed to the truth. I could no longer delude myself. It was ridiculous to think that Gran had *ever* believed I was her granddaughter. There must have been a dozen different ways in which she was able to distinguish between the real Ursula and me. How could Ursula and I ever have thought for one moment that Gran would be taken in? The notion was completely ludicrous. That I could now see with total clarity. But why hadn't she challenged me? Wasn't she the least bit concerned about the disappearance of her granddaughter? Did she think I had murdered her? And now that her son-in-law was suddenly and very conveniently dead, surely she must wonder what I might have in store for her.

I spent as much time as I dared calming myself down, then went into the kitchen where I grabbed some Stilton, walnuts, and stuffed dates and hastily arranged them on a serving platter.

"I forgot we had this as a savory, Gran," I said, carrying the tray in and setting it in front of her.

"Oh, how lovely," she exclaimed.

I was aware of her old eyes on me as I busied myself bringing out some small plates and napkins. I heard the intake of her breath as she prepared to speak and my stomach tightened. Whatever I expected next, it wasn't these words.

"You know," she said. "I think we should have a little celebration. Isn't there a bottle of rather good champagne about somewhere?"

I was as nervous as a racehorse, and I thought I probably

looked like one as well, all staring eyes and flaring nostrils.

"I - I believe there is, Gran," I managed to stutter.

"Why don't you go and fetch it, my dear?"

I was glad to again escape from the room for a few minutes, and confess I took a swig out of the brandy bottle before I went back with the champagne wrapped in a white cloth and two exquisite, crystal flutes. I managed to uncork the bottle without spraying the entire room and poured us both a glass. As I handed Gran hers where she sat on the sofa it seemed to me that her smile was full of secrets.

"Well, what shall we toast to, Ursula?"

My heart turned over. I lunged about in my mind for something safe and reassuring.

"To your continued good health, Gran."

"How sweet of you," she said, and with a slow, deliberate movement clinked her glass against mine. After taking a sip, she gave me a quizzical look, and raised her glass again. Terrified of what she was going to say next I also lifted my glass. "To absent friends and relatives," Gran said.

"To absent friends and relatives," I repeated, like an automaton.

As smiled, I thought I detected a slight satirical light in her eye.

"Do you have someone you wish to toast, Ursula?"

"Only you, Gran," I said, and I truly meant it and prayed that she knew I did.

"Thank you, my dear," she said.

RAPTURE OF THE DEEP

"How awful to think that if we hadn't encouraged him to come on the cruise -" Helen sighed, shaking her head, "- he'd still be alive."

"He didn't have to come," Mac replied without looking up.

"Of course not, but I still can't help feeling responsible."

Mac set his empty eggcup aside and reached for the *New York Times*.

"Do you think Neil and the girls blame us?" Helen asked.

"No more than they blame us for Naomi's death."

"That's a bit different, Mac. Naomi died of cancer." Helen's eyes strayed to the window. On the other side of the snowy deck the land fell away into a wide valley. The morning light was diffused through a mist, stained pink by the reflection of the sun's rays on the snowy caps of the western mountains. Salt Lake City glittered in the distance with a cold beauty.

"How can they blame us when they encouraged him to come with us." Mac rattled the newspaper.

Helen got up and strolled to the windows. She peered

disconsolately at the deck where the barbeque, draped in its black plastic cover, was topped by the fresh snow that had fallen in the night — depressing evidence of a late, winter storm. In fact the entire winter had been depressing along with the pre-Christmas cruise which had been designed to cheer them up. They usually took two vacations during the long winter months. Thank goodness Mac hadn't suggested another cruise. She was a long way from shaking off the effects of the last one. Her shoulders drooped disconsolately. Nothing would ever fill the gap in their life now dear Bertram was dead.

It had been such a lovely cruise at the start. They had all basked in the tropical sun, either on the decks of the *Royal Countess* or on some lovely Caribbean beach. Oh, those beaches! Every island had its own particular color of sand, everything from pure white through cream and rose to silver-flecked ebony.

The six of them, Jane and Oliver Davis, Naomi and Bertram Prentice and she and Mac, had been promising themselves a cruise together for a couple of years, and it was Naomi's sudden death, at sixty-two in September that had mobilized them into the realization of life's cruel inconstancy, spurring them to take the cruise while they still could. It had taken a lot to persuade Bertram to join them; but when his son and daughters had added their support, he'd reluctantly agreed.

Right from the beginning Bertram was besieged by guilt. He just could not rid himself of the feeling that it was not quite right to be whirling around the Caribbean when his wife was in her grave. He confided this to his companions when the ship left Miami amid the usual circus of excitement, and so remained quietly in his stateroom. He appeared for dinner, then secluded himself for the whole of the next day, emerging again only for dinner. The same thing happened the following day. Only on the third day at sea did he join his friends on deck and begin tentatively to involve himself in shipboard activities.

Helen and Jane were solicitous, doing their best to see that he felt comfortable. They stopped their husbands from pressuring him into participating in activities or events that he just wasn't ready for, like boisterous deck games and evening cabarets. For Bertram it would have been painful to sit in a nightclub, eyeing half-clad nymphets, listening to slinkily-clad singers belting out songs with lurid lyrics, and putting up with questionable jokes from second-rate comics. But he did agree to quiet drinks in the Hibiscus Lounge where a pianist softly played while crooning old songs from the golden years of radio.

It was a long cruise, more than a month, and soon the five of them settled down into a routine of eating, drinking and Bridge, balanced by calisthenics and a five kilometer walk around the deck every day. When the ship put into port, they went ashore to do the touristy things; visit the sights, drift into upscale bars for martini lunches, shop, and generally do everything that was expected of American tourists. At the end of the day, they returned to the ship to rest and prepare for dinner and the evening fun.

It must have been on one of those stops that Miranda Delamare came aboard. Helen said it was at the Caicos but Jane disagreed. She was sure it must have been before that because they arrived at the Caicos on Friday, and she was positive that Miranda said she had seen the movie that was shown Thursday. But if that was so, she must have been on board at least two days before because their previous stop had been Tuesday. Not that it mattered, of course. What mattered was that Miranda was suddenly on board and had crossed paths with Bertram.

Their encounter contained a marvelously disturbing quality which thrilled Bertram even as it perplexed him. It was a moment he wanted to keep to himself and so never shared it with his friends. He had taken to strolling alone around the deck just before he retired for the night. He would stand at the stern and marvel at the clarity of the moon out here away from the smog, and the breathtaking beauty of the network of stars as fine as lace, or gaze down far below at the exquisite patterns formed from the silver foam on the black water which swirled from under the great, white bulk of the ship. The scene was never the same two nights running as the ship ploughed its way through the tropical seas, but it was always magical and would have been perfection had Naomi been by his side. Bertram was not only saddened but constrained by her absence. Without her he could not freely revel in the beauty around him or the joy of living.

Then one evening, when he turned from his commune with the sea and the night sky, he saw a woman, or rather, became aware of a vague presence, the sense of another being. At first there was no more than a shadow, hardly discernible from the shadows around it, but gradually it deepened in intensity until it became the outline of a figure. Perhaps because of a slight change in the ship's course or a sudden illumination by the moon's rays as they pierced through a cloud, the figure emerged like a will-o-the-wisp and she was a woman. A light breeze lifted the soft folds of her white chiffon dress causing it to float around her like the mist on an Irish marsh.

She was some distance off which allowed Bertram to secretly observe her subtle, sylph-like movements as she moved slowly back and forth. Although fearful of being thought a voyeur, he could not help but surreptitiously watch her. He was transfixed, captivated by her ethereal quality. She was obviously waiting for someone and while he didn't really want to know who it was, he still found himself unable to take the steps to leave, and so he waited with her. She seemed lost in a reverie, unaware of him, and except for the movement of her dress stood so still that the radiance of the moon appeared to pass right through her.

After what felt like several minutes of this, Bertram was made uncomfortable by the thought that she might know he was there, covertly watching her. So he resolved to go. Besides, there was a chill in the air, and he could not afford another bout of the pneumonia that he had suffered after Naomi's death.

A glance at the illuminated face of his watch brought a quick, puzzled frown to his pleasant face. His usual nightly routine saw him retiring to his cabin at about eleven, but according to his watch it was one a.m. Bertram stood immobilized by the confusion.

"Is something wrong?" a soft, husky voice asked, startling him. He had not heard or been aware of her approach. "I'm so sorry. I didn't mean to startle you." She placed a gentle hand on his sleeve.

"Oh no, please don't apologize." Bertram found himself gazing into her upturned face, pearl-like in the moonlight. "I was far away."

"Yes, you were." There was concern in her expression. "Do you feel quite well?"

"Yes, I'm fine," he assured her. "It's just that I seem to have lost…"

She tilted her head, concerned. "What?"

Bertram pulled himself together. If he told this lovely young woman that in less than fifteen minutes he had lost two hours of his life, she would think it was his mind he had lost. And though he didn't know why he should care, that was not the impression he wanted to make on her.

A sudden tremor shot through him, and again she was all concern, moving her hand to touch his skin.

"You're very cold."

"Not really," he rather weakly protested.

"I think we should go inside for a nightcap," she said, slipping an arm through his and urging him gently forward. "I like the Slipper Room best, don't you? It's so cozy and quiet. By the way, I'm Miranda Delamare."

Bertram introduced himself haltingly because he was still baffled by what had occurred. One minute he'd been standing on the deck, a man past retirement age, a lonely man, a widower, reflecting on the loss of Naomi, and now here was this young, gorgeous woman hanging on his arm. And the two of them were about to share a late-night drink in the Slipper Room, the most intimate of all the public places on the ship — a room where couples gathered who wished for a certain amount of privacy because they were unable to take advantage of their cabins. And the thought suddenly occurred to him…*What would his traveling companions think if they saw him?*

But they wouldn't see him would they because it was now in the early hours, and they would be safely asleep in their cabins, readying themselves for their early morning jog, followed by a breakfast hearty enough to wipe out the beneficial effect of their self-imposed exercise. Reassured, he allowed the lovely Miranda to lead him not only into the Slipper Room but into an alcove in the shadows where they were served with brandies by an unconcerned waiter who, had his life depended on it, would not have been able to describe the couple to a prosecutor in a courtroom.

When Bertram next looked at the time, it was three o'clock. He could not have said where the last hours had gone. He was aware only of being enfolded in a warm glow created by Miranda's smoky eyes and the murmur of her voice, as soothing as the whisper of the sea on a beach, and the exciting touch of her body close to his. Throughout it all, and through the days that followed, he asked himself many times why this lovely creature was bothering with him.

But he had no answer.

When Helen, Mac, Jane and Oliver became aware of this unusual friendship - which Bertram was able to conceal for nearly a week with Miranda's complicity - they posed a slightly different question to each other, not so much what does she want with him as what does she want from him? Although in all their minds they had the answer. They knew all about shipboard predators and had no illusions.

Before Bertram was discovered, he and Miranda shared wonderful moments of privacy when his companions were taking their afternoon naps, or socialized with new acquaintances on the ship. It did not for one moment occur to Bertram that Miranda was unusually compliant with his suggestion that they initially avoid his friends. He'd been so long out of the dating game he was unaware that any modern young woman would have been highly insulted to be kept away from her admirer's associates and would have most emphatically refused to co-operate. But Miranda seemed happy to stay clear of the noisy bustle of shipboard life, preferring to sit in some quiet spot encouraging Bertram to tell her everything about himself which he did with a great sense of relief. And as he unburdened his guilt for being alive and well and even cheerful, Miranda absolved him of his regret that his thirty-year marriage with Naomi had ended with her death before he and she were able to travel as they had always promised themselves they would do when Bertram retired.

It was inevitable, however, that Bertram's friends would finally chance upon the two of them together. Helen was the first to spot them. She had caught sight of Bertram strolling the deck a step or two behind a vibrantly, beautiful young woman in white shorts and a white halter top. Helen made no connection between the two until the woman turned her head, and still walking, said something to Bertram. For one awful moment Helen thought that Bertram had made an inappropriate remark to upset the woman and was about to intervene when she was astonished to see the woman reach out and take Bertram's hand in her own, drawing him closer to her. In an overtly solicitous gesture Bertram bent his head, and Helen thought she saw him place a light kiss on the woman's temple but dismissed the idea as ludicrous as they were swallowed up by the crowd.

The encounter not only perturbed Helen but sharpened

her awareness of just how vulnerable Bertram was, and that realization rattled her. He was a good-looking, distinguished older man who was also exceedingly rich which made him a prime target for any little gold-digger on the prowl. Moreover, Helen felt responsible because she had pressured him to come on this cruise therefore putting him in the position of being preyed upon, as she was sure he was, by this woman. It was such an old story she couldn't imagine why she hadn't considered the risk. In any case, she resolved to speak to Bertram about it before confiding in Mac or the others. As it happened the opportunity for an intervention did not arise. That same day, as if fate had decided to forestall Helen's good intention, Bertram came into the open with the relationship and brought the young woman forward to introduce her to his friends.

The evening started off oddly because Bertram didn't appear for dinner which worried the women. After Jane had sent a grumbling Oliver go to Bertram's stateroom to check on him, she remarked that she was concerned because Bertram had not been himself for the last few days. She noticed that he'd been distracted and vague, and had read somewhere that this condition could be red flagging an imminent stroke. Helen considered mentioning that she had seen Bertram with a young woman but thought better of it. She wanted to get Bertram's take on that incident first. When Oliver returned, even more disgruntled at having traipsed around the ship on a useless mission, he reported that Bertram was nowhere to be found. However, a steward had told him that Mr. Prentice had dressed for dinner and left at the usual time. That was even more puzzling because it was unlike Bertram to absent himself from the evening meal without an explanation.

Carrying on as usual, the quartet of friends, as had become their custom, moved to the Hibiscus Lounge after dinner for *digestifs*. And shortly after they had settled themselves with their drinks Bertram entered through the high, gilded archway with

Miranda Delamare on his arm. Jane, Oliver and Mac literally stared with their mouths open, while Helen immediately recognized the young woman Bertram had kissed that afternoon. With an unpleasant lurch in her stomach, Helen watched them approach and sensed through some deep, primitive instinct, that something was dreadfully wrong.

With a broad, proud smile on his face, Bertram presented the stunning, young woman whose diaphanous, white evening dress enhanced her pale beauty and fragile figure. With hardly a moment to recover from the shock of this unexpected development , Bertram's friend's managed to welcome her that evening, and, as Bertram so obviously wanted it, into their intimate circle. It was, after all, only for the duration of the cruise.

In the event, Miranda proved to be somewhat elusive, preferring to spend much of the day in her own pursuits and insisting that Bertram enjoy his holiday with his friends, which endeared her to him even more profoundly. She never joined them for a meal but occasionally had an after-dinner drink in their company before leading Bertram off to wander around the decks to enjoy the starry, tropical nights. This arrangement, unconventional though it appeared to Helen, served to convince the others that Miranda's intentions were honorable. It could be that she was not a gold-digger, they ventured, somewhat cautiously, but rather a nice, innocent young woman taking a kindly interest in their bereaved friend.

It may have been simply a kindly interest on her part but Bertram clearly was smitten with her — on this they were all in agreement; and, yet, he seemed to accept that nothing could come of the relationship. It was obvious that he could not introduce Miranda, who was younger than his own daughter, into his family so soon after their mother's death. He was pragmatic enough to understand that. However, important questions still presented themselves — what was Miranda's agenda, where was she from, what was her history? And why would a woman of such charm and beauty, who could have any rich, *young* man she set out to captivate, be interested in hanging around a man old enough to be her father?

His friends could not ask Bertram the final question, but in answer to all the others he told them that Miranda lived on the west coast, had been in New York all winter and was taking the cruise home because she was paranoid about flying, but if Miranda had boarded the ship at Miami, why hadn't any of them noticed her earlier? Of course, there were nearly two thousand passengers on board so perhaps it wasn't that odd, especially considering that the four friends rarely saw her except when she was in their company. Mac had caught a glimpse of her at the pool one day. She was cutting through the water with such incredible grace and remarkable speed that he stood and watched her in awe. Back and forth she went, not at all inhibited by the other people who awkwardly splashed around her. She was clearly a serious swimmer and effortlessly avoided the dilettantes. When she finally emerged and saw Mac, she gave him a friendly wave, retrieved her terry-cloth robe, slipped it on and moved off in the opposite direction. In a moment she was gone, and Mac had mused that she certainly couldn't be called intrusive.

Helen also felt somewhat mollified when she discovered that Miranda had never invited Bertram to join her in her stateroom. He didn't even know where it was. Miranda, on the other hand, sometimes walked him back to his cabin after one of their late night promenades but only as far as the door. What Helen didn't know was that once or twice Bertram had summoned up his courage to invite Miranda in, but with a dazzling smile and that light touch on his arm, she had politely declined him every time.

The night before they were due at Port of Spain, Helen invited Miranda to go ashore with them. The shopping was reputed to be wonderful, and they thought it might be nice to spend an hour or two on the beach, but Miranda prettily refused. She had letters to write and it was good to do that chore while the ship was docked so that they could be mailed right away.

It was late that night when they were back at sea and Bertram and Miranda were in their usual place leaning on the ship's railing, that he believed he heard the sound of low, sweet singing. There was always music on board ship but this was very different. It was not coming from the direction of the cocktail bars, the cabaret or the ballroom, and it was not the sort of music played in those rooms. This singing was unearthly. At first he thought it was Miranda, but soon saw that it was not, and indeed, the music seemed to be drifting up from the sparkling display of phosphorescence in the water below.

"What is it? You look perplexed," Miranda said, smiling at him.

"Can you hear it?"

She tilted her head towards the public rooms opening onto the promenade deck. She heard dance music, laughter, and the regular sounds of a large group of happy people enjoying themselves, floating out on the night air. "I can hear a lot of things. What in particular?"

"I don't know, an angel singing, perhaps?"

He urged her to listen again, but she shrugged and shook her head. And then all of a sudden the music was gone, but its haunting quality lingered with Bertram throughout the night. His sleep was restless, and every time he awoke the lilting strains were in his head or just outside the porthole, he couldn't say which.

At the next port Bertram went ashore at the urging of his friends, but because Miranda wouldn't go he didn't enjoy the experience. The whole time he was away he longed to return to the ship. His eyes was drawn to it from wherever they were in the little seaside town. The others were uncomfortably aware of his disquiet and just assumed he wanted to be with Miranda or at least near her, nearer than he was. To his credit he stuck it out. He went in search of her when they returned to the ship, but couldn't find her anywhere. He was tense throughout dinner, so the look on his face when Miranda later appeared in the Hibiscus Lounge was like a lost child reunited with his mother.

"Where is this going to end?" Helen murmured, as Miranda carried him off.

Four pairs of eyes were riveted to the backs of the retreating couple. Couple! They were so close together that every time Miranda moved her head her shimmering hair brushed against his shoulder. As they walked through the archway and his arm went around her waist, and the hearts of his friends sank. They did not speak their fears. Helen, who from the first had sensed something was wrong, kept her counsel.

As Bertram and Miranda strolled, arm in arm along the deck that night, he mused on how delightful it would be to hear that lovely seductive song again and wondered if Miranda could sing it to him.

"You know I would if I could, darling," she laughed. "But remember, I didn't hear it." She squeezed herself against his side.

Then, shortly after they reached the aft railing, the music was there. It drifted across the water, rising and falling in sweet waves of bliss reaching deep into his heart. Such rapture as he had never known suffused his entire being, filling his soul with a joy so powerful it was almost a religious experience.

But Miranda couldn't hear it.

Disappointed, Bertram asked her to lean towards the railing to better catch the sound. "But the music cannot possibly be coming from there, Bertram," she teased. "There's nothing out there but water."

"But it is," he insisted anxiously. "Come on, let's go down a deck. Maybe you'll hear it better."

"But I can't hear it at all."

Shaking her head with an indulgent smile, Miranda allowed him to take her hand and lead her to the companionway, hurrying past dozens of *chaises-longs* stacked against the walls, until they reached the stern. "There!" He turned to her triumphant. The music was much louder. "You must be able to hear it now."

Miranda shook her head, the moonlight caressing her pale hair. "You don't know how much I'd love to be able to say that I can," she murmured softly. "But, I'm sorry, Bertram, I can't."

Much later that night, early morning, really, as he lay in bed in and out of sleep, the low, sweet refrain haunted both his restless dreams and his waking moments. What puzzled him most was that Miranda was unable to hear the music. He felt strangely wounded that they could not share the experience, as if he had been deprived of something important. Furthermore, he was sure that it would uplift her soul as it had his, and he desperately wanted her to feel it as he did. As shafts of pale light fell across his bed heralding the dawn he got up, dressed and went to the aft deck. Early morning joggers were out, calling to one another, panting and laughing. He tensed with irritation. How could he possibly discern the sweet sound of his music with such noise going on? He remained edgy and distracted throughout the day, unable to concentrate on anything. In a frenzy of impatience he longed for the night.

Jane and Oliver remarked on his strange mood but put it down to a mixture of grief and guilt from falling in love with a woman less than half his age so soon after Naomi's death. Helen, however, was nervous, afraid for his mental state, and decided to confront Miranda.

"If you can find her alone." Jane's tone was ironic. They were lying on deckchairs in the sun. "I've never seen her unless she's with Bertram."

"I have," Mac observed without opening his eyes.

Jane's carefully shaped brows went up. "Oh? Where?"

"At the pool." Mac now stirred himself. He yawned and stretched. He rose heavily and hitched up his shorts. His gaze went to the nearby entrance to the Poseidon Room where the most lavish of the buffet lunches was served. "Saw her swimming there a couple of days ago, like a fish. Anyone ready for lunch?"

"I'll catch up with you." Helen was not in the mood to eat. Having decided to intervene with Miranda before she lost her nerve, she broke away from the others and made her way to the pool. After establishing that Miranda wasn't in the water Helen sauntered among the sun worshippers. There was no sign of her.

"Hello!"

Helen jumped and spun around. Miranda was right behind her, luscious in a white bikini.

"I'm sorry. I didn't mean to startle you," Miranda apologized, with her engaging smile.

"That's all right." Helen pressed her hand against her thumping chest. "I was looking for you, actually."

"Splendid, let's sit and have a chat."

"How about I order us of one of those?" Helen asked as a tempting looking drink went by on a tray.

Miranda shook her head. "Thanks, but not before I swim."

"Mac says you're a wonderful swimmer."

"Not really." Miranda shrugged. "I just love the water." She smiled, gazing at the merrymakers in the pool, then turned to Helen. "Why were you looking for me?"

Helen had formed no approach. Put on the spot she fumbled for words. "Umm…well, to be truthful, we're all a little concerned about Bertram, and since you're spending a lot of time together, we wondered if you would you give us your opinion of… well, of his state of mind."

Miranda's eyes widened. "His state of mind? I'm afraid I don't understand."

Helen moved awkwardly. Already she wished she hadn't started this. "Well, he's behaving somewhat differently from what we're used to and seems to be terribly distracted. Has he mentioned anything about being worried?"

"No, but he talks often about his late wife."

Helen was amazed. "He does?"

"Oh yes, he misses her very much. Do you know that he thinks that if one of them had had to die, it should have been him? He feels guilty because he thinks he could have made her life happier and could have done more to prevent her death."

"But that isn't true," Helen protested.

"I've tried to tell him that. Bertram is a very caring man."

"He is also quite vulnerable at this time of his life, Miss Delaware."

"I am well aware of that." She suddenly turned her head and looked directly into Helen's eyes. "I know where you are going with this, but you can rest assured that there is nothing romantic between us. Bertram is old enough to be my father. We're simply friends." Miranda gave Helen a sweet, but distant smile. "I think I'll go in for my swim now."

When Helen told her friends about her conversation there were mixed reactions.

"He thinks he could have made Naomi happier?" Jane exclaimed. "He did everything in the world for her. There was simply nothing more that he could have done."

Helen agreed. "I won't argue with that, but you know he thinks he should have taken her to Switzerland as soon as she became sick. It sounds as though he believes that might have saved her."

"Well it wouldn't have," Oliver observed. "She was treated by the finest oncologists in the U.S.!"

"It's what Bertram believes that's important," Jane reminded him. "It is very sad if that is his true feeling."

"So, what do you think?" Oliver pressed. "Is she a gold-digger?"

"You know I thought that before I spoke to Miranda, but now I'm not so sure."

"Really? What is her motive then?" Jane asked, curiously.

"I think she may genuinely like him, that she enjoys being with him. I believe it is innocent."

"You can't possibly know that from spending ten minutes with her," Mac declared, his attitude indicating that they should leave the matter be.

"No, but suppose she wants companionship without the hassles of a shipboard romance," Helen persisted. "This way she doesn't have to go into the nightclub and the bars by herself where she would no doubt be approached by every lecher on the ship. This way she has Bertram's protection. It is the perfect set-up for her."

"I thought we were concerned about Bertram, not her," Jane responded curtly.

"Yes, but it benefits Bertram as well."

"Not if he's smitten," Oliver put in. "And there's no good going to come of him going down that path."

Helen nodded, and sighed. "You're right, of course. It's so difficult, especially seeing that he is snatching a few days of happiness."

"Is he happy?" Oliver queried sardonically. "He looked to me to be in better shape when we boarded this ship, than he does now."

"I'd agree with that." Jane added. "And if you ask me he's picked the wrong girl to share his troubles with." She looked at Helen. "What do you think — should one of the boys speak to him?"

This suggestion immediately brought loud protests from both the men.

"Why not?" Jane demanded, affronted by their reaction. "He's your friend! Don't you care about him?"

"I care enough to leave him alone," Mac retorted. "The man has his own life to live. He can take care of himself. He's not a kid."

"Oliver?" Jane appealed to her husband.

"I'm with Mac. If I were in Bertram's shoes, I wouldn't want anyone interfering, and I don't think we should."

Helen and Jane exchanged glances. Were they interfering where they weren't needed or wanted? When the two men had gone off, Jane asked, "What else did she say?"

"Not much, except that she assured me she has no romantic interest in him."

Jane snorted, "All that does is confirm our suspicions on that score. It is far from meaning that she has no interest in his bank account."

"Well, as I said..." Helen shrugged and didn't say anymore.

The women were reluctant to give up on their concern for Bertram, but in the end they resolved that the boys were right. They would not interfere. It was Mac's view, propounded when he was alone with his wife, that they were all making far too much of simple emotions that were heightened by the romance and adventure inherent in shipboard life.

Shortly after Helen's talk with Miranda the *Royal Countess* put into port for two days signaling a welcome break in the tension. Not expecting Bertram to accompany them, the four friends felt guiltily apprehensive when he appeared at breakfast and said he'd like to join them.

"Miranda's writing letters," he said.

"Hasn't she heard of email?" Mac muttered to Helen.

As soon as they were on shore, everyone's spirits lifted and they thoroughly enjoyed all the glorious adventures the island had to offer. Everything seemed to be fine again. Bertram was relaxed and happy, offering no comment about Miranda the whole time which was a relief to the others. So, it was with some regret that they boarded the ship for departure forty-eight hours later.

All was well until Miranda failed to put in an appearance at the Hibiscus Lounge to collect Bertram as she always did. As the evening dragged on uneasiness crept into the group. Bertram began to show signs of stress, which slowly increased to the point where it was palpable. Even his physical appearance seemed to deteriorate. His skin became pallid beneath the tan he'd acquired. His right eye began to twitch, and the hand reaching out for his glass shook. Conversation waned, and still she did not come. A deadly gloom descended over them. Of course his friends felt deeply for his obvious distress, but they were simply incapable of dealing with it. When the atmosphere became too unbearable, Jane suddenly leapt up and tapped Oliver smartly on the shoulder. "Come along, Honey, it's been a long day, and if we're to win the Bridge tournament, we should be getting to bed."

Oliver agreed with alacrity.

"Coming Helen?" Mac held out a hand to assist her up.

Helen glanced from him to Bertram who sat despondently staring into his third brandy. "Well…" Her reluctance to leave him alone was clear to Bertram. He glanced up and gave her a wan smile, at the same time heaving a great sigh.

"Don't worry about me, Helen. I'm going to turn in any minute."

The Bridge tournament had been scheduled to coincide with the open stretch of water between Jamaica and the Yucatan Channel which the cruise ship would traverse over the next couple of days. At the last moment Bertram withdrew from the tournament with the excuse that his concentration just wasn't up to par, and so his friends did not see him at all that day. They found the tournament was a welcome distraction, and the post-mortem on the day's games enlivened their dinner conversation.

Bertram tried to show an interest, but most of the time his

eyes never stopped flickering around ever hopeful that Miranda would appear. They moved to the lounge. As the evening wore on with no sign of her, he became afflicted with a tremor which shook his body. Mac later told Helen that he looked like a man about to have a heart attack.

"I bet the damned girl disembarked in Jamaica," he grumbled as he climbed into bed. "Ask the purser in the morning. He should know."

Helen waited until evening before she went to the Purser's office, just in case Miranda showed up during the day. She and Jane went on a tour of the ship, at one point posting themselves at the pool for half an hour, but there was no sign of her.

"Miranda Delamare?" The purser asked, turning to consult his computer.

"Yes, Delamare." Helen nodded.

"Could that be spelt with an E? Delemare?" He checked the computer again, going through all the variations of the spelling. "Just let me double check with passport control." He did that online but nothing emerged. "Well - " he said at last, "- not only does it look as though your friend didn't leave the ship in Jamaica, it appears that she was never on board."

"Never on board!" Mac exploded when Helen repeated this to him.

"Zip me up, will you, please, Hon?" Helen sighed, stepping into her cocktail dress. "He looked at all the records. I watched him. Everything is computerized."

"Yes and computers are only as good as the person who enters the data."

"But there isn't likely to be an error with passports and visas as well."

"I think it makes it more likely," he responded ironically. "Are you nearly ready to go?" Mac was far more interested in dinner than a vanishing woman. "Maybe she's using an assumed name."

Helen stopped checking her hair and stared at his reflection in the mirror. "Why Mac, of course, that must be it! You clever old thing!"

"Can we go now, please?"

Helen picked up her up purse and sailed past her husband. "But why would she be using an assumed name?"

"Because she's married and wants to keep that little gem of information to herself."

Bertram sent a message saying that he was having dinner in his cabin and would join them for breakfast the following morning. This gave Helen the opportunity to pass on what she'd discovered to the others. There was no-one with the surname of Delamare on board. "So she's traveling under a assumed name," she told them with a knowing look.

"Well, that explains a lot," Jane commented astringently "Is anyone going to tell Bertram?"

Mac shook his head. "No need. She's no longer on board so we should just forget it."

Helen eyed him reproachfully, and the rest ate their *Surf'n Turf* in gloomy silence. Bertram's unhappiness had not exactly ruined their holiday, but it had cast a pall over it that no amount of Bridge and food was able to dispel. The women were particularly sympathetic to their friend's circumstances and hated to see him suffering so badly. It was with amazement, therefore, that they stared at him the next day when he bounded into breakfast with a joyful gait and beaming smile. He was a man who had been handed a new lease on life.

"You look wonderful, Bertram, honey," Helen said, standing up in her enthusiasm and giving him a hug. "What have you been up to?"

"I've been swimming."

"Swimming?" Jane exclaimed. "I didn't know you liked to swim."

"Neither did I," Bertram laughed, sitting down and looking

hungrily at what they were eating. "But Miranda persuaded me."

His companions reacted with varying degrees of confusion. A look went around. Helen spoke first. "Are you saying that you've been swimming this morning?"

"That's right," he said gleefully.

"With Miranda? We thought she left the ship at Jamaica," Jane ventured.

Bertram's demeanor changed. His happiness didn't diminish but he looked somehow abashed. "She did leave." He cleared his throat, awkwardly. "I didn't mean to imply that she was with me. I was swimming alone."

Jane leaned forward and placed her coffee cup carefully in its saucer. "Well, I'm sorry to say this, Bertram, but it wasn't very courteous of her to go off without saying goodbye."

"I'm afraid I'm to blame for that. She was going to, but then I said I would convey her respects. And she was in a bit of a rush so…it was really my social faux pas."

"Oh." Helen cast a sidelong glance at Jane. They were thinking the same thing. Miranda had left the ship because she had discovered that they were suspicious of her and she couldn't afford to let them to find out who she really was.

That night Bertram secretly met Miranda at the rear of the Lido deck.

"Did you tell your friends that I left the ship?" she asked.

"Yes, but I still don't understand."

"You will, darling, I promise, soon, and everything will be wonderful." She gave him a brief goodnight kiss and begged off their usual walk to take care of something important.

"Can't it wait?" Bertram pleaded. "I haven't seen you for so long."

"So long?" Her laughed tinkled out into the night air. "A few hours, that's all."

"Where were you?"

"Arranging things for us, darling," she murmured, and kissed him again. "Be patient."

So thrilled at having her back again Bertram was full of nervous energy. He could not go back to his cabin yet, and the sea air was so invigorating. He went alone to the lower deck and walked to the stern. It had now become his favorite place on the ship, and the starry sky that night was so magnificent he felt giddy looking at it. The moon threw a brilliant shaft of silver light over the charcoal ocean lending the water a rich satin gleam, disturbed only by the spangled wake of the *Royal Countess* as she plied softly and silently towards Mexico. Then, with a sigh like distant ghosts, the chorus began its siren song, drifting on the soft breeze and drawing him into its alluring mystery.

How long he stood there he did not know, but he felt drunk with the elixir of the gods. And when the music finally stopped, he returned to his stateroom so elated that he was unaware of the deck beneath his feet. It was only then that he realized it was two a.m. The hours had passed as if they were minutes.

Miranda sent him a message to meet at the pool in the early morning, a time when only the joggers had emerged from their cabins, and the two of them swam joyously together without being disturbed by any other passengers. He also swam alone that afternoon, much to his friends' astonishment, who were curiously puzzled by his expert strokes, for which he had no explanation himself. He'd always been a poor and reluctant swimmer but was now able to skim through the water like a dolphin.

That evening at dinner Bertram was filled with such an air of elation and anticipation that it swept over the others in waves. Had they been in port, Helen would have sworn that he was planning to jump ship and elope with the alluring Miranda, but she was not even there. It occurred to Helen that the two had arranged to meet at the end of the cruise and that accounted for his celebratory mood.

Again that night Bertram secretly met Miranda on the Lido deck. She was particularly radiant and her hair and eyes were more luminous than ever. The floating gossamer fabric of her dress appeared to be shot through with rivulets of silver, making her appear so fragile as to not really be there at all, a holograph, rather than a substantial being. As they walked towards the stern, she suddenly stopped, gasping. She clutched Bertram's arm as she tilted her head to listen. "Is that it?" she breathed. "Is that the music, darling?"

"You can hear it," Bertram whispered, through tears of joy.

"Yes, I can. Oh Bertram, how beautiful it is."

"It's so wonderful that you can hear it."

"And I've got wonderful news for you, darling too," she murmured, slipping her arm through his. "My divorce is final."

He almost collapsed — his head was in a whirl, his heart pounded.

"I just picked up the email from my lawyer. The decree absolute was granted yesterday. Oh, Bertram, we can be married when we get to Veracruz, can't we?"

Bertram was so overcome he was unable to answer. He wrapped her in his arms as tears streamed down his cheeks.

"I'm so happy!" Miranda exclaimed. "Let's celebrate!"

"Yes!" Bertram managed to recover his voice. "Champagne for everyone on board!"

"No, not champagne, darling. Let's celebrate with a swim!"

He laughed, taken aback. "Now? Is the pool open?"

"No, not in the pool, darling" she urged. . "In the ocean."

"In the ocean? What do you mean?"

Her lovely face rose eagerly up to his, and she kissed him exquisitely on the lips. "You're a marvelous swimmer. I taught you, remember?"

"Yes, but, how can we swim in the ocean, we're not in port."

"That doesn't matter. We can just as easily swim from here, believe me."

"I don't understand."

"You will. You trust me, don't you Bertram?" Miranda cuddled up to him. "My soon-to-be husband."

He was utterly transfixed by her, and those words took his breath away. When she lifted a hand to brush away his tears, he caught her fingers and passionately kissed them. "Yes, of course I do!" he exclaimed recklessly. "I'd trust you with my life."

"Come on. Let's do it," she purred, tugging him towards the steps.

With gentle murmurings, she guided him to the deck below and a tiny place jutting out from stern where the shadows were blacker and it was much quieter, save for the tantalizing music that drifted across the water to them.

"Come on," she extolled. "There's a metal ladder on the hull. We can use that to get down to the water."

For a moment Bertram hung back, still uncertain if she was serious. Was this a test of his trust in her?

"It's all right, darling. Everything will be fine," she smiled.

Not totally reassured he allowed himself to be led to the railing. It was alien and sinister in this area of the ship where they should not be, far away from the light, fun and noisy companionship of the shipboard. He couldn't see the ladder.

"Come on, darling," Miranda urged. "Like this!" Laughing, she let go of his hand and kicked off her silver sandals. With a sudden lithe movement she slipped over the railing, then tucked her feet on the edge of the hull and clutched the rail with both hands. The wind caught her hair, and her dress billowed out like a sail suddenly unfurled from its mast. And for a moment, Bertram felt as if he had never seen anything as lovely as this. It never even occurred to him that she was in terrible danger.

Excitedly she urged him to follow her lead. "Come, let the music sweep you away."

Bertram's clamber over the side of the ship was not nearly as graceful as that of his lovely companion. The rail itself was so cold that it felt as if it were burning his hands, and he couldn't find the footing she obviously had. She kept insisting that there was a ladder, but for the life of him he couldn't locate it, and his feet slithered down the steep side of the hull, helplessly flailing and dangling there. It meant his arms bore the burden of all his weight, and in a sudden profound panic he knew he could not hold on for very long that way.

Swimming? She had said they were going swimming, but how could he swim in his heavy clothes? She might be able to swim in her diaphanous dress, but his suit, his leather shoes and all his garments would make him sink like a stone. He would drown! He saw that now. He broke out in a terrible sweat and just as nausea began to rise up in his throat, he felt her arm around him, an arm as strong as a man's and heard her soft voice whisper in his ear.

"Let go, my darling. Let go and we'll always be together."

He tried desperately to turn and look at her, but he couldn't risk losing his grip on the rail.

"Don't struggle, darling, just trust me." As her voice flowed over him, it suddenly lost that wonderful quality which had lured him on. It was new a voice he'd never heard before. The soft murmuring became a growling until, "Let go of the rail!" it commanded with a terrible, ugly, vicious shriek. And all of the delicacy which had drawn him to her became sharp, discordant and unbearable — like the screech of a nail dragged across glass, joining with his own shriek as her steel pincers attempted to rip his hands from the railing. "Let go you old fool! Let go!"

The nightmare was upon him now. Gone was the beautiful, young woman with her gentle, smoky eyes, her tender look, her charming smile. His throat constricted in a scream of terror for next to him, levitating near the rail, was an unspeakable monster, stinking and repugnant, who poured a stream of venomous invective that seared Bertram's flesh and tore at his soul. The creature's cavernous, dripping mouth emitted unearthly, gurgling sounds to strike horror into the heart of its victim, and its breath reeked with a stench so filthy it was beyond the scope of human description.

The roaring in Bertram's brain threatened to burst open his skull as he recognized the imminence of his death, and unable to protect himself he felt the once adorable Miranda pry his fingers loose from the rail. His fingers broke like matchsticks, releasing a final tormented scream, silenced only when he was swallowed up by the sea.

SENDING POST CARDS

Bob didn't start worrying in earnest until that night when he returned home from the golf course. He came breezing in for dinner and seeing only two places set asked where Maureen was.

"She hasn't arrived yet," Faith answered.

"Has she called?" Bob asked, aware of his wife's stiff shoulders. She always held them like that when she was stressed.

"No."

"She's twenty-four hours late, Hon."

"Well, it's a long drive, and you know what she's like. She may have given one of the other guests a ride home."

"Have you tried calling her?"

"I thought it was too soon. You know how she hates to be monitored."

After a moment's uncertainty he nodded and went off to have a quick shower. When he reappeared he poured them both a drink, but he couldn't disguise the anxiety he felt. He put his glass down, went to the phone and dialed Maureen's cell. She might hate being monitored but there were limits. After several rings a recorded voice announced that the subscriber was unavailable. He hung up. "I'm going to call Donna."

"Perhaps we should wait until morning."

"No. I'd like to get some sleep tonight."

Faith chewed her lip. Bob's anxiety was not alleviating her misgivings. "Okay," she acquiesced.

Bob understood her hesitation. "I know Maureen won't like it, but..." He dialed and in a moment grimaced. "Answering machine. Hi Donna, it's Bob, would you give us a call when you get in?"

Faith and Bob ate an uneasy dinner then took their cream lab, Basil, for his evening walk, or rather, he took them. Basil followed his nose around Greenvale estate, the upscale retirement community which had been the Hendersons' home since Bob had taken an early retirement at fifty-five. They strolled past the select villas in their park-like settings of flowery gardens and perfect lawns, past the tennis courts where friends waved to them. Sometimes, on their evening walk, the Hendersons would go into the clubhouse and have a social drink but tonight they went straight back home. As they approached their own drive, they anticipated the relief of seeing Maureen's Jeep Cherokee parked in front of the garage but were disappointed.

The light on their answering machine, however, was blinking. Bob walked over and hit the play button. Donna's voice, breathless and harried as always, resounded through the living room. "Sorry I wasn't here when you called. We're home now. I'll try again later. The wedding went well. No major disasters, but Sally was really sorry Maureen couldn't make it. Well, we all were, of course. Talk to you soon."

Faith and Bob stared at one another.

"What does she mean?" Faith asked.

"Damned if I know," Bob said, picking up the phone and dialing her number.

"Put it on conference," Faith whispered.

They seated themselves on either side of the console.

Donna answered immediately. "I was just about to call you."

"We're on conference, Donna," said Bob. "Faith is here."

"Oh, hi Faith."

"Hello, Donna. We got your message."

"Is something wrong? You sound worried."

"Well, you said you were sorry Maureen hadn't made it to the wedding and - "

"Yes, well, we all were. You know how fond we are of Maureen, and Sally was so looking forward to having her here. Sally will be sending - "

"Donna!" Faith cut her off. "Maureen did go to the wedding."

"What? Sorry, Faith, I didn't catch that."

"Maureen did go to the wedding!" Bob emphasized.

"Well, perhaps she started out - " Donna replied cautiously, "- but she never showed up."

Faith and Bob stared at one another struck dumb.

"Are you there?" Donna's voice wavered, then spoke aside to her husband. "It's Bob and Faith. They're on conference."

White-faced, Bob cleared his throat. "Donna, is that Richard you're speaking to?"

"Yes, he's right here with me. What's going on?"

"That's what we'd like to know," Bob said.

"Maureen left here last week," Faith went on, tensely. "What day was it, Bob?"

"Thursday."

"Yes, she left here Thursday."

They listened to Donna and Richard whispering without being able to discern the words.

"What is it? What?" Bob demanded.

"She didn't arrive," Richard answered.

Bob began to sweat. "Did she call you? Did she say her plans had changed?"

"No, we haven't heard from her since last weekend when she phoned from your place and said she was coming. We thought it was a bit strange when she didn't arrive, but we didn't worry about it because...I mean, well, you know how unpredictable Maureen is."

Faith and Bob had no answer to that. They did know how unpredictable their daughter was. Faith began to shake. "Is Sally there?" she asked in a trembling voice.

"No, Honey, she isn't. They've left on their Mediterranean cruise."

"Did Sally say anything about Maureen not showing up?" Bob asked.

"No. I'm afraid she and Greg have already phoned today; so we won't hear from them again until the next port, if then. You know how it is – it's their honeymoon, and..."

Bob jumped in. "When you do speak to Sally again could you ask if she has any idea what happened, if Maureen mentioned making a side trip or meeting someone on her way?"

Both Donna and Richard spoke, "Of course, we will."

A few more words were exchanged — neither party hearing what the other said — then Bob and Faith hung up.

"I'm going to see the sheriff," Bob said.

Tears streamed down Faith's face. "Oh, Bob. No!"

"Got to do it, Hon." Bob put his arm around her. "You stay here in case she calls or shows up." As he reached the door, Basil heaved himself up and padded after him, his doggy eyes anxious. "Sorry, buddy, you've had your walk."

Night had fallen. Across shadowed lawns, golden lights glowed from distant windows. Harris County Sheriff's Office, as stylish as the neighborhood it served, was discreetly screened by a tall hedge, its close-clipped lawn enhanced by a fine Colorado blue spruce.

The deputy on duty, Will Collins, knew Bob Henderson and was surprised to see him. There had been a rash of B & E's lately, and if this was another it would have been better if Bob had stayed at home and called 911. Will frowned and shook his head. *People never learn.*

"What can I do for you, Bob?" he asked.

"It's Maureen, Will, she's missing."

Collins wasn't expecting this. His brows drew together. In this small community you could practically count the population on two hands, and Greenvale had never had a missing person. He ran a check through his head. Maureen Henderson was a woman in her twenties, good looking, athletic, a runner. In fact, he'd seen her running around the village most days with her mass of copper-colored hair tied up on top of her head. She'd run in the New York and Boston marathons and had only been back in Greenvale a few weeks. Come to recuperate from one of those new illnesses with initials, FMS or CFS, whatever, and had to give up her job and rest. *Weird way to rest, all that running!* She'd been interviewed on the local television channel which is how he, like everyone else, learned all those details.

"How long has she been missing?" Collins asked, pulling out a pencil and a pad.

"Since last Thursday."

"Last Thursday? That's six days."

"Yes."

"Why haven't you reported this before?"

"We've only just found out. She went off to La Junta to attend a girlfriend's weekend wedding and was due back yesterday. We thought nothing of her being a bit late but when she didn't arrive home today, we started to feel concerned. So we phoned the parents of the bride, and they said Maureen never got there."

"Did she fly?"

"No, she drove."

"On her own?"

"Yes."

Collins' expression said it all. "Not a great idea these days."

Bob didn't want to hear that. "Maureen can take care of herself. She's been living on her own in New York for seven years."

"Does she carry a gun?"

"Not to my knowledge."

"You said it was a weekend wedding, it doesn't take two days to drive to La Junta."

"She was going early to spend time with the bride. They've been friends since high school."

The deputy tapped his pen in a puzzled staccato. "Have you looked to see if there is some clue, something that she left behind which would give some indication of her plans?"

"No, we haven't. Her plan was to drive straight to La Junta and back again."

"So you should look through her things before we go any further. Do that and let me know if you turn anything up, and we'll go from there. Okay?"

Bob nodded and got up, his mood a small degree lighter at the thought of doing something constructive. When he got back home, they went directly to Maureen's room. Basil followed them upstairs and after walking around to check things out to his satisfaction he flopped down in the middle of the mushroom carpet. Maureen had always been fanatically neat as a child and an obsessively neat teenager. That had not changed in adulthood. That day, as always, all was in order in her room. Everything was in its place. She had even stripped the bed and sent the linen down the laundry shute before she left.

Faith and Bob went through the room and en suite with a fine toothcomb. In her dressing table drawer they found her passport and other documents, but no diary, no notes, nothing particularly personal. So far as they could ascertain Maureen had taken her wallet, her daybook, and her check book, just things she would need for a short visit.

Bob called Collins with this information. "There's absolutely nothing to indicate what happened or where she might have gone between here and La Junta."

"Well, maybe she didn't go to La Junta," the deputy suggested.

"So, what happens now?"

"We'll begin checking the hospitals and accident reports. And I'll need Maureen's dental records."

"She doesn't have a local dentist."

"Can you get them from New York?"

"Well - " Bob was doubtful but said nothing. He didn't want to admit to the Deputy that they knew very little about their daughter's life in New York City. She was a very private person. Secretive, some of the relatives espoused. But that was nothing to do with anyone outside the family, including law enforcement. "I'll see what I can do," he said.

By morning all the appropriate police departments and hospitals between Denver and La Junta had been contacted. No road accident involving Maureen Henderson or a Jane Doe had been reported. In addition, no Maureen Henderson or a Jane Doe had been admitted to any hospital within the area under inquiry. So the search had been extended to the Highway patrol which was already carrying out a reconnaissance of the one hundred and eighty-six mile stretch of highway Maureen would have traveled.

As Faith and Bob waited they began to realize just how little they did know of their daughter's life since she'd left home right after college and made her way to New York. She had left her job three months before so no-one there would be likely to have any useful information to give, and they had no knowledge of her friends there.

"What about friends around here?" Collins asked, when he

came over a day later to tell them the result of the I-25 search was negative so far.

Bob shook his head. "She didn't have any."

"There aren't many people around here her age," Faith pointed out defensively. Collins nodded amiably. She was right. The Hendersons were the youngest residents in the retirement community. Most others were in their seventies and older.

"What about this Sally?" Collins asked, checking the notes he had made when Bob reported his daughter missing.

"Sally was an old friend of hers," Faith said. "We were neighbours in Seattle. They moved to resettle in La Junta. Maureen hadn't seen her for a while but was excited about going to the wedding and wanted to get there early. The girls had a lot of catching up to do. What happens now, officer?"

"A routine missing person alert will be issued." Collins picked up his hat, ready to leave. "And I'll contact the La Junta police — have them talk to Sally as soon as she gets back from her honeymoon."

'Routine missing person.' Already a statistic, Faith thought.

Bob walked Collins to the door. "Will you continue searching the highway?"

Collins nodded and dropped his voice in deference to Faith who was watching from the living room. "We'll broaden the search to routes 24, 50, 71 and send out an APB."

Even when the information highway was fully in gear it still seemed to Faith and Bob that not enough was happening. They were assured that the relevant police departments were routinely following all the official procedures in such a case. Reports flowed in and reports flowed out of the Harris County Sheriff's Office. Sightings were investigated, leads were followed up on, but nothing substantial materialized.

Faith wanted something put on television and called the local TV station which had interviewed Maureen about her running. That station complied and ran a small sound bight on her which other stations did not pick up. As the days passed the Hendersons felt their loss was being dismissed as unimportant, and their anguish disregarded. Angry and frustrated, they resolved to take matters into their own hands. Two weeks after they had reported Maureen missing, with absolutely no developments, they drove to La Junta to see Donna and Richard. Together the four hashed and rehashed Maureen's plan to drive to the wedding. When Sally called from the Mediterranean and was questioned about her phone conversation with Maureen prior to the wedding she said that she had given no indication that she intended making a side trip or that she might stop off and meet someone. Sally said, yes, she'd been upset when Maureen didn't arrive but that was Maureen, always changing her mind and doing her own thing.

The Hendersons were distraught, baffled and frustrated, but there wasn't much more they could do, except arrange to search every inch of the I-25 themselves looking for some clue, any clue to their daughter's incomprehensible disappearance.

It took some organization and a lot of help from friends and family, but for the next month search parties drove and searched every inch of I-25. They didn't have the resources of professional search and rescue units, so their check of the ravines, precipices, valleys and rock faces had to be done from the roadside. Hours were spent scanning the terrain through field glasses but all to no avail. There was simply no trace of Maureen or her car. By the middle of October the weather at the high elevation turned from summer to winter and they were forced to give up.

The snows came. It was a forlorn time. At Christmas, Bob and Faith's son and second daughter arrived at Greenvale with their families. They all tried to make the best of it, but festive did not enter into the holiday. Thoughts of the missing woman never went away and that, of course, stirred an underlying restlessness never overtly acknowledged but felt by all, a conscious need to do something more. So, on the twenty-sixth, while Faith amused the grandchildren, the rest of the family set out as soon as the plows had cleared the highway and drove in a convoy to La Junta. If anyone spotted what seemed to be a peculiar shape in the snow, they stopped and scanned the site from the road. Though they did not speak it, they all had the same thought, that the snow might give up the outline of a crashed car. But there was nothing. After a brief stop for refreshment in La Junta, they drove back at the same pace, checking the east side of the highway. But again they were disappointed.

As the weeks passed, with no word of Maureen, the consensus grew that she must be dead, that her car had crashed down a steep precipice into such heavy forest that it would not be visible from any angle. But disappearance was not the same as death. In death a chapter ended, and shattered as it was, the mind could accept and find a certain closure within. Here there was no peace because the family would be in limbo until they knew what had happened to their daughter, sister, sister-in-law, aunt. So many lives were affected. Faith's worst fear was that Maureen might have been abducted and was still being held captive by some psychopath, and that she was enduring unspeakable suffering and mental torture.

That winter the light went from the Bob and Faith's life, replaced by fear and unbearable uncertainty. Their son, who still lived in Seattle, begged them to sell up in Colorado and move back to the Pacific Northwest, but Faith would not hear of it. So long as Maureen was still missing they would stay close to the place where she had vanished. Even though Bob said that they must accept she was dead, Faith could not, would not, and was desperate for more action, not less.

Summer arrived and passed.

Winter came again and went.

Time eventually blunted their grief and allowed Faith and Bob to work out new routines to get them through the bleak days and hopeless months. They no longer tensed when the phone rang or jerked when there was the sound of an unexpected car in the drive. Life would never be the same but gradually, reluctantly, they adjusted.

One summer afternoon, twenty-three months after Maureen disappeared, Basil heaved himself off the paving of the back patio, and glancing across at Faith where she was pottering around a far flowerbed, the dog gave a short bark of warning. Faith looked up to see Basil padding off around the side of the house. Putting down her hoe, Faith pulled off her gardening gloves and followed him.

Will Collins, no longer deputy but risen to sheriff of Harris County had left his prowl car on the road and was walking up the drive. The Hendersons hadn't seen him in quite a while, and Faith's stomach shriveled. The sheriff was trying to give nothing away but she was too perceptive for that. She began to shake. She swallowed hard, "You've found her, haven't you?"

Collins wished her husband were there. "We've found a vehicle which matches the description." He almost flinched at her gasp. Out of the corner of his eye he saw the dog raise its head and stare at him. "The plates are missing, but we don't have much doubt that it's her Cherokee."

Faith folded her arms tightly across her chest, trying to hold herself together. She wanted to ask about Maureen's body but she couldn't force the words out.

This was lucky for Collins who wasn't going to say anymore without Bob being there. "What time are you expecting Bob home?"

Faith glanced up at the clock. "He should be in the clubhouse now, but he usually stays on for lunch."

"Better give him a call."

In less than ten minutes Bob pulled into the driveway.

"The thing is," Collins said quietly. "There is no body."

Faith burst into tears, and Bob took her in his arms, looking questioningly at Collins over her head.

"The vehicle was discovered by a hydro surveying crew deep in a ravine not fifty miles along I-25."

"But you searched the entire I-25!" Bob cut in. He couldn't keep the criticism out of his voice even though he knew it wasn't justified.

Collins shrugged. "It's a helluva way down. It didn't come to rest easily. The boys say it bounced off the cliff face right into the gully. It's concealed from the road by an overhang. It's going to take them awhile to get it out of there. She must have been going some speed to land up where she did."

Faith pulled away from Bob and went to the other side of the room covering her face with her hands.

"I'm going out there," Bob said harshly.

Collins glanced uncomfortably over at Faith. "Look, Bob, that wouldn't be a good idea. As I said, there's no actual body."

"What the hell do you mean by that?"

Collins lowered his voice. "There are – bones."

"Oh, God!" Faith wailed.

"It's been nearly two years." Collins muttered to Bob, and didn't add, 'and there are animals in the terrain'. "If you could give me a personal item of hers which she would have handled, for fingerprint identification, you understand. Forensics are out there checking the vehicle."

Bob's body sagged. "Okay, just a minute." He went upstairs and came back with her passport.

The Henderson's son and surviving daughter flew in immediately. By the time they arrived, the Cherokee, or what was left of it, had been lifted out of the ravine and taken to the highway patrol compound. They went with their father to view it. Faith did not. One plate was found when the surrounding area was searched and now it lay on the twisted driver's seat. The passenger seat was unrecognizable. The paper documentation had disintegrated, but there was no doubt that this was

215

Maureen's car. The skeletal remains located near it had been taken to the morgue and awaited a positive identification. They went from the compound to the coroner's department where DNA swabs were taken. Bob was told that when all the forensic tests were completed and the coroner signed off on the body, it would be released to the family. Collins would notify him at the appropriate time.

At home Faith sat in the garden in a tide of helplessness, Basil her faithful companion beside her. Somehow over the last few months it had been almost possible to believe that none of this had happened, that Maureen was still in New York leading the life she loved. It was nature's way of softening the terrible blow perhaps, but now everything came flooding back — the horror, the despair, the anguish.

Would the coroner be able to tell if Maureen had suffered? she wondered. If he could say that she had died instantaneously, it would make it easier. Well, perhaps, just a little. She could not bear to think of her daughter lying out there in the mountains for nearly two years, not fifty miles away, possibly alive for days waiting to be found. The very idea made her feel sick. As the tears flowed, Basil got up and put his head on her knee, then raised it to gaze at her lovingly. She leaned forward and gathered him in her arms, crying into his fur.

By the time Bob and her other children had returned from the accident site, Faith had pulled herself together. She would cry again, many times, but now there were things to be done. Maureen would soon be home with them and that was an answer to one of her prayers. Now her daughter must be laid to a proper rest.

It was over…or so she thought.

Two days later the sheriff hitched up his pants and strolled over to the clicking fax machine. Thinking of his lunch, he pulled the sheet out and began reading it. A minute later he called Deputy Lovat into his office. "Report's just come in from the medical examiner's office on the Henderson woman."

"Coffee?" Hugh Lovat asked and veered to a side table.

"No, I have to go out."

Lovat poured himself a coffee. "The Hendersons'll be able to get on with the funeral now."

"Don't bank on it."

"Eh?"

"It isn't her."

"What?"

"It's a woman, but it's not Maureen Henderson. Wrong DNA." The sheriff stabbed a stubby finger at the print-out. "And the skeletal remains are the wrong size. This woman was a lot shorter than Henderson."

"Sounds mighty suspicious, Will."

"I'd better get over to Greenvale, can't let them bury someone else's daughter."

The DNA result signaled a new nightmare story for Faith and Bob. Told that the remains were not their daughter they were instantly transported back to the time of Maureen's disappearance, plunged into the horror of what amounted to a second disappearance, going through it all again. It was a blow from which Faith did not believe she could recover. Why was she being made to suffer this way? Preparations for the funeral were already underway, notices sent out. All this had to be cancelled. Faith could not deal with it. A neighbour volunteered to do what was necessary. Nor was Faith able to face any more questioning from the sheriff and his deputies, but questioning there had to be and so it fell to Bob.

Collins watched Bob closely across the desk, waiting for his reaction to the new mystery. Finally Bob spoke, "Okay, it can't be Maureen's car. It can't be. Someone planted the license plate to make it look as though it is."

Collins pondered that, as though he was seriously considering it as a possibility "Why would anyone do that?"

"I don't know, but it must be the case. You agree that the plate wasn't attached to the vehicle, that it was found some distance off."

Collins hitched his chair closer to the desk and leaned forward to open a file. "The engine number is consistent with the Jeep Cherokee your daughter purchased from Ridley Motors in Queen's, New York in April 2001." He eased himself back in his chair which creaked under his weight. "Also - " He paused. "Also the fingerprints in the car match those from the item belonging to your daughter that you gave us. I don't think there's any doubt it's your daughter's vehicle, sir."

"Then where is my daughter?"

Collins took his time to answer. He had to be careful. This was a curious business. Anything he said could be used against the department. Nowadays, with the media playing the role it did, they, and the public, were quick to jump on the deficiencies of whatever law enforcement agency was involved in a case. Criticism of how an investigation was handled could come out of the simplest thoughtless remark from the police to a member of the public. 'Loose lips sink ships' was becoming as apt as it had been in the forties. There was no doubt in the sheriff's mind that although this body wasn't Maureen's, she was dead. He was not, however, about to air that view to her distraught father.

"I just don't know where Maureen is, Bob."

Bob was in despair. "Then what do we do now?"

"We reinstate all the procedures for a missing person."

"That wasn't a helluva lot of use last time!"

"It's the starting point."

There didn't seem to be much else to say, but Bob was reluctant to leave. His sense was that modest though it was, this was the nerve centre of the investigation; and if he hung around long enough, he might discover something which would be of use.

"What about the remains at the crash site. Have they been identified?"

"I can't tell you anything about that. I don't mean I won't, I just don't have the information. The DA's office in Denver is taking charge of that part of the investigation. They'll attempt to identify the deceased from the bones. You understand the difficulty. She's a Jane Doe and without a control sample of DNA, how can a match be made? It's only if she is on record that that might lead somewhere."

"What about dental records?"

"I'm sure they're working on that, but that's a bit like the chicken and the egg. Unless this Jane Doe is in a data base somewhere we're not going to be able to use her teeth to id. her and the chances are she isn't." Collins rocked in his chair. "Consider the stats, Bob. Thousands of people disappear every year either by accident or design. Most are reported, but not all. Some are recovered dead or alive, many are never traced. That could be because they don't want to be found or because they're now reduced to bones lying in some unknown location, such as we have here."

Bob did not derive any comfort from those words."Is Denver going to keep me informed?" he asked shortly.

"If an identification is made I reckon they'll want to know if you knew this other woman and how come she was driving Maureen's vehicle."

"It was obviously stolen."

"Right." Collins didn't want to go down that road with this distraught father. A simple vehicle theft was one thing, but the unreported theft of a vehicle whose owner had disappeared off the face of the earth was another. "You can rest assured the case on your missing daughter is still active."

"My son wants us to begin a search of our own."

"That's within your rights, Bob. Any support that can be given to the official investigation is always welcome."

"So it's all right with your department?"

"Sure."

"We want to post her photograph again in Denver and La Junta in all the malls, supermarkets, theatres, community centers."

"Sure, you go ahead."

The climb back from the second disappearance was indeed too much for Faith Henderson. The first step, getting past the sudden halt of preparations for the funeral, was not successful, and from there she stumbled, not forward, but backward and eventually became mired. Deeply depressed, her very existence became a struggle. Bob grew desperate. He could barely function with Faith in the state she was in. As he fought to put their shattered life in some sort of order, knowing he couldn't watch Faith twenty-four / seven, he asked her older widowed sister, Laura to come and stay with them for a while. Laura's presence gradually brought some semblance of normalcy into the Henderson household, but Faith did not regain her interest in life. She complied with whatever was arranged and went quietly along with Bob and Laura like an obedient little child in the company of adults, and the days gently passed.

Dean Calistro screwed up his face as he listened to the voice on the other end of the line. "But that's absolutely impossible!" he refuted. He stood at the window of his Beacon Hill brownstone and stared over Boston Common at the gleaming gold leaf of the State House Rotunda. "My sister is on a sailboat with her husband. They're on a round the world trip. I've just had postcard from them. So how can she be dead in Colorado?"

As soon as he hung up he dialed the precinct back, fully expecting to hear that there was no Detective Siskin in that division. But in this effort, Dean was defeated. Detective Siskin was working on the Martel file, and Dean's appointment with him at ten the next morning was confirmed.

Dean wasn't worried, but he was vexed, more than vexed, outraged! There had obviously been some major foul-up within the police department. One thing was certain, he would not submit to the DNA testing the detective had requested and said so to the officer the next day who tried to take the swab. Dean demanded to speak to Detective Siskin.

The man who stood up when Dean walked into the cramped office shared by half a dozen plain clothes officers, was tall, rangy and cordial. He had a tired face which spoke of the frustrations of his job, and thinning grey hair was a further testament. He offered Dean a coffee which he refused.

"You need to get your facts straight, Detective," Dean jumped in aggressively. "I don't know what kind of mistake has been made within your department, but I can tell you I don't appreciate getting a call out of the blue telling me my sister is dead! There's no way the bones you've found can be hers. Erin and her husband are sailing around the world. There is no way, no way, - " he repeated for emphasis. " – that she has ever even been to Colorado!"

"Mr. Calistro." The detective folded his arms on his desk and leaned on them. "I appreciate your outrage and I understand your confusion - "

"There is no confusion, Detective! I don't know how many other ways I can put it, but that skeleton is not Erin's!"

"It isn't just a case of the bones," the detective asserted quietly. "Fingerprints have been lifted from the preserved material found in the car. Erin Martel's fingerprints."

"It isn't possible!"

"That's what the investigation shows."

"No, wait, how do you know — about the fingerprints, I mean? Erin doesn't have a record."

"They're on file from when she worked - " Siskin put a pair of steel-rimmed glasses on his nose and bent his head over a print-out in front of him, "- in Washington, at the Senate. She was an intern when she was at university, right?" He looked up and regarded Dean steadily.

Dean was disbelieving. "Yes, that's right."

"They were matched in a routine scan sent out by the Denver police department."

"But there has to be a glitch somewhere!"

"It's possible," Siskin nodded. "That's why we asked you to come in for the DNA sample."

Dean's mind began to race, but there was nothing he could latch onto from his turbulent thoughts. He heard the other man's voice and tried to focus on it. "What?"

"You said your sister is on a cruise?" Siskin repeated.

"No, no, not a cruise," Dean corrected savagely. "She and her husband are on their own sailboat! The Seahorse. I keep telling you, they're doing a trip around the world. They've just left the Mediterranean. I had a card from them only a couple of days ago mailed from the Canaries."

"Do you have that card?"

"Not with me," Dean exclaimed tersely. "It's at home, along with all the other cards they've sent me since the fall of 2002. Do you want to see them?"

Siskin rose. "Let's wait for the DNA result." He led Dean out of the squad room and down the hall to an anteroom and left him there in the care of a technician. Siskin made his weary way back to the detective's room. He didn't know what was going on in the Calistro family and didn't care. If the DNA result was positive, there was no argument. Those bones out there in Colorado belonged to Erin Calistro Martel. How they got there when the owner of them was supposed to be at sea on the other side of the world was of no interest to him at all. If there *was* a case, it was a cold one and, thankfully, not in his jurisdiction. Let Denver take care of it.

Detective Keith Yorke, a veteran of the Denver Police Department, received the report from the Boston lab that the DNA test result from Dean Calistro of Boston, Massachusetts, matched the skeletal remains found along the I-25. The bones were officially identified as Erin Martel's. It was she who had by accident or design driven off the interstate two years before. Yorke logged into the Martel file and added the new information. The local coroner was informed. The bones could now be returned to Boston and the woman's family. Before he went off duty that afternoon the formalities were completed. Case closed.

It had become a weekly ritual. On Wednesdays, when Faith thought Bob was on the golf course, he drove the fifty miles along the I-25 to stand at the edge of the highway and look down over the rocky bluff into the dark ravine where the Cherokee had come to rest. That spot on the highway was the last place his daughter's car had been, so he continued to be drawn there, unable to tear himself away from the point where the vehicle had gone over the edge.

The site had almost recovered from where the heavy machinery had churned up the edge of the highway to haul up the vehicle from the depths. The steep precipice and the forest growth were hardly damaged. Someone had told Bob the crew thought there might be another vehicle further down the mountainside, one which could have been involved in the accident, but this proved not to be the case, so the two car accident theory had been dropped. Will Collins had never believed in that theory anyway. He said that if that had been the case, there would have been evidence of it on the road surface at the time of the accident. But there was no such evidence. In fact, there was no evidence of any accident at all, and the investigators had concluded that the Cherokee had been deliberately driven over which would account for no skid marks, at a specially chosen place to keep it hidden for a considerable time.

How could that be? It was a puzzle which would not let Bob rest. Over the next few weeks one scenario after another washed through his mind. Had Maureen known this other woman and had arranged to meet her? Or had she picked her up as a hitchhiker? Was is possible that Maureen had not died from the crash but had been able to stumble away and had become lost in the mountain wilderness and eventually died from exposure? If that was the case the chances are they would never know.

October approached again. Soon the weather would bring Bob's private vigils to a halt, but he vowed to continue to visit that spot until the snow came. One day when there was a hint of crispness in the sparkling mountain air, a rental car pulled up a little distance ahead of Bob's parked Altima. Bob turned from the railing, the railing which had been installed by the Department of Highways following the retrieval of the Cherokee, and waved the approaching man off. "I'm fine," he called out. "No problem."

"Glad you're okay," Dean Calistro called back"- but that isn't why I stopped. I just wanted to look at the…" He gestured over the railing. "Majestic, isn't it?"

"Yes," Bob agreed.

They stood some distance apart, watching blue and purple cloud shadows softening the dramatic landscape of steep hillsides and mysterious trenches, all heavily treed, impassable for the most part, and in the distance the high mountains — the beautiful and infamous Rockies, fronted on this eastern side by the Sangre de Cristo range.

A patrol car appearing around the bend passed them, then halted and made a U-turn to come back and draw up behind Bob's Altima. Will Collins climbed out and strolled over, frowning, "Anything wrong, Bob?" As he spoke he was glancing suspiciously at the other man standing a few feet away.

"No, everything's fine, Will."

Overhearing this Dean stared, then approached the other two men. He looked at Bob. "Excuse me, are you Bob Henderson?"

Bob was startled and perplexed. "Yes." Who was this man who knew his name. He'd never seen him before.

"I'm Dean Calistro." Dean offered his hand.

Both Bob and the sheriff were stupefied.

The sheriff moved first. He stepped forward and took Dean's hand. "Will Collins, Harris County Sheriff's Department. You're the brother of the victim?"

"Yes. I wanted to come before but, well, I couldn't get away, and I just…I just wanted to see this place for myself." He turned to Bob and held out his hand. "How do you do?"

Bob shook hands but couldn't form any words.

"I'm still having a hard time - " Dean began, then broke off to bend his head and light a cigarette.

"I know what you mean," Bob managed to choke out.

"I still don't think it's her," Dean said fiercely. "I keep trying to tell everyone it isn't but they refuse to listen to me."

"Why are you so sure?" Will asked curiously.

The question riled Dean. "This accident occurred almost two years ago, and my sister wasn't even in this country, never mind out here! She had left New York harbor on a sailboat with her husband, and they're still sailing around the world."

Collins looked Dean in the eye. "Do you mind if I ask a couple of questions?"

Dean inhaled his cigarette, shrugged and nodded.

"First, did your sister know Maureen Henderson?"

"Not to my knowledge" Dean turned to Bob. "I'd never heard your daughter's name until this happened. Had you heard of my sister?"

Bob shook his head. "No."

"That don't mean they didn't know one another," Collins stated.

"I guess not," Dean agreed, reluctantly. He threw the remains of his cigarette on the ground and squashed it under his shoe.

There was an awkward silence, each man stretching to find the link between these two women.

Dean brought out his cigarettes again. "What's Maureen like?"

"You say 'is'," Bob picked up immediately.

"Well, we know it wasn't her down there so there's no reason to believe she's dead. How old is she?"

"Twenty-nine."

"What's she like?"

A small smile pulled at Bob's mouth. "Independent. Maureen's been independent since she could walk."

"What does she do?"

"Work, you mean? Marketing executive. For the seven years prior to - to this, she lived and worked in New York. She's been on her own since she was nineteen."

"By that do you mean she's not married?"

"Yes. She did have a partner for a couple of years, but we never met him. A couple of months before she - she disappeared, she got sick and had to come back here to convalesce. What about Erin?"

"Also lived in New York." Dean lit another cigarette and almost immediately threw it down and stepped on it. "She's married happily to Alton. They're a great couple. They'd been planning to sail around the world since they became engaged. They'd wanted to do it for their honeymoon, but they didn't have the money then. A relative of ours died a couple of years ago and left Erin and I a nice little sum each. She and Alton are using hers for their dream trip. They bought the Seahorse and off they went. So..." he turned to the sheriff. "No matter what the DNA indicates, I've proof Erin could not have been within miles of here when this accident happened."

"Proof?" Collins' brows shot up.

"Yes," Dean almost shouted. "I told the Boston police this. At every stop Erin and Alton have made they've sent me a card from that port, telling me how they are and where to expect to hear from them next."

"Is that right?" The sheriff stuck his hands in his pockets.

"Yes, ever since they left, a card from every port."

"When did you get the last one?" Collins asked.

"A week ago, from Cape Town. Got it right here." He patted his pocket.

If this was true, Bob suddenly thought, even if there had been some mix-up in the lab and this man's sister was still alive sailing around the world, she had to be in some way involved in Maureen's disappearance. His flesh began to creep, as though he were in the presence of some alien force. He found himself physically repulsed whether by this man who had appeared out of nowhere, or by the ghost of that woman who had died down there, whoever she might be, he did not know. Flooded by the belief that this man's sister whose prints were in the Cherokee had engineered Maureen's disappearance or death, or both, he was galvanized into action. He strode off abruptly, got into his car and left.

Dean stared after him. He understood. He too found the scene, the atmosphere, the circumstances surreal, and he asked himself what he was doing here. What was the use of it?

Collins glanced thoughtfully after the disappearing Altima, then regarded the motionless figure of Dean. Whatever the divergent opinions of the two men, brother of one, father of the other, these two women must surely have known one another. They had both, at some point, been in that Cherokee, of that there was no doubt. Fingerprints and DNA from both of them were present in the remains of the vehicle.

"I'd be interested to talk to you a bit about those postcards, sir."

Dean shook himself out of his reverie. "I'd be happy to tell you, Sheriff." He took out his cigarettes and offer the pack to Collins.

Collins shook his head. "I'm a cigar man."

Dean lit up. He stood alongside the sheriff and gazed at the vista of uncompromising escarpments and ravines, forest and mountains, beautiful but oh so hostile. "The Boston detective wasn't interested in anything I had to say. I signed a statement that detailed how my sister and her husband have been gone for over two years now, and how I've been receiving the postcards from them. He just brushed it off as irrelevant."

"That would be because of the fingerprints and the DNA match."

"I don't believe that the labs are infallible, Sheriff. I think that was illustrated in the OJ case. Contamination of samples is commonplace. So that, in combination with the postcards convinces me that there has been a catastrophic mistake in this case."

"There's just the two of them on board?" Collins asked. At Dean's nod he went on, "She's quite an adventurous woman, then, to undertake a trip like that."

"Yes." Dean allowed himself an affectionate laugh. "You wouldn't think it to look at her."

"How's that?"

"She's a little thing and quite diffident. She always has been, but Alton makes up for that. He's got enough get-up-and-go for twenty people."

"It was his idea, then, this round the world sailboat trip?"

"No, no, not so far as I know. Erin has always been enthusiastic, and you can tell from her postcards she's having a great time."

"Can I take a closer look at that last card?"

"Sure." Dean took it from his inside pocket and handed it to him. "I've brought them all with me. I was hoping the Denver police department would take a look at them, but the officer in charge there said the case is closed." He threw his half-smoked cigarette down in the gravel with a bitter gesture.

After reading the card Collins said, "I'd like to have a look at the others if you've no objection."

Dean was immediately alerted. "Do you have an idea?"

Yes, the Sheriff had an idea all right but not one he was willing to impart just yet. "Where are you staying, at the Greenvale

Inn?" It was the only hotel in Greenvale.

"Yes, but I've got a flight back to Boston tomorrow."

"Why don't you get the postcards and come over to the county sheriff's office. It's on Spruce Avenue, two blocks over from the Inn."

Within an hour Dean was in the Sheriff's office seated across his desk. There was silence as Collins picked each postcard up in turn and examined it intently. Laid out on a row on the desk top he was able to trace the long, meandering sea voyage of the woman who was supposed to be dead. The last card was indeed from Cape Town, mailed two weeks before, and in it Erin wrote that next stop would be Durban. Inspecting the postmarks Collins remarked, "If I remember my grade school geography, Durban is quite aways around the coast. It would take them, what, three weeks, or so in a smallish sailboat?"

"It's hard to judge." Dean reflected. "If they left when they said they would, yes, but not if they lingered in any ports along the way."

"Well." Collins gathered up the cards. "I thank you for this, Mr. Calistro."

"Do you have any ideas?" Dean's jaw was stiff with tension.

Collins handed the postcards back. "I'd like to give it a bit of thought."

"Do you have my address in Boston?"

"It'll be in the files."

Dean took a business card out of his pocket and laid it down. "Just in case," he said.

Collins escorted Dean out and watched him walk to his rental car. He didn't go back inside but lit a cigar and stood in the twilight, lost in thought. Postcards. Postcards from Montevideo, Rio, Caracas, the Mediterranean, the Canary Islands, St. Helena, Cape Town and more in between. Next stop Durban. You needed a passport for a journey like that. A passport, yes. He went inside and into the evidence room, more of a locker really in a detachment as small as Greenvale where there was rarely any serious crime. He pulled a cardboard bank box off the shelf and opened it. There it was. Before he took it out, he pulled on a pair of latex gloves. It should have been given back to the Hendersons. Forensics had only needed it to lift her fingerprints, but it had been forgotten. Now Collins inspected it more fully. He opened it and then nodded his head. Expired. He put it back in the box and stripped off the gloves. Deep in thought he strolled into his office and lowered himself into the chair at his desk. After a while he arranged his large, rather clumsy hands over the keyboard and opened a database on his PC.

Bob didn't tell anyone about the encounter with Dean, but it nagged away at him. He considered telling Faith but didn't want to risk upsetting her any further. Still, for several days he brooded on the man's adamant claim that despite all evidence to the contrary the woman in the ravine was not his sister - because of those postcards. Well, anyone could mail postcards, Bob thought.

Anyone could mail postcards. Glowing with health, her body golden against the pure white of her halter top and slacks, the woman smiled at her man. *My man!* His arm slipped around her and they ploughed their way, ankle deep in sand, along Durban's fabulous beach. Miles of thick creamy sand edged the clear blue surging surf where nets kept the sharks at bay. Heaven, this is heaven, she smiled, and we deserve every minute of it. All that planning, and in the end it had been so damned easy!

It took no persuasion at all to get Erin to accompany Alton to Denver on that last little business trip before they left for their long awaited odyssey. She thought nothing of that stop in the early morning hours on the part of the highway he had chosen, where the Cherokee was waiting. The pad of chloroform over her face, her limp body thrust behind the wheel of the Cherokee, and over the edge, down into the deadly precipice. The plan only stumbled when the vehicle didn't catch fire. It had a full tank of gas. She had filled up in La Junta before driving out there. It was a setback. They had counted on the body being burned beyond recognition. There was no time to do anything about it, they couldn't afford to be seen on the 1-25. Still, two years had passed without a hint of suspicion. They couldn't understand it but they took it! "Maybe all the identifiable bits were eaten by coyotes," she had joked to Alton.

Alton, her old love, her only love, whom she had almost, but not quite, forgiven for marrying another woman when her back was turned, sending her into a decline that almost finished her.

"Lucky coyotes," he had joked back.

Safe, they set out for South America, Europe, then Africa. She smiled as she thought of them sending all those postcards, Alton signing both names — Erin and Alton, the happy couple. Alton had one in his hand right then, a brilliantly colored photograph of lovely, flowery Durban with its magnificent sea shore. She took it from him and read what he had written, 'Hello Dean, we're staying in Durban for a while. Too perfect a place to leave. Next stop Majunga, all our love, Erin and Alton'.

Arms entwined they went up to the promenade and found a mailbox. She tossed the postcard in, and they exchanged a laughing kiss.

"Maureen Henderson?"

She spun around — involuntarily, too late to stop herself.

Two tall, blond men. Clothes too formal for the beach. One of them held out his warrant card and smiled. "Immigration service."

MISSY

The most astonishing thing to her was that the sky had not changed. There it was looking just as it had when she left London two days before.

In the early fifties a flight from London to Central Africa required an overnight in Nairobi. In addition her journey was extended by a few hours because of a problem in Cairo; some political crisis which prevented the plane from landing there. Instead they went on to Khartoum. It was night when they landed but suffocating hot. Everyone was ordered off the plane by surly men in army gear carrying rifles, into a Quonset hut. In the hut there were things for sale, bazaar-style, and someone came around with orange juice. She refused it having been told to drink nothing abroad but boiled water. But at least they left the baggage alone. The following week passengers experiencing the same diversion to Khartoum had their baggage opened, belongings searched and things taken.

Her name was Sophie Moore, she was eighteen, and had accepted an invitation from her maternal uncle and his wife to join them in Africa, not at one of the glamorous towns around the coast, but at a mining camp on the copperbelt. Remote. Isolated.

Landing in N'dola she found herself in a whole new world, already observed as totally different from anything and everything she had ever known, except for the sky.

The Douglas C-47 carried only a small number of passengers who stepped around her when they descended the metal steps to the dusty runway, and hurried through the heat to a drab building, nothing more than a small corrugated hangar. She stayed where she was, looking around at the flat landscape baking under the noonday sun, plumes of red dust rising whenever a movement stirred the ground.

The flight crew came down the steps and passed her. The stewardess touched her arm and nodded towards the airport building.

After a minute Sophie followed them.

By the time she reached the hangar the few passengers and crew had been processed and were gone. Her uncle was waiting for her on the other side of the makeshift customs barrier. He waved across the trestle table, beaming. She grinned at him, relieved that he was there. All through the flight from Nairobi she had been worrying about the possibility of him not being there. What would she do in the middle of Africa totally alone, virtually penniless, with nowhere to go? But he was there, grinning at her.

"Is this all you've got?" he asked when her passport was stamped and she joined him.

She glanced at her valise with its matching square cosmetic case with the handle on top. They were all the rage with model girls in 1953, so naturally the young and trendy had to follow suit. "Yes."

Tommy Ramsay leaned down and kissed both her cheeks. "It's great to see you, Soph. How are you?"

"Fine, and you?"

"Yes. Good flight?" he asked , leading her out of the air conditioning into the heat of the day.

"Yes." It was the first time she had flown so she had no idea whether it was a good flight or not, and actually it was three flights, but who was counting. "Where's Aunt Moira?"

"She decided not to make the drive. Mad dogs and Englishmen, you know."

The landrover, looking not much different from the one he swanned around North Africa in during the war, was the only vehicle in the parking lot. He threw her suitcase in the back. "Not a very comfortable ride, I'm afraid."

He was right. Once out of N'dola, the roads between the settlements, cut through the bundu, were nothing more than two narrow strips of black top between high stands of elephant grass against an unending backdrop of straggly cordwood trees. As they rattled along Sophie felt as though she were in a hamster wheel. They were moving but nothing in the landscape changed. They met few vehicles for which she was thankful. In order to pass each had to move over to use only one paved strip each. Clouds of choking red dust rose from wheels under the offside wheels and there was much squealing of tires. It was a scary exercise because they were traveling at speed and no-one slowed down.

Sixty miles from N'dola the bulk of the massive copper mine rose out of the landscape, looming over the mining camp huddled around it.

Camp made it sound like tents – army tents, but it wasn't like that at all. Short unpaved residential streets were laid out on a grid pattern across which large identical bungalows faced one another. Most of the town's housing belonged to the mine, provided for employees– the white ones, that is. Black mine workers lived in compounds. Black domestic servants lived in huts in the grounds of the bungalows.

Tommy turned down Fourth Avenue. Even before they got to the fifth bungalow Sophie had spotted her aunt. She was sitting in a wicker armchair on the broad clipped lawn with tea set up beside her. A man lounged in a deckchair a couple of feet away.

"I see she's got company," Uncle Tommy said, pulling into the gravel drive alongside a landrover indistinguishable from his. Leaving Sophie's bags in the vehicle he took her over the grass to her aunt. Moira looked up, squinting against the sun. "So, you're here."

There didn't seem to be much else to say to that except, yes. *Just popped in from London.*

The man had risen. He was dressed, as was Tommy in what Sophie was to come to know as the habitual daytime costume of the colonial male; short-sleeved, open-necked khaki shirt, baggy khaki shorts to the knees, long socks and leather sandals, a cross between the officers of the Egyptian campaign and scoutmasters.

Ray, as he was introduced to her, did not wear underpants, as she soon saw when he collapsed back in the low deckchair and, with a flourish, placed his left ankle on his right knee.

At some kind of command a black servant, dressed exactly like the two white men, appeared carrying two more garden chairs.

"Sophie, this is N'sunga, my head boy. N'sunga, this is Missy. You will look after Missy very well."

"Yes, B'wana."

"Take her luggage from the landrover and put it in her room."

"Yes, B'wana."

There was, Sophie related in her diary later, something totally unreal about that tea party on the lawn.

As she ate a slice of rich chocolate cake and drank black tea – no milk was allowed in the Ramsay household - she observed a side of her aunt she had never seen before, a curious middle-aged flirtatiousness, directed, of course, at the lounging visitor. As this went on Sophie glanced at her uncle. It didn't seem to bother him. He smiled at Moira's innuendos, and chuckled at Ray's puerile jokes.

After an hour Moira rose saying it was time for her nap, and swinging her hips at Ray, went into the house. A minute later Ray heaved himself up and Tommy followed suit. They walked across the lawn to the vehicles in the drive. There they stood and talked for a minute. They were too far away for Sophie to hear what they were saying but it seemed to be amiable. Ray got into his landrover and reversed out of the drive. As he passed along the rough gravel road he raised a hand in a farewell salute.

"I expect you want to settle in," Uncle Tommy said to Sophie. "I'll show you your room."

As they strolled up to the house she took in the lush greenery, impressed at how different the mining camp itself was from the dusty red bundu beyond the camp limits. She supposed it was an oasis, and discovered that it was; manmade, by the mine. She was to come to learn that the mine was god. The mine provideth and the mine taketh away.

"What's that?" she asked, pointing at a large grassy mound with a door in it in the next garden. "It looks like an Anderson shelter."

Uncle Tommy laughed. "It's an ant hill."

"What? An anthill, but it's enormous."

"You'll see them everywhere, in the camp and out in the bundu. Most are much bigger than that one. It's abandoned, of course, so the Taylors hollowed it out and are using it as a garden shed. They're Canadians, the Taylors, I mean, but out here all white people are called Europeans regardless of where they come from. We had a couple of anthills as big as that on this property but I had them leveled. I wanted to grow our own fruit and vegetables. Now look, Sophie, this is as good a time as any to clue you in a bit. In this house we eat no meat, and drink no milk, for the simple reason I don't believe either is safe, so when you make friends and go out to eat I'd like you to observe that practice, and never never drink anything cold except for champagne, that's safe enough. I'd stay away from the beer too, unless you've opened the bottle yourself."

"I actually don't drink, Uncle. I'm only just eighteen."

"Well, you'll probably have to start out here or you'll go thirsty. Ask for champagne. It won't be from France and the alcohol content will be very low. Mostly it's pink. Peel any fruit you are given. If it's already peeled don't eat it."

She nodded, and as they passed around the house she saw the extent of his produce garden, everything from banana and paw-paw trees to mangoes and guava vines, but not English fruit like apples or cherries. There were rows of potatoes, carrots and onions.

"That's an avocado," he said, pointing to a large tree with spreading bows. "It was already here when we moved in, of course. It's quite a mature tree. Do you like avocados?"

"I've never tried them."

"You'll find they're addictive, but that's okay, we've got plenty. Your aunt and I pretty much live on fruit and vegetables. Except for her cakes and desserts. She's a marvelous baker, you know."

"Yes, I remember."

He took her on a tour of the house, giving the bedroom he shared with Moira a miss as she was in there sleeping. The rooms were large and dim, made so by the wide covered veranda encircling the bungalow which kept the sun off, and which was the most lived in part of the residence. The house was refreshingly cool because there was no glazing in the windows, only screens.

"We don't need glazed windows," Uncle Tommy said. "It never gets cold here, and the rain can't blow in because of the overhang. We get some pretty spectacular storms in the rainy season."

Her bedroom was very charming. N'sunga, or someone, had unpacked her suitcase and hung her clothes in the wardrobe. Her underwear had been folded up in a dresser drawer. It gave her a strange feeling.

"I'm going to shake up the boys," her uncle said. "Have a rest. We meet on the veranda for sundowners at six. Dinner at seven."

When Sophie emerged at the designated time Moira was already ensconced on the veranda in a cushioned wicker chair with a cocktail in her hand.

"Help yourself," she said, pointing backwards.

Sophie went through the French doors into the lounge. The cocktail cabinet, which now had a key dangling from the lock, was wide open revealing a sparkling display of crystal and every sort of liquor. She hunted through until she found a bottle of sherry and poured herself as small amount.

"We have to get a few things straight," Moira said without preamble, when Sophie rejoined her. "To begin with, you can drop the aunt and uncle."

Sophie was taken aback, not sure she had heard right. "Pardon?"

"I said, you can drop the aunt and uncle. I have no intention of broadcasting to the entire camp that Tommy has a niece as old as you."

"Oh, all right."

"And secondly, I expect you to get a job right away. It isn't our intention to support you."

"No, of course, I understand that."

"I'm glad to hear it. Tommy did not exactly consult me before he wrote and asked you to come out here to live with us."

"Oh, I'm sorry."

"So I'd appreciate it if you'd not intrude on my life too

much."

This was not an unexpected remark coming from Moira. She'd never made any secret of her dislike of her husband's family, and everyone knew the reason why. Her rudeness just had to be absorbed. "I'll get a place of my own as soon as I can," Sophie said.

"You can't. White women don't live alone out here. It isn't safe. The mine provides housing for bachelors but not for female employees, so you're stuck, I'm afraid, and so am I."

Tommy came from across the lawn then. He got himself a beer and sat down, stretching out his long legs. The women of the camp changed for the evening meal but men rarely did so. They sat down in their khaki, unless it was a formal dinner and dance, in which case they changed into tuxedoes.

"So how did you like Nairobi?" Tommy asked.

"I liked what I saw of it, which wasn't much because we were so late getting in."

"Why didn't you fly via Wadi Haifa?" Moira asked, on a note of criticism. "We always go by Wadi Haifa, don't we, Tommy?"

He didn't answer that, asking instead, "Which hotel did they put you in?"

"The Colonial. The airline crew were there. They were in the bar for a nightcap. The stewardess was so beautiful. She was wearing a little black dress with a glittery embroidered waistband, you know, that traditional Indian design."

Tommy laughed. "Still love fashion, then, just like your aunt."

"I've told her to drop the aunt and uncle," Moira said, holding out her glass for a refill.

"It was fun sleeping under the mosquito net," Sophie said. "But I got such a shock when I woke in the morning and saw a man walking around my room."

"What man was that?" Tommy enquired, coming back with Moira's drink.

"A servant, I discovered. He'd brought in my tea."

"Why were you shocked?" Moira asked.

"I thought they'd send in a maid, a woman."

"Not on this continent, my dear. Do you see any women servants in this house?"

"No, actually."

"Boys do all the domestic work, so you'll have to get used to it. Have you brought any evening dresses with you?

"Yes, one."

"You'll need a few more than that. I hope the one you've brought is suitable. We have a dinner dance at the hotel on Saturday night. It's quite an important occasion."

A gong sounded in the house.

As they walked into the dining room Tommy said, "Oh, I almost forgot," and brought out a small key from his pocket which he held out to Sophie. She thought it must be the house key but it looked a bit small for that.

"We don't lock the house," Moira told her. "There'd be no point when you've got half a dozen servants in the place. They could let every thief in Africa in while you're away, and probably do in many cases," she added, nastily. "Anyway, the screens can be cut with a pocket knife."

"It's the key to one of the refrigerators," Tommy explained. "The one full of bottled boiled water. Our drinking water. Make sure that you always lock that fridge again after you've gone there. We can't afford to have the water contaminated."

Sophie didn't ask them how it would become contaminated.

By the end of the week she had the promise of a job on the mine and had met two neighbour girls of her own age. There were only a few white teenagers in the camp, male or female. Most were either back in Europe at university, or had abandoned the copperbelt for more exciting surroundings as soon as they were of working age.

Sophie's pale green chiffon evening gown, copied from one

of Princess Margaret's, passed Moira's inspection. Curiously, though, it seemed to Sophie that the approval was grudging, as if Moira would have liked to find some fault with the dress, and to have claimed that it was totally unsuitable for the important occasion. Had she done so it would not have been a matter of running down the street and buying another dress, for there were no dress shops in the camp, only dressmakers. Would she have forbidden her to go to the ball, Sophie wondered?

She found it a little strange to be driven to a red carpet event in a paramilitary vehicle with Tommy in a dinner jacket and she and Moira in long gowns and high-heeled evening sandals. On the way she was prepped by Moira as to how she should behave in the company of the party they were joining. "They are our very dear friends," Moira warned.

It took but five minutes to drive to the only hotel, the Grand Windsor, a typical colonial structure with an immense pillared lobby open to the outside like a breezeway. Among the public rooms was a lofty bar and a ballroom so huge it could accommodate dozens of tables around the perimeter and still leave a major space for dancing.

No-one *was* dancing, however, even though the orchestra was in full swing. This was sundowner time. Serious drinking.

"There they are," Tommy said, and taking Sophie and Moira on either side of him led them to where their friends were already comfortably seated at a prime table on the edge of the dance floor; two couples in their thirties, and the young sister of one of the wives, a girl the same age as Sophie.

The men rose at their approach, and Tommy proudly introduced Sophie to the group. Hands were shaken. As everyone sat down the man called Tiny whose young sister-in-law lived with him and his wife, said in a tone full of innuendo, "Now you've got your niece here you're going to discover the hazards of having a pretty young girl under your roof."

"She's not my niece," Moira immediately snapped.

This rebuttal brought a loud whoop from around the table. "She already doesn't want to own you, Sophie," Tiny roared.

Sophie was mortified. With a flushed face which, unbeknownst to her, enhanced her fragile beauty, she dropped her eyes and twisted her fingers in her lap. If Tommy was as embarrassed as she was by Moira's comment he did not show it. He asked them what they would have to drink and called a waiter over. He ordered another round for everyone else. All the women were drinking champagne, the men, whisky.

"Did you get all the names?" the young girl asked Sophie with a broad grin.

"Not one," Sophie admitted shyly.

"Well, I'm Jane Green and that's my sister Catherine Beaumont." She giggled. "The one who deliberately riled Moira, which he always does, is my brother-in-law, Ian, but we call him Tiny because he's so big. The other couple are old friends of Catherine and Tiny's, Daniel and Peggy Frobisher. We knew them in England."

"And I'm Sophie, Tommy's niece."

"But not Moira's," Jane laughed.

Sophie shrugged uncomfortably. "Sorry about that. Tommy is my mother's eldest brother. How long have you been out here?"

"Eight months."

"Are you here permanently?"

"I don't think anyone is here permanently," Jane said satirically. "Why, are you?"

"I hope so."

"Are you going to apply to the mine?"

"I've already got a job. I start on Monday."

"Gosh! That was fast. What will you be doing?"

"Reception to begin with. What about you? Do you work for the mine?"

"Oh yes. Everyone does. Every European, anyway. That's

why we're here. I'm in the share transfer office. It's actually just across the road from here. We're not up at the big house like you privileged crew."

"Who's privileged?" Peggy Frobisher asked across the table.

"Sophie," Jane answered. "She's got a job in Reception."

Daniel looked at Tommy, "How did you pull that off?"

"Hugh Lowden owed me one."

"She starts on Monday," Moira said with satisfaction in her voice.

"It didn't take you long to push her out, Moira," Tiny laughed.

After another round of drinks, dinner was served, and when that was cleared away the dancing began. Since neither Sophie nor Jane had escorts the three men at the table assumed that they would partner the girls in turn. In the event, they were to be disappointed. The ballroom was full of unattached men who kept Sophie and Jane in a constant whirl until three in the morning.

After that night some of the young men began breaking trail to the door of number five, fourth avenue. Sophie, heeding the warning not to disrupt Moira's life, expected to be hauled over the coals for the disturbance but Moira's reaction was just the opposite. She greeted the young men cordially, more than cordially, enthusiastically, always asking them in for drinks or tea depending on the time of day.

"She's hoping you'll pick one of them and get married next week," Jane teased with a laugh.

The two girls had become friendly over the month following Sophie's arrival.

They didn't often see each other at work because Jane rarely had an excuse to leave her office on the main street and go up to the mine but they had begun meeting after work either at the mine club or the Grand Windsor, the only two places in the camp for the white population to socialize. The days were hot and remained so until the sun went down about six. Because the evenings were dark office hours were different from England. Work began at seven in the morning and finished at three so that the employees had some hours of daylight in which to relax on the golf course or the tennis courts or at the pool.

"No doubt she is hoping that," Sophie agreed mournfully. "I don't know why she agreed to have me out here. She's made it crystal clear that she doesn't want me, and I'm just a nuisance."

Jane agreed with a sympathetic smile. "Tiny and Catherine have said the same. They were surprised when Tommy told us you were coming. Besides that, Tiny couldn't understand why you would want to live with them. Tommy's all right, even if he is a bit wet but Moira is awful. How did he ever come to marry her?"

Sophie shrugged. She didn't know. "I don't want to live with them. I thought I could get a place of my own."

"White women don't live alone out here. It just isn't done."

"I know that now."

"Is Tommy spending more time at home now you're here?"

It was common knowledge that Tommy worked many hours of overtime a week, which, as a mine manager he was under no obligation to do, but as his alternative was being at home with Moira his decision seemed quite logical to everyone who knew them.

"No, he doesn't come home until six and he works every weekend."

"Piling up the lolly. Tiny and Catherine thought he was bringing you out here because he's so lonely."

"Could be, but he still spends a lot of time away from home."

"How do you and Moira actually get on?"

"We don't. She has no time for me. Or our side of the family. She has already told me to my face that there is only one lady in our family and that's my grandmother."

"Are you serious? What a bloody nerve."

The girls lay back in their *chaises-longue* and closed their eyes. The waning sun was still hot but bearable. Jane's skin was tanned to a smooth brown. Sophie was still pale but her fair hair had begun to bleach to an even lighter shade. Moira tried to make her wear a hat. Catherine said that Moira wasn't concerned about protecting Sophie from sunstroke as she claimed, she was envious of Sophie's blonde hair.

"Pity Catherine and Tiny haven't got room to put you up," Jane murmured. "It would be nice for me to have you live with us."

"That wouldn't work even if they had room, Moira would never speak to them again."

"Yes, well, that would be a welcome bonus. By the way, there's a tweet in the tree that the cerebral but adorable Matthew Wyatt has been leaving his card at five, fourth avenue."

"Adorable, is that what he is?"

"Don't you think so?"

Sophie lifted and dropped her shoulders. "I don't know."

"Well, eligible, anyway."

"What makes him so eligible?"

"His father's money, my dear. Don't be too quick to dismiss it."

"Matthew's nice enough but I'm not interested in him."

"I'm not much interested in Stan but I'm going to marry him."

Sophie's eyes popped open. She lifted herself up onto one elbow and stared at her friend's languid form. "You are going to marry Stan?"

"Yes. He asked me last night."

"Why didn't you tell me?"

"I just have."

"But – but no-one has said anything."

"You're the first to know. He's is supposed to pick me up from here at half four." Jane sat up, blinking. "What's the time now? We're going over to Roswell's to pick out a diamond."

Roswell was the only jeweler in the camp. He made almost everything to order from diamonds bought directly by his customers from an associated mine in the Cape.

"Do you mean you haven't told Catherine and Tiny?"

"Stan is coming to dinner tonight. We'll tell them then."

Sophie pulled her knees up and wrapped her arms around them. "Are you really not interested in Stan?"

"What?"

"You just said you were not much interested in Stan but you were going to marry him."

"That's right."

"You mean you're not in love with him?"

"Love? What's that got to do with it? How many couples in this camp do you know who are in love?"

"I don't know anybody yet."

"Take my word for it. Forget love. Marry for money. Unless you have expectations of your own."

Sophie didn't have any expectations that's why she had been eager to move to Africa. She'd graduated from a good English High School but her parents wouldn't pay for further education. She wanted to go into law, but it wasn't an option. Her parents claimed that no sooner had she got her degrees than she would get married and it would all have been a waste of time and money. If she could earn the money herself she could get her own education, and there was money to be made on the mine.

Jane said, "The added advantage of Matthew is that he is smitten with you."

"Don't be silly."

"You know he is."

"I'm not interested in him. When's the wedding?"

"August."

"That soon?"

"Why would we wait? Anyway, we don't want it in the middle of the rainy season."

"So it will be here then, not in England."

"Stan doesn't get leave until next year, and he has two more years left in this contract after that, so we'll be here for a while. I'd like you to be my bridesmaid."

Sophie smiled. "I'd be honoured."

"Idiot," said Jane.

One day shortly after that when Sophie was on the reception desk Tiny came by. Like Tommy he was one of the senior managers and often had business in the offices. He was affable and raffish, one of those huggy-bear types; a big man, tall and broad with sparkling blue eyes and a cheeky smile, full of an attractive self-confidence. He invited Sophie for coffee. There was nothing surprising in that. He was a friend of the family. Nonetheless Barbara Murphy, the other receptionist, eyed Tiny speculatively, particularly when he put his hand under Sophie's elbow and guided her masterfully along the hallways to the cafeteria.

Tiny bought their coffee and chose a seat far away from tables that were occupied.

"So, you're managing to survive, are you?" he asked, with a broad grin.

"Well - " She shrugged.

"Moira keeps you under lock and key most of the time I hear."

"No, that's not true."

His gaze made her blush, and he laughed at her. "You shouldn't be so pretty."

Her colour deepened. She lifted her coffee cup to hide her embarrassment.

"When was the last time Moira saw you? She must be kicking herself for letting you come out here."

"Why? Moira is a very attractive woman."

"For an over the hill harridan, yes."

"That's not kind."

"If anyone could be kind about Moira they'd win a Nobel Prize." Laughing Tiny gulped his coffee. "It's obvious she was good looking when she was young, but that's the key, you see, and she knows it. Stay young and beautiful. Like you. When we saw you walking into the ballroom that first time we said, oh-oh, here's trouble."

"Trouble?" Sophie squeaked.

"Your presence, sweetie. The *belledames* of this camp, and there are plenty of them, don't want their noses put out of joint by an influx of young lovelies."

Sophie couldn't help giggling. "I don't know what you're talking about."

"You'll find out." He changed the subject. "Has Tommy taken you to see the slag being poured?"

"The what?"

"So he hasn't. Okay. Tomorrow night. We'll come and get you after dinner, about eight, all right?"

Bewildered she gave a tiny shrug. "Okay."

The following evening Moira left for choir practice, driving her own small car. Tommy said he'd intended going back to the office for a couple of hours but he wouldn't if it meant leaving Sophie on her own.

"It's all right," she said. "The Beaumonts are taking me to see the slag being poured. Whatever that is."

"Oh good. Yes, I should have taken you myself before now. I'll be back by nine."

At eight a car horn sounded. The lights of the Beaumonts car flashed.

"Where're Catherine and Jane?' Sophie asked, standing by the open passenger door.

"Get in."

"Yes, but where are - "

"Get in, Sophie!"

Responding to the urgency in his voice she slid into the seat beside him.

"Close the door. I don't want your aunt bombarding me."

"She isn't here. She's gone to choir and Tommy went back to the office."

Tiny's relief was obvious. He laughed outright as he reversed out of the drive.

"Where are Catherine and Jane," she asked again.

"They didn't want to come. They've seen the slag poured a hundred times."

He drove her to the edge of camp to what was obviously a lookout some distance from a huge hill of tailings. Other vehicles were drawn up in the moonlight. "We don't get out very much in this town," Tiny grinned.

Very soon a giant conveyor carrying huge buckets of molten debris began to move and as the buckets reached the top of the hill they tipped and sent the fiery waste down its slopes. It was a spectacular sight. So spectacular that Sophie didn't notice that Tiny's arm was lying along the back of her seat. When the show was over it was a natural thing for his arm to slip from the seatback to her shoulders. He gave her a squeeze.

"Let's go have a drink."

"Oh, I don't think I should."

"Why not? You're afraid of what Moira might say?"

"No."

"What then?"

If she had said, because you're a married man, it would look as though she thought that this was a romantic assignation, and of course, it wasn't. He was simply a family friend. He took her silence to mean okay, and the next thing she knew they were in the lobby of the Grand Windsor. At least there was nothing underhanded about it. They sat at the bar, out in the open where anyone and everyone could see them, almost as though they had met there casually. When he dropped her off at home he didn't get out of the car, but as she opened her door and made to leave he leaned over and kissed her cheek. It was just a friendly gesture but it sent a flurry of excitement through her and, thanking heaven it was dark so he couldn't see her consternation, she left the car and hurried to the veranda without a backward glance. Luckily neither Moira nor Tommy was back. She went directly to her room but was intercepted at the door by N'sunga.

"Missy, B'wana come for you," he said in his broken English.

"B'wana, which B'wana?" She wasn't expecting anyone.

"He wait, then go."

"Who was it?"

"He write note." N'sunga held out an envelope.

She took it. "Thank you. Goodnight."

"Goodnight, Missy."

Sophie went into her room and switched on the light. The note, written on Moira's letterhead, was from Matthew Wyatt, scratched down after he had waited for her a while. It said that he had to leave but would she come to the dance with him at the mine club on Saturday night? If so, send a boy around in the morning to let him know. Mine houses had no telephones.

Well, at least it was a chance to wear the new evening dress she'd had made by Catherine's seamstress. That had annoyed Moira who informed Sophie that she should be using her dressmaker - where, of course, she could monitor what her niece chose.

Tommy and Moira were going to the dance too but Matthew picked Sophie up in his car, which was a deal more comfortable than the land rover. He didn't want to sit with the Ramsays, the Beaumonts, and the Frobishers but as soon as they entered the ballroom they were swept into the group and there was no way of getting out of it. Jane was there with her fiancé, Stanley Richardson, a serious man, who in his mid-forties had not been married before.

It was not an evening that Matthew enjoyed. Not only did all the men at their table ask Sophie to dance, but much younger men who were at the dance without dates asked her as well. He was just there to dance with the old women, he thought disconsolately as he stared over Catherine Beaumont's head, propelling her about the floor while her husband danced with Sophie. Matthew had never liked Tiny. He was too big, too self-confident, too amiable, too attractive to the ladies.

"What did Moira say when you told her you'd seen the slag being poured?" Tiny asked, looking down at Sophie with a grin.

Sophie was staring at the white front of his evening shirt. Even in her high heels she wasn't tall enough to see over his shoulder. His arm was strong around her waist. He was a good dancer, almost lifting her off the ground in the turns, making the movements effortless for her. Their clasped hands were pressed against his chest.

"I didn't tell her," Sophie admitted in a mumble.

"Why not?"

"I don't know. The subject didn't come up."

"Did you tell Tommy?"

"No. I actually haven't seen much of him this week. He's off as soon as he's had dinner unless they are going out together, which it seems they don't do very often."

"No, they never have, but Moira has her distractions."

"You mean Ray?"

"Ray and others."

Sophie pulled away a bit to stare up into his face. "Really?"

He laughed. "Don't tell me your family doesn't know."

She looked away. "There were whispers when they lived in England but no-one told us children anything."

"Poor old Tommy," Tiny smirked. "He should have left her years ago. Nobody can understand why he hasn't."

"I think he loves her, Tiny."

"Christ. That would be a miracle."

On Monday morning Tiny walked into reception and again took Sophie off for coffee. He did the same thing on Thursday. On Saturday night there was, as always, informal dancing at the mine club. Tiny was there drinking with some friends when Sophie and Matthew walked in. To Matthew's chagrin Tiny immediately crossed the room to ask Sophie to dance. They were dancing when Jane and Stanley came in. After that Tiny didn't approach Sophie again.

The plans for Jane's wedding began in earnest. She and Sophie spent hours pouring over dress patterns and fabric swatches sent from England. "I hope you have no objection to blue," Jane said. "Because it will have to be pink carnations. There's absolutely no choice. You've probably noticed that there's no florist here. All the flowers for weddings come from Donald Kincaid's pathetic little nursery and he can't grow anything but pink carnations."

"Pink carnations are nice," Sophie murmured.

They were lying by the pool drinking Pimms.

"Mm. By the way, I came up to the mine today."

"I didn't see you."

"No, you weren't at the desk. I didn't know the girl there. She's new to me. She said you'd gone off with your fancy man so I didn't wait."

"My fancy man?"

"I expect Matthew is finding he has more business up at the mine than he ever had before."

"Matthew?"

Jane laughed at her discomfort. "It looks as though he's your fancy man whether you like it or not."

Sophie didn't answer.

When she got home she was told that Matthew was coming to dinner, and when Moira emerged from her bedroom she was wearing a low cut cocktail dress and a sequined bauble in her hair. The table was beautifully set with a bowl of Donald Kincaid's pink carnations in middle. Whatever her faults everyone had to admit that Moira knew how to entertain. Of course, it helped that she didn't have to do any of the work herself, only shout orders at the houseboys who scampered about following her directions, and were there to clean up afterwards no matter how late it was.

Afterwards, on the dusky veranda, Moira placed herself beside Matthew on the sofa, the spot he had expected Sophie to occupy. Tommy put a record on and the conversation turned to a concert being presented at the hotel the following week. Anne Zeigler and Webster Booth were on a tour of Central Africa. Everyone was going.

By ten Tommy couldn't stop yawning and said he was off to bed. Early start in the morning. He always got to work an hour before anyone else.

At eleven, when it was clear that Moira had no intention of leaving Sophie and Matthew alone, Matthew got up to leave. "Walk me to the car?" he suggested to Sophie.

At the bottom of the veranda steps he pulled up short and suddenly said, "Sophie, will you marry me?"

She was astonished. It was a strange question to ask someone you'd never even kissed. Then she thought she'd misheard. Perhaps he hadn't proposed. But he had. He took her hand. "Will you, Sophie. I love you."

Those words made her shudder. He didn't exactly repulse her but she felt no physical attraction to him. "Um, I – thank you, Matthew, but, I don't think I'm ready to get married."

"Oh," Matthew was crestfallen. He stood for a moment, then nodded, and sighed, "Well, goodnight, then."

"Good night, Matthew." She stared after him into the black, velvety night. In a moment she turned and mounted the steps onto the veranda where she was frightened half out of her shoes by Moira suddenly appearing and spewing out a torrent of words. "Are you completely and totally out of your mind, girl!"

Sophie recoiled in shock. Moira was literally coming at her with bared teeth, screaming, "You are proposed to by one of the most eligible bachelors in this camp and you tell him you don't think you are ready to get married! You must be retarded. Yes, I was listening! Of course, I was listening and I couldn't believe my ears. Do you think you will have so many marriage proposals you can afford to turn Matthew Wyatt down? What makes you think that men will be lining up to marry you? God knows you don't seem to have a brain in your head. And let me tell you this, there is no place in society for an unmarried girl with no profession. When you get back to England you'll end up skivvying in someone's house or working for minimum wage behind a haberdashery counter. You'll never have a decent home of your own. You'll be scraping for a few pennies for the rest of your days. Without a husband you are nothing!"

As Moira's words sank in Sophie felt the tears swelling her throat. Moira was verbalizing all the fears that had tormented her since her parents had rejected giving her further education. But to have to marry for the reasons Moira was spitting out. It was awful to contemplate.

She stumbled unhappily through the rest of the week. Tiny called by Reception as usual, but Matthew stayed away until the night of the concert, so she thought he had dropped her. The plan had been for them to go together and, to her astonishment he came to pick her up. They left early enough to have a drink before going into the ballroom which had been set up like a theatre, and he behaved in his usual gentlemanly manner, just as if she hadn't turned down his marriage proposal.

Sophie had not expected to enjoy the concert and she didn't. The sort of semi-classical programme the famous couple were performing had no appeal for her yet, even though there were some notable absences among the people they knew, mostly husbands, there was a huge turnout. She didn't think Matthew and Tommy were thrilled to be there either, but they did their duty and sat obediently on either side of Moira. In the intermission there was a mad rush to the bar, and an overflow into the lobby and the grounds, where knots of people stood around with their drinks, talking and laughing. This was really what they had come for.

Sophie went to the powder room. On her way back to join Matthew who was waiting with a champagne cocktail, a hand came out of nowhere and gripped her arm. Her gasp of surprise was lost in the volume of noise from the crowd as she found herself being pulled into a dark anteroom. Then she saw Tiny laughing down into her face. "Oh, you scared me!" she exclaimed. "What ever are you doing here?"

"Looking for you."

"What do you mean?"

"I knew from Jane you'd be at this concert and I came along to say hello."

Her brows drew together as she gazed at him uncomprehendingly. "I don't understand."

"Don't you? Perhaps you'll understand this." And with a swift movement he gathered her up in his arms and kissed her full on the lips.

Sophie was stunned. When he put her back on her feet she stumbled and would have fallen. Speechless, she stood staring at him as if he'd just landed from Mars.

"Now you'd better go back before the others miss you," he said, and laughing he disappeared into the shadows.

When she rejoined the others Sophie was sure that they must all be able to tell what had happened, but they took no notice of her. She had only been away as long as it took to pay the visit and come back. She drank her champagne as voices buzzed around her, and sat through the rest of the programme in a daze. That night she lay sleepless, reliving that sudden and unexpected kiss which had both excited and dismayed her. It was not as though she had never been kissed before. She'd had a semi-boyfriend in England. True she had very rarely been alone with him, her mother and grandmother both being watchful chaperones, but when the two of them did manage a few minutes of privacy his embraces were chaste, very unlike Tiny's passionate kiss.

Tiny did not put in an appearance at the Reception desk at all the next week for which she was thankful, but Matthew came around to the house every night. She found herself glad of the distraction, and also very relieved that he did not make any romantic moves. Well, that would have been difficult because Moira did not leave them alone. Each night after dinner Tommy and Matthew passed each other; Matthew arriving and Tommy going back to the mine. Each night, drinking and smoking, Moira sat beside Matthew on the veranda sofa regaling him with stories of her youth.

One evening Ray appeared on the lawn below. He emerged from the darkness like Lawrence of Arabia out of the desert. Moira had no choice but to invite him to join them which she did in a cold voice with a disagreeable look. That didn't trouble Ray. He lounged in his chair in his usual pose displaying himself, presumably as a lure to Moira, for he showed a remarkable lack of interest in Sophie.

When Matthew was leaving he asked Sophie if she would go to the dance with him on Saturday night. "Of course she will," Moira exclaimed, blowing a stream of smoke into the air. "Tommy and I will be there too. We'll all go together."

Glancing rather longingly at Sophie, Matthew took his leave.

Moira stubbed her cigarette out and lit another one. "You must be quite mad, Sophie," she badgered in a tone as disparaging as her look.

"Why, what's she done?" Ray asked in surprise.

Moira ignored him, continuing to address Sophie. "How long do you think he is going to hang around waiting for you?"

"Matthew?" Sophie said, irrelevantly. "I don't expect him to wait for me."

"That's good, because he won't. As I told you before, there aren't many bachelors as eligible as him in this place. You'd do well to snatch him up while the opportunity exists."

"What you talking about, Moira?" Ray interjected. "This camp is full of bachelors. It's the women who are missing."

"I did use the word <u>eligible</u>, Ray. We are not concerned with bush rangers and navvies."

"Not everyone works on the mine," he muttered.

"Fancy that, Ray!" Her voice dripped sarcasm. She eyed him derisively. "I've lived in this camp six years, there's nothing you can tell me about it. You'd better be on your way, hadn't you? Dorothy will wonder what you're up to."

"Oh well," Ray heaved himself up. "Goodnight, then."

"I tell you one thing, my girl," Moira said grimly before Ray was even down the veranda steps. "If I were a couple of years younger I'd give you a run for your money."

Sophie frowned. *What was she talking about?*

"He wouldn't have to ask me twice to marry him."

Marry him? Matthew? She was old enough to be his mother!

"I'm not in love with Matthew," Sophie said.

"Oh, don't be so pathetic! Love has nothing to do with it. You marry for position, for security! Hasn't your mother taught you anything?"

"She's never said anything like that."

"Frankly, I don't think she's told you much about anything, or perhaps it's simply that you aren't very bright, Sophie."

Sophie was out of her element. "I don't know."

"You should be snapping him up while you have the chance."

"Well - "

"Do it, my girl. If you don't, you'll live to regret it. Mark my words!"

At the Saturday night dance Moira was gaily flirtatious, as sparkly as her diamond pendant, a twenty-year anniversary gift from Tommy, and her sequined gown. She was particularly attentive to Matthew who was having trouble getting one dance with Sophie so popular was she, and in the ladies "excuse me" he was furious that Moira came up and took him away from Sophie.

Sophie was immediately snatched up by someone she didn't know who pressed her to his body as did most of the men. But not Tiny. He didn't do that. When she found herself in his arms he held her firmly but not close, although he did rest their locked hands against his chest. She didn't speak. She was still embarrassed by the kiss.

"How have you been this week?" he asked, looking over her head as he moved her deftly around the crowded floor.

"Fine."

"Fancy another look at the slag being poured?"

He must have felt her tremble. "I don't think that's a very good idea."

"What if I promise not to make any advances?"

"Even so."

Later in the powder room Sophie said to Jane, "Some of these men are gross."

Jane laughed. She laughed at everything. "What are you talking about?"

"When they're dancing with you. They press up against you when they're - you know."

"Oh, you have to get used to that!"

"I don't want to get used to it. I hate it."

Jane was concentrating on repairing her make-up. "Get yourself engaged then you won't have to dance with anyone else."

"Oh, don't you start."

"Moira been at you, has she?"

"She's pressuring me to say yes to Matthew."

"That surprises me considering she obviously fancies him herself, though she can't honestly believe he could possibly be interested in her."

Sophie shrugged. "I don't know."

On Monday Tiny called at the reception desk. "Got time for a coffee?"

"I can't. Barbara's having hers. I can't leave until she comes back."

Tiny glanced at his watch. "Pity. Tell you what, why don't you drop by the house after work for a sundowner."

"Oh, I don't know."

"What do you mean, you don't know, you meet Jane most days, don't you? She's told me you are in no rush to go home and we all know why. Come on, you'll enjoy it."

"Are you sure Catherine won't mind?"

"Of course she won't mind. Don't be so wet."

"All right."

Sophie took her time walking from the mine to the Beaumonts' house. She'd got to know Catherine since she'd become friends with Jane, and she liked her, but Catherine was ten years older than she, a married woman, with very different interests. Sophie didn't know what she would say to her.

Tiny was waiting on the porch. He looked uncharacteristically anxious. "I didn't know if you'd come," he said, relaxing and beaming at her. She couldn't help smiling back, he had such a bubbly personality, always happy, very different from the sad people she lived with. He took her into the lounge and asked her what she wanted to drink.

"A Pimms, please."

A houseboy meandered into the room. "Get lost, Amrit," Tiny said. The boy wandered off again. It amused Sophie. Moira was always ranting at Catherine for the way her domestic staff behaved. *Totally undisciplined, Moira accused. They'll murder you in your beds.* Sophie looked around. The pocket doors into the dining room were open. She could see through to the kitchen. Aside from a couple of slouching houseboys there didn't seem to be anyone about. "Where's Catherine?"

"She's in Chingola visiting a friend."

The flesh crept on Sophie's scalp. "She's not here?"

Tiny gave a hearty laugh. "What's the matter?"

"Where's Jane?"

"She's gone to play golf with Stan. That should be something to see."

Sophie put her glass aside. "I can't stay here without Jane or Catherine."

"Why in heaven's name not? Do you think I'm going to rape you?"

She was shocked. "No, no, of course not."

"Well then."

After a minute Sophie picked up her glass again but she wasn't comfortable. Tiny kept up a flow of conversation to which she responded in monosyllables, but some of what he said made her laugh.

She stayed where she was for half an hour and then said she must go.

"No, you don't have to go," Tiny said.

But she stood up and walked to the door. "I do."

Without being aware of his movement she found herself wrapped in his arms and the recipient of another of those kisses. She didn't protest. She couldn't protest, it was far too lovely an experience, but as soon as he stopped she struggled out of his embrace. "I have to go."

"There's no need. I promise to be good."

"It's not right, Tiny. You're a married man."

"Nothing's going to hurt Catherine. It's just a bit of fun."

A bit of fun? Was that what she was, then? A bit of fun?

She left with a pounding heart, her mind in turmoil. She was aware of the garden boys watching her walk down the drive, one was sitting on the grass leaning his back on the veranda supports, the other lying on a garden bench. The neighbor across the road was in a swing chair with a newspaper on her knee. She wasn't reading it. Averting her face Sophie turned onto the gravel road and hurried away as fast as her high-heeled sandals would allow.

She didn't expect Tiny to come into reception the next day but he did and was leaning on the counter laughing when Tommy appeared. "Hello," Tommy exclaimed upon seeing him. "What are you doing in this neck of the woods?"

Tiny was unflustered. "Bit of business with Hugh Lowden."

"Ah. Got time for a cup of tea?"

"Yes, sure." Following Tommy across the lobby Tiny turned and winked at Sophie.

Tiny dropped by Reception every day the following week. Sophie went for coffee with him only once. At the other times he stood chatting and laughing until he was forced to leave to allow Sophie to get on with her work.

Since Jane had become engaged and no longer wanted her company Sophie had got into the habit of meeting Matthew in the mine club after work. It was better than going home to sit with Moira, and worse still, Moira and Ray. Because of the nature of his job Matthew sometimes got delayed and she would sit on the wide shady veranda with her Pimms watching people splashing around in the pool, or, if she went around to the other side of the veranda, playing tennis, which is where she was that day.

"Tennis, anyone?" It was Tiny, being facetious, grinning down at her. "Mind if I join you?"

Her face flushed. "No, of course not. I'm waiting for Matthew."

"God knows why," he said lowering his large frame into the lounging chair. "The man's a wimp."

"No, he's not, Tiny."

"Yes, he is. Trust me. I know about these things. What are you doing tonight. Seeing him?"

"No."

"What then?"

Sophie shrugged. "Nothing."

"What sort of nothing?"

"Nothing. "

"So come over to the hotel for a drink."

She lifted her glass. "I'm having a drink here."

"I mean after dinner."

"With you and Catherine?"

"Sure."

She gave him a suspicious look. "Catherine will be there?"

"Sure she will."

Sophie glanced beyond him. "Here's Matthew."

Tiny stood up and turned. "Hi."

Matthew nodded unhappily. "Hello, Ian. How are you?"

"Not bad for an old man." He turned to Sophie and gave her a sly wink. "Cheers."

She did go over to the hotel after dinner. There was nothing else to do. Tommy had gone back to work and Moira had been picked up by a friend. Sophie presumed it was Ray, she didn't bother looking out to see, so she took Moira's car. It was allowed but Moira kept a tight rein on it, as she did on everything in the household.

Despite Tiny's assurances, there was no Catherine.

"She begged off with a headache," he said leading Sophie to a seat in the bar lounge.

"You should have let me know."

"How was I supposed to do that?"

"You could have sent a boy over."

"You think he would have done it? He'd've skived off to visit a friend. Anyway, I'm letting you know now. She can't come."

"Then I'm going."

"Okay." He signaled a waiter over and ordered them both drinks. "Have your drink and go, but I'd like to know why."

"Because you're a married man."

"I'm flattered that you look upon me so romantically, little girl."

Sophie blushed. "I don't."

"Look, this is a public place. There are people all around us. What is wrong with two friends meeting by chance and having a drink?"

The gender difference? The age difference? Everything.

"But we didn't meet by chance. It was arranged, and Catherine was supposed to be here."

"Relax, Sophie! Life's too short for all this angst. You've got to live in the minute!"

An hour flew by and then she insisted of leaving. Tiny escorted her through the open hotel concourse where the usual lounge lizards were sitting around with drinks watching people come and go. He walked with her to the car and in the shadows took her face in his hands and kissed her tenderly. "You're very sweet, little girl," he murmured, and kissed her again.

Sophie broke away and without a word dived into the car and drove off. She prayed that neither Moira nor Tommy was home, and neither was. N'sunga was in the garden smoking. She had started to run to the house but slowed down when she saw him and muttered a hurried goodnight. In her room she lay down on her bed and cried.

There was no-one to talk to, no-one to go to for advice. She had no experience in her life to draw on. Was she making too much of the encounters with Tiny? Were they really just the meetings of friends as he insisted? If so, why did he kiss her in that way? How old was he anyway? Mid-thirties at least. Catherine was eight years older than Jane and younger by at least five years than Tiny, so he had to be. But none of that really mattered, what mattered was that he was married and even if they had done nothing really wrong, she had responded to his attention, and was thrilled by his kisses so that had to count as his cheating on his wife. But how to get out of it without making a fuss? He and Catherine were close friends of Moira and Tommy, as she and Jane had become friends. Back and forth she went, her thoughts flying around in confusion settling on nothing. Her mental anguish brought her no satisfactory solution. In the end she saw only one way out, and that was to marry Matthew.

She fell asleep that night as perplexed, unhappy and lonely as she had ever been in her teenage life, but determined to tell Matthew that she would accept the engagement ring she knew he had already bought.

The next day some of her resolution deserted her. She did not love Matthew. There was no chemistry between them, and the thought of spending the rest of her life with this man whom Tiny characterized as a wimp began to scare her. She would leave it for a few days.

"So, you got home all right last night?"

Tiny was in front of her, resting his arms on the reception counter and staring at her with a twinkle in his eye.

She smiled. She couldn't help it. He was so jolly, and they hadn't done anything wrong.

"Come on, let's get a coffee," he said, and, compliant as always, she went with him.

"Where's Sophie?" Tommy asked, going into Reception a minute later.

Barbara looked up. "Gone off with her fancy man. Where else would she be?"

Tommy thought it was a joke but she wasn't laughing. Her head was bent over the work she was doing. He frowned, not understanding. "Where would that be?"

Now Barbara looked up. "The cafeteria, that's where they meet. At least when they're in this building."

264

Now Tommy was thoroughly bewildered. "Who're you talking about?"

"Sophie, and Ian Beaumont."

"Ian? You mean Tiny?"

"I reckon that's what his friends call him. I don't know him personally."

"What was that about a fancy man?"

Barbara's face reddened but not in embarrassment. "I called him that because he's always stuck here flirting with her," she said harshly.

"I think you've got it wrong," Tommy accused.

"Okay, if you say so," Barbara muttered and went back to her work.

Sophie didn't think anything of it when Tommy strode into the cafeteria. Across the table Tiny was making her laugh as usual, and glancing up she said 'hi' to Tommy, and pushed out a chair for him to sit down.

Tommy eyes were on Tiny. "What are you doing here?"

"Having a coffee, what about you?"

"I came over to see Sophie." He turned from Tiny and looked at her. "There was a letter from England in the mail this morning that looked official. I thought it might be important. Immigration, or something." He took an envelope out of his pocket and handed it to her, then gave Tiny his attention again. "I thought you used the cafeteria in the Ross Building. I don't think I've ever seen you over this way before."

"You saw me here a couple of weeks ago."

"Did I? Oh, right. I remember," Tommy said thoughtfully.

He sat down and had coffee with them, then escorted Sophie back to her desk.

Sophie was surprised when Matthew came to meet her from work that afternoon. "I thought we might have tea together," he said, giving her one of his small, pale smiles.

She shrugged. "Okay."

The only place to have tea was at the hotel. They sat on the terrace where a light breeze lifted the edges of the snowy tablecloth. "Is this some special occasion?" Sophie asked, a little afraid he was going to propose again, and still waffling about what her answer should be.

"Well, I - " Matthew looked flustered. "No, um, well, Tommy gave me a call and thought it might be a good idea to - " His voice trailed off.

"To take me out to tea?" she supplied, with an amused look.

"Well, yes."

A waiter came with the tray, and without thinking Matthew poured. "You've never told me about your life in England. Did you have a boyfriend?"

"Sort of." She squinted into the distance. "My mother and grandmother were quite strict. They let me go out with one of the boys I knew but I had to tell them exactly where I would be and I couldn't stay out any later than ten."

"And did you? Stay out later than ten?"

"No, of course not." She lifted a shoulder and tilted her head, almost apologetically. "It was a bit awkward if we were going to a dance but there wasn't anything I could do about that."

"Did your boyfriend mind?"

"It wouldn't have mattered if he had. I don't know why he bothered with me really."

"I do," Matthew said, with a spurt of animation. "You're a nice person – and you're very pretty."

"Moira doesn't think I'm either. She's constantly criticizing me for having no personality, and she says I definitely haven't inherited my mother's good looks."

"She's just jealous."

They sipped their tea in silence for a while. Then Matthew said, "You know, Sophie, I wish you would think some more about – well, about my proposal."

"You said you wouldn't mention it again until I did."

"Seriously. I mean, if we were engaged people would know that you aren't -" He broke off, looking uncomfortable.

"What? Aren't what?"

They both looked up as a shadow fell across them. It was Tiny, large and friendly, grinning down at them. "Mind if I join you?"

Matthew did mind. He minded very much. "Sophie and I were just discussing -"

"Thanks," Tiny said, lowering himself into a chair and signaling the waiter to bring another cup and saucer. "I'm dying for a cuppa. I've just got off work. So, what are you two young'uns up to?"

"We were having a discussion about - " Matthew began.

"Nothing," Sophie cut in. She didn't want anymore talk about getting engaged.

"So I'm not interrupting anything," Tiny said, giving the waiter a nod to pour his tea. "That's good."

"Actually," Matthew exclaimed boldly. "You are."

"Oh!" Tiny assumed a clown like expression then burst into laughter. "Sorry!"

Matthew went pale. He stood up with a pinched face. "I'll call around and see you later, Sophie," he said, and hurried away.

Even before he was out of earshot Tiny snorted, "I don't know why you waste your time with that idiot."

"He's actually very nice. What are you doing here, anyway?"

"I just happened to be passing."

When Sophie and Tiny walked into the parking lot an hour later they did not see Matthew sitting in his car. But he saw them. He watched white-faced as Tiny kissed Sophie, not on the forehead, not on the cheek but full on the mouth – a long kiss.

He sat thinking in the car after Sophie had walked off and Tiny had driven away. So he didn't take her home. Matthew thought that was significant. It had to mean that Tiny didn't want Tommy or Moira to see them together. He felt a sudden and powerful surge of rage against Ian Beaumont which left him gasping.

He went round to the house that night.

His hope that Moira was out was a vain one, and he was forced to put up with an hour of her heavy-handed flirtatiousness, and then when it looked as though Sophie was going to excuse herself and go to bed he quickly stood up and said it was time he was leaving. "Will you walk to the car with me?" he asked Sophie.

As they crossed the lawn he chewed his lip for a minute then said, "Look, Sophie, I – er – just thought I ought to tell you that Ian is being a bit obvious."

"Ian?"

"Tiny."

"Tiny? I don't understand."

"I think you do, you can't be that naïve." It was too dark to see her face. There was no moon.

"I don't. What do you mean?"

He lost his nerve. "I think you should, well, be careful, that's all." He got in the car and drove away.

But it was too late.

When Jane had returned from golfing that afternoon she had found Catherine in tears. That evening was hell. The next morning Jane stormed up to the mine and marched into Reception. With her eyes flashing fire she strode to the counter, reached over and slapped Sophie on the face so hard Sophie almost fell to the floor.

"And to think that you were going to be my fucking bridesmaid," Jane screamed, and marched out again.

"Oh," said Barbara, unable to hide her satisfaction. "I'll bet that stings."

The situation was as bad at home. Sophie was too ashamed to go to the club to swim as she intended and went straight home.

Tommy was standing by the avocado tree with his arms folded, staring into space. Moira was pacing the veranda.

"Don't you dare stand there and tell me you aren't having an affair with him!" Moira screamed.

"I'm not," Sophie protested.

"Stop lying! I've checked with Barbara Murphy. She says you're always leaving the reception desk to go off with him. Even you saw that, didn't you, Tommy."

"Well, only the once – or twice," he muttered.

Sophie glanced at him, now slouched uncomfortably in a wicker chair. She tried to send him a silent appeal but he wouldn't look at her, or at Moira.

"She's been meeting him all over camp!" Moira spat at Tommy.

"I haven't been meeting him," Sophie said, in tears. "We just happened to be in the same place at the same time."

Moira let out a screeching laugh, "That's rich! How was it you just happened to be in his house when Catherine was away in Chingola?"

"I thought she was there. Tiny invited me to go for a drink with them both."

"So Tiny lied to you, is that what you're claiming."

"Yes, he did."

"Let me tell you something, my girl. Tommy and I have been friends with Tiny and Catherine for eight years and I don't take kindly to a – a – stupid girl coming out from the UK telling me that Tiny is a liar."

"I didn't say that."

"It sounded remarkably like it to me. So you thought Catherine would be there, did you? And what did you do when you found that she wasn't? Did you leave right away? What's the matter, cat got your tongue?"

"No, I – I wanted to leave but Tiny - "

"Forced you to stay? Of course. So you hung around there for close to two hours."

"No, it wasn't that long."

"But it doesn't take long, does it?"

"Moira!" Tommy exclaimed.

The blood rushed into Sophie's face. "It wasn't like that, Moira." She appealed to her uncle. "It wasn't. I haven't done anything wrong."

"No wonder you wouldn't have anything to do with Matthew," Moira sneered. "God, I couldn't imagine even you being stupid enough to throw away the opportunity to marry someone like Matthew for a sordid affair with a married man twice your age."

"I have not been having an affair with Tiny!" Sophie insisted.

"Perhaps you call it something different, but it amounts to the same thing, seducing a man away from his wife."

"I didn't."

"But you did, Sophie. You did. Don't play the innocent, and don't try to say it was Tiny's idea. You must have led him on. He would never have deceived Catherine without encouragement from you. They have one of the strongest marriages in this camp. Tommy will back me up on that. Or at least they did until you started your shenanigans. How you could agree to be Jane's bridesmaid pretending to be so demure, when all the time you were carrying on with Tiny behind Catherine's back is beyond all comprehension."

"I think that's enough, Moira," Tommy said.

"Oh, you do, do you? Well, answer me this, how are we supposed to hold our heads up in this camp after this?"

"It will blow over," he said.

"There is only one way it will blow over, and you know what that it! So do it!" With that she stormed off, and a minute later they heard her bedroom door crash shut.

Tommy rose heavily and went into the lounge. He came back

with two brandies. He gave one to Sophie and sat down near her. "Sophie," he said gently. "I want you to be quite honest with me. Is what is being said true? Have you been meeting Tiny?"

"Not meeting, exactly."

"Barbara Murphy called him your fancy man. Why would she do that?"

Sophie bowed her head. "She shouldn't have. He – he isn't – wasn't my fancy man."

"But you can't deny that there is some romantic involvement. You've been seen kissing him."

"Not really. He was kissing me."

"Moira was told that it didn't look as if you were trying to stop him."

"Who told Moira that?"

"Sweetheart, this is probably my fault for not explaining to you when you first arrived that this place is like an English village. Nothing can be hidden."

"There's nothing to hide, Uncle – I mean Tommy."

"Oh yes, there is. Those kisses should have been hidden. Well, no, I shouldn't say that. Those kisses should never have happened. I can understand you being attracted to Tiny. Women always are. He's a bit of a lad. But you shouldn't have encouraged him, Soph."

"I didn't encourage him. I really didn't."

"Your aunt spoke harshly to you but what she said is true, love. Tiny would never have made advances, without, well, without encouragement from you. Men don't do that. You're young, you don't know these things." He moved uneasily. "She's also right when she says that it's going to be difficult for her, for us, to, well, face people. This is such a close community."

Sophie stared into her brandy snifter. "I'm sorry."

"I'm afraid there is only one way that the matter can be put to rights, Sophie."

"How?"

"I'm afraid you will have to go back home."

Sophie was shocked. "But I don't want to go home."

"You should have thought of that before."

"There's no life for me in England, Uncle, you know that. It's why you suggested I come out here, to get a good start, to make some money so I can further my education."

"Yes, I know all that."

"I love Africa. I want to settle here. I thought that when I have the money I could go to Johannesburg or Durban to study. I want to go into law, and there's no opportunity for me to do that if I go back to England now."

"These were all things which were a possibility before this business with Tiny."

"But it isn't fair. I didn't ask him to deceive Catherine. I didn't lead him on."

"Well, if that's what you say, but you didn't stop him, either, which amounts to the same thing."

He tossed back the rest of his brandy and stood up. He rested his hand briefly on the top of her head. "I'm sorry, love, but there it is."

ISBN 142510581-5